STORM CHASER

STORMS OF BLACKWOOD BOOK THREE

USA TODAY BESTSELLING AUTHOR
ELLE MIDDAUGH

STORM CHASER

STORMS OF BLACKWOOD BOOK THREE

Edited by: Hot Tree Editing
Published by: Moon Storm Publishing LLC
Cover Designed by: Cover Reveal Designs

To anyone who feels like they're
stuck between a rock and a hard place...
It will get easier.
You will find a way out.
Stay strong.

CHAPTER 1

LEXIS

THERE WERE A MILLION PLACES I COULD'VE FOUND MYSELF IN when I finally opened my eyes.

The same red sex room I'd blacked out in. The towers, prepped and ready for torture. The dungeons. The gallows. *Elysium.* To name just a few.

I never once thought I'd wake peacefully in my room as if nothing had ever happened.

Sunlight streamed in through my big arched windows, warming my face. I sat up, glancing curiously about the space. The plum-colored silken sheets were tucked perfectly all around me, as if I hadn't moved at all in my sleep. The sitting room was tidy; all evidence of the sweet treats I'd snacked on before the ball had been removed, and a fresh bouquet of flowers had been positioned on the glass table in their stead.

What the fuck was going on?

The last thing I remembered was fighting the Storm King —all of us falling, one by one. He'd taken us down with such sickening ease, making me absolutely certain there'd been magic involved somehow. I didn't know if he'd been actively trying to kill us, or if he'd just been teaching us a lesson, but either way, the fact that we'd lived meant... Crissen had saved our lives. *Again*.

But had *he* survived? Or had we drained him dry in our attempt to cling to life? Would the bond even allow that? For some reason, I had a feeling it was an all-or-nothing sort of thing, and if one of us survived, then all of us did. Or at least, I hoped that was the case.

I pulled the white cotton nightgown out from my chest, realizing two things at once. One, someone had cleaned and redressed me. And two, the strange stab wound the Storm King had given me was completely gone.

Flinging my sheets from my body, I stood up and walked to my window, peering down at the massive fountain of the Greek gods below. It was strange how things could seem exactly the same but feel so irrevocably different.

The first time I saw that fountain, I'd been arriving at Blackwood Palace to meet the princes. The only thing I hated then was poverty; the only thing I feared was losing my pet sloth. I'd marveled at its magnificence and beauty.

Now, it just looked dull. The water spewing from the mouths, hands, and breasts of the gods seemed stagnant and slightly green. Now, I hated all sorts of things—especially the Storm King—but poverty was the farthest thing from my mind. Now, my greatest worry was losing anyone I ever loved at the hands of the wicked king.

He'd already taken so much....

A knock sounded at my door, and as I spun around, I saw a young servant girl standing in the open frame.

"Good morning, Your Highness. I'm here to prepare you for breakfast."

My brows furrowed in sarcastic surprise. *Breakfast?* The Storm King had damn near killed us, and now we were going to eat breakfast and chat about the weather as if nothing had happened? The man was fucking insane.

"How about you bring breakfast up to my room? And while you do that, I'll prepare *myself* for the day ahead."

Hopefully that'd consist of a hot bath, then getting the fuck out of the citadel.

She smiled sympathetically. "Sorry, Your Highness. I have strict orders from His Majesty, the king. We have foreign dignitaries arriving today, and everyone is to look their best and be on their best behavior—especially you and the princes."

The princes. My heart filled with joy and excitement at just the mention of their titles. "Are they awake too?"

I had no idea how long we were asleep or how long it'd taken us to heal. I was under the impression that this was the very next day, but now that I thought about it, I couldn't actually be sure. It might've been *weeks* for all I knew.

"Yes, Your Highness," she said, twisting her apron with willowy fingers. "They're being prepared for breakfast as we speak."

Suddenly, there were voices in the hallway and the stomping of angry feet.

"*I said*, get out of my way," one of the voices demanded. Rob.

"We can dress ourselves, *thank you very much*," another voice said. Cal.

A moment later, four hulking bodies crammed into my doorway and poured into my room. Clad in nothing but soft bed pants, they were a breathtaking sight to behold. All that smooth skin and those delicious rippling muscles... I sighed contentedly, taking in deep lungsful of their delicious spicy scents, allowing their allure and familiarity to calm me like a high.

"*Out,*" Rob ordered the servant girl standing wide-eyed and uncertain in my room. Not to be told twice, the poor girl quickly fled into the hallway once more. "And shut the door behind you."

It closed quickly, and Rob flipped the lock.

A moment later, I was hefted up into his burly, tattooed arms, his tongue plundering my mouth in the most delicious way. Our lips parted suddenly, and I had a single moment to breathe before Cal's lips came down on mine. His kiss was demanding, pouring out all his fear and worry and love. Then gentle hands ran up my spine and pulled me away. Ben's lips replaced Cal's, his hand restraining my chin, his tongue stroking mine in a way that made me dizzy with lust in an instant. When I came up for air, Dan turned me around and crushed me to his chest, his fingers raking up and down my sides as his tongue danced with mine.

Instead of being passed to another prince when our kiss was complete, Dan simply sat me down on wavering legs. That's when I finally realized something was very wrong. There should have been *five* Storms crammed into my room, *five* Storms kissing me, not *four*. One of my beloved princes was missing.

My mouth went dry. "Where's Ash?"

"That's exactly what we were about to ask you," Cal replied, features grim. A lock of blond hair dipped down into his blue eyes. "I haven't seen a little bird flitting around anywhere. Have you?"

I shook my head slowly, allowing the full weight of that statement to sink in. If Ash wasn't around in bird form... then where the fuck was he?

4

Ben's brows furrowed, and his brown eyes narrowed in thought. "How long have we been out?"

"I don't know. I just woke up," I admitted, and all the guys nodded their agreement. "Does anyone else find that a little... odd? That we all just happened to wake up at the exact same time?"

"Not at all," Ben said, pinching his bottom lip with a sun-kissed hand as he paced around my room. "I'd bet a mountain of jewels that the Storm King planned this. Drugged us somehow. Kept us unconscious until the exact moment he wanted us to wake."

Well, that wasn't terrifying or anything. Who knew what sinister bullshit he could've been up to while we were comatose?

Rob marched to the door and unlocked it, flinging it open quickly to reveal the terrified faces of the servants waiting out in the hall. "How long have we been passed out?" he demanded.

Their eyes went wide, but one of the men stammered, "T-Two weeks, Your Highness."

"Oh, my gods," I whispered, covering my mouth. I stared at the servant guy. "What was King Zacharias up to while we were sleeping?"

He shook his head. "N-No idea, Your Highness. He was away on business. He only just returned this morning. That's why he ordered us to... w-wake you."

"And how, exactly, did you do that?" Ben asked, more curious than accusatory.

The female servant held out her hand, revealing a tiny vial of clear liquid. "He told us to give you each three drops of this. He said you'd wake in less than fifteen minutes, and he was right; you awoke in less than three."

"May I?" Ben asked, holding out his hand.

The servant girl quickly relinquished the vial to Ben, then backed out into the hall once more.

The Sand Prince lifted the little bottle up into the sunlight, and my lips parted as I watched the liquid inside shimmer and sparkle in all the vibrant colors of the rainbow.

"Fascinating," Ben muttered, staring intently.

"Did the king tell you what this liquid was?" Dan asked, his sea green eyes locking onto the servant girl, who immediately blushed at his attention.

"No, Your Highness. He would never entrust us with information like that."

Sighing harshly, Rob shut the door in their faces once more and locked it tight. Then he leaned back into the wood, ran his hands through his ebony hair, and growled in frustration.

Dan turned back to us, nervously worrying his lip. "What are the odds that the king's *'away on business'* status had something to do with Ash?"

"Probably better than we'd ever care to imagine," Rob replied, sounding gentle instead of brash for once. He scratched at the dark stubble along his jaw and sighed.

Had the Storm King found Asher flitting around? Had he figured out who he was? Kidnapped him? Tortured him? Buried him alive? Or worse?

My thoughts were a graveyard of unholy possibilities.

"What if Ash was the *business*, because Ash was *the egg*," Ben surmised, "and the Storm King had no idea it was actually him?"

"No," Cal decided at once. "We made that fake and never once did anyone have possession of it except for me. There's no way he could have shifted and replaced it somehow without me knowing."

"No way?" Ben asked curiously. "I assume you cleaned up for the ball. Did you take the bag with you into the shower?"

Cal's lips thinned, and his eyes narrowed. "Are you accusing me of losing our brother?"

"Not accusing," Ben clarified, "just pointing out facts. He very well could have snuck into your room and done the deed while you were momentarily distracted. I wouldn't put it past him."

Cal sighed and ran a hand through his golden blond hair. "I was only in the shower for a second."

"It's all right, bro," Dan said, patting Cal on the shoulder. "If Ash really did take the place of the egg, then that shit's on *him* and no one else."

A knock sounded faintly at the door. "Your Highnesses, please. We really must get you ready for breakfast now. The king will not be pleased if you're late."

Rob's lip curled, but he opened the door yet again. "Who exactly are we having breakfast with?"

"Just His Majesty this morning," one of the other servants spoke up. "But the foreign dignitaries will be arriving tonight for dinner. Now that Timberlune and Hydratica have declared war upon us, His Majesty is scouting for allies. Representatives from Eristan, Valinor, Rubio, and Werewood should all be arriving within a few hours."

"Gods fucking damn it," Rob grumbled, pinching the bridge of his nose.

Cal sighed. "It makes sense. Fortifying our defenses is probably exactly what *I* would do. But that means we're stuck playing his games once again. We need these allies as much as he does. If not, it's *our people* who will pay the price. *Our people* who will be slaughtered in a senseless war."

Dan rolled his pale green eyes and scrubbed a frustrated hand across his face. "Well, here we go again, then. It's like our childhood reincarnated. Take a beating, witness some torture, then act like it didn't affect us in the slightest."

"Let's just get through breakfast," I suggested, rubbing a

hand up Dan's smooth, bare arm. "We'll take this one step at a time, until we can somehow get the upper hand."

All the guys agreed and retreated to their respective rooms to prepare for breakfast.

"I'm afraid we no longer have time for your bath, Your Highness," the servant girl apologized. "We'll just have to make do with styling your hair, applying your makeup, and dressing you in a suitable gown."

Bam.

Out of nowhere, tears welled in my eyes and the small smile dropped right off my face. Gemma used to be the one picking out my gowns. The one prepping me for another day of bullshit at the palace. Without her and her wise words of encouragement, how was I going to make it through the days to come? She was always the light in the midst of my darkness, my home away from home. Now that she was gone, where the hell did that leave me?

"Sorry, Your Highness," the servant apologized uncertainly. "I didn't realize the bath meant so much to you. I suppose I can try to steal some time away from your hair in order to fit it in."

Gods, she'd read that situation all sorts of wrong.

I wiped my tears and shook my head. "No, we can skip the bath."

Hell, I used to skip baths for weeks back in Blackleaf because I didn't have time to get to the river when I was mining for jewels all day and half the night. And even if I *did* have the time, I almost never had the coin for soap.

The servant girl grabbed a brush and started tugging on my hair, blissfully unaware of my heart breaking right before her. Or maybe she just didn't care? Either way, now that Gemma was on my mind, all the grief I'd suppressed that night had come rushing back.

I'd selfishly dragged her to the palace with me, but she

had adjusted beautifully, making friends with the servants and learning everything she needed to in order to help keep me on track. She'd listened to my trivial complaints, and while she totally laughed at half of them, she still took the time to help me figure them out. She encouraged me to follow my heart and pursue all of the princes. And she suffered torture at the hand of the king, simply for being my friend.

At least the torment was over. Never again could he hurt her on behalf of my failure; if nothing else, I should be happy for that. I didn't know if I believed Elysium was even real anymore, but if it was, I knew she'd be there. She was the best of the best, the most deserving soul there ever was for an eternity of peace and happiness.

"I love you, Gemma," I whispered, too quiet for even me to hear. "I will make him pay for what he did to you, I swear it."

I would kill the king... even if it was the last thing I ever did.

 EMMA

THE SOUND OF SEAGULLS CALLING AND THE CRASH OF THE SURF woke me slowly. Sunlight gently filtered in through my open windowpane, swathing me in a thin blanket of warmth. I smiled as I opened my eyes.

The bed was empty, aside from me, so I knew Tristan was already up and manning the fishing nets. It had been weeks since our tiny boat landed across the sea, weeks during which I honestly wondered if we'd survive.

We did, though—*survive*—and we managed to build a cute little shack too. Okay, fine, *I* built it, and it was hardly a shack, more like a small beach house complete with a stilt foundation—I'd scoped out the nearby villages to get a feel for the construction in the area. It was a good thing my background had been in carpentry, because as adorable as Tris was, he couldn't hammer a straight wall or fit a square corner to save his life.

We eventually decided that *he* would fish, hunt, and garden for our food, and *I* would craft things out of wood and sell them in the nearby villages for money—which, here in Hydratica, meant pearls. So far, I'd only sold a table and chairs, but it had gotten us five pearls, and I was pretty damn proud of myself for that.

We were really doing it. We were setting down roots in a foreign country, and we were surviving. I was beyond happy; I was freaking blissful.

I hopped out of bed and skipped into the living room. Since Tristan and I now lived on a beach, I'd decided to decorate the house with a nautical vibe. I'd constructed all the furniture out of salty-gray driftwood, sewn the upholstery into varying shades of blue, and hung a wooden captain's wheel on the wall above the fireplace where a near-constant pot of fish stew hung boiling over the flames.

Through the kitchen window, I saw Tristan mooring his little boat and hauling a net full of fish, crabs, scallops, and oysters onto the dock I'd recently made. All those years as a stable boy had left him stacked with brawn, and I could tell his years as a fisherman were going to be just as good to him. As I tied on my stained white apron, I watched his muscles flex and tighten under the weight of the netted sea creatures, and a lock of his dark hair dipped into his eyes. My lips part in awe. The sight of his magnificence would never get old; I would always feel like a horny little teenager when it came to him.

Flinging the front door open, I ran over and launched myself into his arms, causing him to drop the net onto the freshly cut boards of the dock. Thankfully, he'd already tied it off, otherwise my enthusiasm might've lost him an entire morning's work. Oops.

"Sorry!" I apologized, squeezing him even tighter.

He chuckled and squeezed my butt, kissing my neck up to my jaw then finally my lips. "No apologizes from you, beautiful. I love seeing your smiling face first thing in the morning."

Did I mention I was in love with him? Because I so totally was.

"You want to check the oysters for pearls?" he asked.

I smiled wide. "You know it!"

Since Hydratica's currency consisted solely of pearls, it was technically illegal to fish for the clammed creatures. Only the monarchy was allowed to collect and distribute them. But we were rebels, illegal immigrants, so we may as well collect a few illegal pearls as well, am I right?

It wasn't like we were trying to cheat their system or anything. We were just doing what we had to do in order to survive. I was sure the royals wouldn't agree with that if we ever got caught, though, so hopefully that never happened.

"Looks like you got a good haul today," I commented, shooting Tris a flirtatious grin.

He hefted the net back over his shoulder and led us up the beach toward the house.

"I did find some interesting things," he admitted, plopping the net in the sand amongst the grassy dunes. "I trawled off the western coast near that one island chain, and I think I stumbled upon an old shipwreck."

I gasped and clapped my hands excitedly. "Seriously?"

Tris nodded, digging through the net to remove a few items that were definitely *not* sea creatures. A spyglass, a compass, an iron ring with a lavender pearl in it, and a small pouch of silvery coins.

"Ooh!" I squealed, snatching the spyglass and compass. "These will be perfect on the wall next to the captain's wheel!"

Tristan grinned. "And I figured we could pop the pearl

out then melt the ring and coins into some tools to help you with your carpentry."

Oh my gods he was amazing. "I love you, Tris. Thank you."

He put an arm around my shoulders and kissed the top of my wavy blonde head. "I love you too, beautiful. Why don't you take those items inside while I cut these up? I know how you hate the smell of raw fish."

I grinned. He knew me so well. "Good idea. I'll take the clams too."

"Sounds good." He quickly sorted his catch into separate piles, and once he was done, I scooped up the clams—along with my pirate treasure—and hurried into the kitchen.

Standing at the sink, I took a moment to stare out the window, watching the waves roll in and spread their frothy fingers across the shore, raking little bits and pieces of sand and shells back into the ocean as it retreated then rolled in again.

Somewhere over there, across the sea, was Alexis and the harem ladies. My dad and my siblings. My friends. My family. My entire old life.

I allowed sorrow to wash over me for just a moment, acknowledging my feelings no matter how painful they were. I couldn't change what had become of me, but I could change the way I reacted to the situation.

Instead of crying over everything I'd lost, I smiled at all I'd gained—peace, safety, and a fresh start. Instead of wallowing over the loss of my best friend, I decided to be grateful for the gift of true love I'd found in Tristan. And instead of allowing the longing for my family to smother me, I took the love I had for them and breathed it back into the universe, praying to those deadbeat gods to bless my family with happiness and good fortune.

It was the best I could do. After all, I was never going back to Blackwood. I'd never see any of them again.

I pulled a knife from my apron pocket and popped the pearl from the ring, depositing the metal circlet in the pouch along with the coins. Then I set my blade to the clamshells, prying them open and checking their squishy cushions for any pearlescent treasure. Of the ten shells, two of them had pearls—one a dusty pink, the other a pale champagne brown. Neither of them were quite as large as the one from the ring, but they were essentially free money, and I sure as hell wasn't going to look fortune in the face and scoff.

When I was finished with the clams, I pocketed my three pearls, gathered my two pirate treasures, and entered the living room. I smiled as I looked around. It really was a beautiful home, an excellent place to settle down and hopefully raise a family one day.

Measuring the wall behind the wheel, I hammered nails into each side so that the new items would sit symmetrically above the hearth. I hung the spyglass on the left and the compass on the right. Together, the three items were absolutely perfect. Not only did they look made for one another in design, but they were also symbolic of a deeper union of ideas.

At least, to me they were.

It was as if our bodies were ships, each sailing our own course through the sea of life, simply trying to stay afloat until the inevitable shipwreck at the end. And these items—a spyglass, a compass, and a wheel—were tools that would help guide us along the way.

The spyglass to see in every direction.

The compass to know which way to go.

And the wheel to steer us onto the right path.

Tristan and I were on the right path. I felt it in my very

bones. For one reason or another, we were exactly where we needed to be.

I sighed and glanced out the window once more toward the sea.

Were Alexis and the others on the right path for them?

Only time could tell.

CHAPTER 3

LEXIS

THE GUYS MET ME IN THE HALLWAY AFTER THE SERVANTS HAD prepped us for breakfast and left, but the only thing I saw was a big brown chimera egg resting ominously in Cal's broad hand.

My eyelids fell shut. So it was true. Ash really had traded places with the fake egg.

Son of a fucking bitch.

Cal went back into his room, probably to re-hide the egg, before coming out empty-handed and shutting the door. "I tore my room apart after Ben mentioned the swap could have happened while I'd been showering. Sure enough, I found it tucked in the underside of my mattress."

No one said a word as the heaviness of his statement settled in. There wasn't much we *could* say. All we could do now was hope that Ash hadn't made a huge mistake, and that he'd return to us as quickly as possible.

Silently, Cal held out his arm and offered to escort me down to the formal dining room.

I slipped my hand through the crook of his elbow and forced myself to smile.

"You look beautiful, Peach," he muttered before pulling my hand up to his lips.

I glanced down at my light and lacy, powder-blue gown, then over to his perfectly fitted navy-blue suit, as if noticing them for the first time. My gaze slowly slid from prince to prince, taking in the gorgeousness each man radiated as they strolled confidently down the wide corridor. Gods, they were sexy.

"Yeah, Jewels," Rob added over his shoulder, hopping on the tail end of Cal's compliment, "you look pretty and shit."

He had a few tattoos peeking out above the unbuttoned collar of his suit, and I wanted to lick them. I forced my gaze away from his tats and up to his stormy gray eyes. "Thanks, asshole. That means a lot coming from you."

He chuckled just as the sound of a door opening and closing echoed somewhere behind us. I turned around, surprised to find Crissen walking alone.

"Hold on," I said, planting my feet in the royal purple carpet. "We didn't wait for him?"

Rob spun around and crossed his burly arms. "Why would we?"

Sighing, I jabbed a thumb at Rob while glancing up at Cal. "He's an asshole. What's your excuse?"

He shrugged, trying to remain impassive. "Crissen's been living here for over a month. I'm pretty sure he knows his way around."

I turned to the sweetest guy I knew. "Back me up, Ben."

Ben smiled warmly and gazed behind us to where Crissen was quickly catching up. "Sailor's right. We should have waited. We're acting like a bunch of dicks."

"Speaking of a bunch of dicks," Dan cut in cheekily, "we still need to get that team tattoo."

"I am *not* getting five freaking dicks tattooed onto my body," I argued, starting to walk once Criss reached us.

"Oh, come on," Dan teased. "We could put the tits in the middle with five dicks radiating out around them like a star or something. Very artistic."

Crissen's brows furrowed, and a tiny smile passed his lips. "I'm sorry, tits and dicks?"

Dan grinned. "It's our team tattoo."

"It is *not* our team tattoo!" I argued again, getting a good chuckle out of the guys. "I still like the rose with five thorns, personally."

"Don't act like *we're* not the roses," Dan teased me.

"How about five roses in a vase?" Crissen asked with a grin.

I turned to him, my eyebrows raised. "That's actually pretty accurate."

After all, I was the one with the "vase" they were all trying to fit their "stems" into.

Everyone laughed except Rob. "Just don't get any cute ideas about it being *six* roses. You can keep your prickly little dick far, far away from Jewel's vase, or I will personally cut it off."

Crissen's eyes went wide, and his cheeks flushed a pale pink. "For fuck's sake, I wasn't even—"

"Save it," Rob cut in as we reached the stairs and started descending. "I wonder what's for breakfast, anyway? I'm starving."

His brash treatment to our newest member was a little upsetting. I understood the fact that they didn't really like each other. I also understood the fact that he was possessive of me and didn't want to share... *again*. But he was being downright rude to the poor guy, and I was starting to feel bad for him.

"You don't actually plan on eating, right?" Ben asked Rob and the rest of us. "After the poisoned wine incident, I certainly wouldn't trust him with an entire buffet."

My stomach grumbled in protest, but damn it, he was right.

Rob groaned. "Gods damn it, it'll probably be something delicious too."

"Yeah, like brain stew," Dan teased, making me fake a gag.

"*Pig* brain," Rob assured everyone.

Cal's grin widened. "Lie."

"*Fuck*, that's disgusting!" Dan cried, shaking his head as if to clear the cannibalistic image that had no doubt crept up. "Those demons were pretty cool though, aside from that."

Rob grinned. "I told you demons always get a bad rap. Just because they possess innocent people and eat human flesh doesn't mean they're evil."

When we reached the bottom of the stairway, I glanced at Crissen, wondering what he must've been thinking about our strange little group.

He merely blinked and shook his head. If his emotions were anything to go by, though, he was both worried *and* intrigued by us. There also seemed to be a hint of longing floating in the air around him, but I wasn't exactly sure what that meant. Hopefully he wasn't yearning to try some brain soup, because *bleh*. Gag a maggot.

When we reached the dining room, the Storm King was already waiting for us. He watched with cunning yet amused eyes as we all found seats far away from him and stood at the backs of the chairs until he lowered himself to the velvety cushion. Reluctantly, we did the same.

"Good morning, children," he said with a pleasant smile that was surely all for show.

Children? If my eyes rolled any further into the back of my head, the guys might think I'd had a stroke.

"Good morning, Father," Cal said, knowing full-well his siblings probably wouldn't reply.

To my surprise, Crissen added a polite greeting as well. "Good morning, Your Majesty."

The Storm King turned to Crissen and folded his hands beneath his chin. "How many times have I told you to call me Father?"

"Sorry, Your—" He paused, smiling sarcastically as he caught himself. "Sorry, *Father*."

Rob glared between the two of them. "Can we just cut the bullshit? What's this about?"

"Nothing, Robert," the king said smoothly. "This is simply breakfast."

He gestured to the side, and two servants entered carrying trays of food: glazed breads, muffins, dumplings, fruits, and nuts. After them, another set of servants rushed in bringing coffee and tea. After everyone was situated, the servants scurried out as quickly as they'd come in. The Storm King took the first bite, signaling to the rest of us that it was time to eat.

"I don't fucking buy it," Rob said, pushing his plate away.

The king narrowed his serpentine eyes. "I wonder what Rosemary would think of your tone?"

At the mention of his mother's name, Rob immediately mellowed out and went silent.

As an act of solidarity—and honestly, self-preservation—I pushed my plate away too. The other brothers followed suit, including Crissen who seemed to be the last to catch on.

The Storm King narrowed his eyes into dangerous slits. "Not hungry?"

"Can you blame us?" I asked flatly. "After the episode with the wine, we'd have to be brain-dead to trust you again."

He stared at us, and we stared right back. It was yet *another* tiny act of defiance on our part, but it seemed like we were gaining ground with each small step we took.

Eventually, the Storm King leaned back in his chair and crossed his hands at his core. "Very well, then. I'll just cut to the chase. I have another mission that needs completing, and this time, I want Crissen to lead it."

Criss's eyes went wide, and his lips parted. "*Me*, Your Hi— I mean, Father?"

The king rolled his cold blue eyes. "Yes, *you*. You're the only Crissen in the room. Hell, you're probably the only Crissen in the entire kingdom. Who the hell names their kid that? Your mother was a ridiculous fucking woman."

Criss's jaw tensed, and I felt mine do the same. He seemed like a really nice guy. I didn't understand why people were always being mean to him.

"What's the mission?" Cal asked from my left. His voice and expression were perfectly neutral, but I knew how edgy he felt. His tension rode the air around me.

Having empathy as my extra power was pretty damn convenient.

"I want you to find the Eye of the Sea," the king drawled cunningly.

"And what's that again?" Dan asked.

"I don't know, Daniel," he said, giving him a scathing look. "You're the *Sea* Prince. Shouldn't *you* be the one to know?"

This time Dan went silent.

Cal cleverly changed direction. "Where is this item located?"

The king shrugged nonchalantly. "Hydratica, I believe."

"You mean to tell me," Rob began, his temper rising once more, "that you want us to go into the heart of enemy territory, in the middle of an international war, just to retrieve some stupid item you want?"

21

The bastard didn't deny it, so I was sure Rob had been correct—Timberlune and Hydratica had already declared war.

"What happened to the last item?" Ben asked in his deep voice. "The chimera egg. Where is it?"

The Storm King cut him a glare. "That's none of your concern, Benson."

Fear for Ash overcame any rational sense, and my temper flared.

I put both palms on the table and leaned a little closer. "What makes you think we'll ever go on another mission for you again?"

"Concern for your mothers?" he asked innocently. "No? That's not good enough anymore?"

We all stayed silent, staring at him with angry stone-like faces.

He grinned. "That's what I thought. So, I took the liberty of setting up a backup plan while you were all... sleeping."

"You mean, while you forced us to stay unconscious," Dan corrected.

The king shrugged. "That's neither here nor there."

"What's the backup plan?" Cal asked, keeping the conversation on track.

King Zacharias sat up and took a long sip of his coffee. "Did you know that orkyda blossoms emit a pollen that is highly combustible when mixed with alicorn dust and dragon fire?"

"Orkyda blossoms are rare," Ben argued. "Found only on the tallest mountain peaks."

"Not anymore." The Storm King smirked.

"Also, alicorns and dragons are both extinct," Ben added.

The Storm King merely narrowed his gaze as his smile widened. "Are they?"

The tanned skin of Ben's jaw ticked, and his nostrils flared. "What are you planning to do with them?"

The king shrugged, making me want to slap that smug-ass grin right off his face. "I've been doing a little renovating. Sprucing up the villages across the kingdom. Planting flowers..."

My mind whirred, making me dizzy. If he'd planted orkydas all over the kingdom, and he'd somehow gotten a hold of alicorn dust and dragon fire, then that meant... he was planning on blowing up his own people. Burning his own villages to the ground.

We could not, under any circumstances, allow that to happen.

"When do we leave?" Cal asked, apparently coming to the same conclusion as me.

"We?" the Storm King asked humorously. "Did you not hear me earlier? This is Crissen's task. The princes of Black-wood need to return to being lords of their castles. We are, after all, at war."

Rob shot his father a disbelieving look. "We're not trusting that dipshit to complete a mission on his own, especially one of this magnitude. He'll fuck it up for sure."

The king scoffed. "As if you five don't fuck up all the time yourselves."

"Go to Tartarus," I sneered through gritted teeth. I couldn't help myself. He deserved to suffer in an everlasting dungeon of torment for all of eternity.

His eyebrows rose, and his smile stretched further. "So brash, Princess Alexis. I see your lessons with Madam Annette have fallen upon deaf ears. Or, perhaps, her teachings simply aren't what they used to be. Perhaps I should have her terminated?"

I had a bad feeling he was planning to do more than *fire*

her. "That's unnecessary. Madam Annette is a great teacher; I'm just a shit student."

Zacharias rolled his eyes. "Shit student. Shit princess. Shit *mother*. Gods only know how many of my sons you've been fucking and you *still* haven't become pregnant."

All the air whooshed out of my lungs like he'd kicked me in the gut.

His features darkened. "Need I remind you that your time is running out? If you do not produce a proper Storm heir soon, then it will be *you* who is *terminated*. Understand?"

I nodded, because I still couldn't breathe. I was terrified of what he'd do to me if I failed to become pregnant, but I was even more terrified of the idea of succeeding. I might've been twenty-four, but I was *not* ready for a baby. And, as amazing as Cal and his brothers were, I was pretty fucking sure they weren't ready to be fathers, either.

King Zacharias finished off his coffee and patted his lips with a napkin. "You may escort Prince Crissen on his journey to Hydratica if you wish, but know this: we are in the middle of a war. If the lords are not on their respective thrones when the time comes for important decisions to be made, then I'll be forced to make those decisions myself."

The implications were clear as fucking day. Let Crissen go alone and wait for all of us to slowly die, or accompany Crissen, but allow the Storm King to make all the important battle decisions.

We each took turns sharing somber glances, trying to read each other's thoughts and emotions through the stoic set of our faces. The overwhelming emotion I was sensing was anger, but it was followed closely by uncertainty and fear, and then after that... determination.

"So, like I said," Cal began, speaking on behalf of all of us, "*when do we leave?*"

The Storm King grinned wickedly. "*Tomorrow.* Until then, I expect you to be on your best behavior. Your servants have your agendas."

Then he shooed us away with a flick of his wrist.

"Now, go."

CHAPTER 4

The servants were already waiting for us outside the dining room door.

Talk about efficient. Rather than being impressed though, I felt disgusted. The Storm King ran a tight ship. I just couldn't figure out why so many people had hopped on board. I mean, the man was a fucking psycho.

The same young servant girl who'd gotten me ready for breakfast approached me as I marched into the hall. She was tall and willowy with long, straight, dishwater-brown hair. Her face was pretty, but simple, with a straight nose and thin lips. She didn't seem overly talkative or particularly extroverted.

While Gemma had been the light in the center of a room, this new girl was just a flower on the wallpaper.

I didn't judge her for it. There was absolutely nothing wrong with being shy or plain. It was just that I was having a hard time not comparing her to my late best friend, and in a context like that, no one would ever match up. She didn't stand a chance.

I sighed. "What's your name?"

"Rochelle, Your Highness." She curtsied quickly.

"What does my schedule look like, Rochelle?" I cringed as the words came out clipped and a little resentful.

I glanced right and watched as each of the princes consulted with their servants as well. Cal and Criss with their arms folded neatly behind their backs, Rob with his arms crossed in front of him, Dan with his hands on his hips, and Ben with a hand on his chin. I loved how each of their personalities shined through even in something as simple as *standing*.

"Breakfast with the royal family," Rochelle said, reciting my schedule from memory. "Followed by etiquette lessons with Madam Annette. Morning tea with the harem ladies. History lessons with Professor Samson. Then lunch with the princes..."

She continued rattling off my schedule, but I already knew it. It was the same order of events as the last time I was there.

Suddenly Cal was behind me, wrapping his arms around my waist and nestling his face into my neck. "I'll see you at lunch, darling. Same place as before."

Darling. It seemed the name I'd called him all those nights ago at Crissen's ball had become the one we would use for each other, at least in front of others.

I grinned and kissed his cheek. "I'll be there."

Which meant I'd be meeting them at the stables, and we'd be riding on horseback to our secret picnic grounds in the woods.

A few moments later, I pushed open the door to Madam Annette's classroom where the same faux dining room was set up and waiting for me.

She was breezing around and checking every minute detail: from the perfect vases of flowers, to the crisp table-cloths and napkins, to the precise layout of the flatware and silverware. The woman, herself, looked pristine and well put together as always with a lacy, intricately sewn dusty rose gown and her white hair piled high atop her head in a fancy updo.

"Good morning, Princess Alexis," she said with a youthful curtsey despite her obvious age.

I curtseyed back, surprised to find I somehow remembered the movements perfectly. "Good morning, Madam Annette. I trust you've been well?"

She smiled proudly at my manners and conduct. "Excellent, Your Highness, thank you very much. Are you prepared for today's lessons?"

I scoffed. "How could I possibly be prepared? I barely woke up an hour ago, and only ten minutes ago learned that I'd be continuing these lessons."

"A princess is always prepared, Your Highness."

Of course they are.

I took a long, slow inhale and forced a smile. "Then, let's proceed."

She bowed her head in my direction.

"As you no doubt noticed back when you met the Timberlune royals, there are varying versions of the royal curtsy that you should know. Each kingdom has their own special variant, their own little quirk or twist they want you to add onto it."

I rolled my eyes. "Yes, Queen Bravia was deeply perturbed that I didn't curtsy to her properly. But I don't particularly give a fuck, considering they're now waging war against us."

Madam Annette quirked an unenthused eyebrow. "Perhaps if you'd curtsied properly in the first place, we wouldn't be in this mess?"

I fucking laughed out loud. "Yes, I'm sure this war is all on me and my shitty curtsying skills."

She grinned. "You never know."

"Ah, but I do," I teased. "It's a princess's job to *know everything*, after all."

This time she chuckled. "I'm so pleased that my lessons have finally started sinking in."

I glanced out the window. It wasn't safe to talk freely within the palace walls, but if we were outside in, say, the garden, I wondered if Madam Annette might... open up? She was a plethora of information, and I was certain she knew things that I didn't. The question was: would she tell me any of it? Was she, or was she not, loyal to the wicked king?

"Would you mind taking this lesson outdoors?" I asked her sweetly. "The fresh air might do my stuffy attitude some good."

She inclined her head and curtseyed perfectly. "As you wish, Your Highness."

We strolled through the halls and out onto the lawn with poise, like two very proper ladies about to enjoy a spot of tea and a few crumpets in the garden. When we were far enough away from the palace walls, I glanced over at her.

"I'm going to tell you some things you probably don't know, so bear with me."

Start small, Lex. Test the waters before you go too deep.

She put on her stoic face and waited patiently while I took a deep breath and rattled it all off at once.

"He beats and tortures the harem ladies to keep his sons and me in line. His guards held the princes and queens at knifepoint while he forced Cal and I to 'consummate our union' in front of everyone. He beat us within an inch of our lives then forcefully kept us unconscious for weeks. Guards helped him—guards who barely earn a living wage. Servants helped him—servants who are routinely beaten. So, my question is *why*? Why help him? Why let him do this? Why support such a wicked monster?"

Way to go, you dumbass. You just dove headfirst into the deep end.

I groaned internally at my own tactlessness.

With wide eyes, Madam Annette dipped into a standard curtsy, then tipped her head back, exposing her neck. "This is the common curtsy of Werewood. They're werewolves, so exposing the neck shows subservience."

So apparently, we wouldn't be talking about any of this. *Great.*

"As a *royal*," she continued, "you would cover your throat with your hand as you dip, like so."

She curtsied again, demonstrating the slight deviance from the first time. "This is how you'll address Prince Rafe."

It made sense. So, I copied her movements with relative ease.

To my surprise, she breezed over and corrected me. Adjusting my posture, tilting my chin, and arching my neck even further. As she leaned in, she whispered, "Perhaps he has so much support because no one has made a stand against him? If one of the princes were to stand up... or perhaps, all five of you…"

My mouth dropped open.

She backed away and immediately demonstrated another standard curtsy, but this time she brought her palms together above her heart. "This is the royal curtsy of Eristan."

Simple enough. I copied her movements with fluid grace.

But again, she corrected me. Lifting my elbows and pressing my palms tighter together, even pushing on my lower back to force my curtsey deeper. She leaned in and said, "I propose speaking with the queens, the servants, and the royal guards. Find out just how willing they are to serve their king, or just how willing they *aren't*."

She retreated with an innocent nod, as if we hadn't just been having a treasonous, double-sided conversation.

"Very good, Your Highness. Ambassador Rasheem is not royalty, however, so you will not be required to bow to him."

"Okay," I agreed, still dumbfounded that she was actually opening up.

"Next is Rubio. They refuse to acknowledge any monarch other than their own queen. So, Captain Akiko will *not* bow to you, and neither will you bow to her."

My brows furrowed, and I crossed my arms. "Then why the hell is Rubio coming here at all? I can't imagine the Storm King wanting to do business with a kingdom who doesn't acknowledge his power and prestige."

Madam Annette folded her hands in front of her—a subtle hint at the gesture *I* should have made instead of crossing my arms. "King Zacharias may do whatever he wishes. Rubio is a kingdom of tribal warriors, highly skilled in combat and extremely resilient. They would make excellent allies."

I rolled my eyes and uncrossed my arms. "What about the last kingdom?"

She bowed, acknowledging my request. "Valinor is a kingdom of big cat shifters—lions, tigers, leopards, etcetera. When they curtsy, they cross their arms in an X across their chest, then curve their fingers to look like claws. Like so."

She showed me the move, and I tried to copy it. Even though I'd just watched her do it, I screwed up the hand gesture. It just felt more natural to keep my fingers straight instead of curled.

Madam Annette grabbed my fingers and bent them. "Straight fingers will offend Princess Veda. You must get this right."

"Oh, great, another princess?" I rolled my eyes.

"Yes," she whispered. "Now, listen. Once you've spoken with everyone at the palace, I believe you'll find there are plenty of allies spread out amongst the kingdom. Find them and rally them."

My brows furrowed as she pulled away and demonstrated the Valinorian curtsey again.

My mind was reeling. We'd been looking for support outside of our kingdom, but it had never occurred to us to look for it *inside*.

I copied her movements to a T, even forced my fingers to curl against their will. "Are you suggesting that making foreign allies is pointless? That I should be concentrating my efforts within Blackwood, instead?"

She smiled and moved her pointer finger in a circle above her head. "One more time from the top! Werewood."

I sighed and performed the Werewoodian curtsey, making sure to cover my neck.

"I wouldn't say it's pointless in the slightest," she whispered to me. "Make *personal* allies. Make *friends* out of these people so that they'll want to support *your* claim to the throne." Then she carried on with her lesson. "Eristan."

I dipped down into the Eristani curtsey, complete with prayer hands.

"You just used a dirty F word," I said flatly.

Her brows rose. "Friends, Your Highness?"

I nodded. "You realize, when I was a peasant in Blackleaf—"

"Which you're not anymore," she reminded me.

"Yes, but when I *was*, I had approximately *one* friend."

Oh, gods, I didn't realize how badly it would hurt to say that out loud. Tears flooded my eyes, but I blinked them away and kept them from spilling.

"And now that she's gone, I have none. I'm not good at making friends."

Madam Annette reached out and patted my hand. "It's not always easy for everyone," she assured me. "But it still

happens for everyone regardless. You'll make new friends—
perhaps even in people you least expect." Then she straightened back up. "Rubio."

I dipped down but couldn't remember what the special
hand gesture was.

She tsked at me. "We do not bow to Rubians, Princess
Alexis."

I glared at her. "You tricked me."

She grinned and rolled her beady little eyes. She was full
of sass for an old lady who was supposed to be prim and
proper. "Valinor."

I bent my knees and crossed my arms, making sure to
curl my fingers like claws.

"Very good, Your Highness," she praised with a smile. "It
looks like our time is up. But, remember this: you will meet
hundreds of people in your lifetime, ones who come and
ones who go. Continue to be yourself, and the right people
will stay."

I smiled and inclined my head, grateful for all her advice.

"Now, off with you," she said, shooing me away. "You have
harem ladies to befriend."

Riiiight.

Because making *friends* with my potential mothers-in-law
was going to be a sweet and simple piece of cake.

CHAPTER 5

*D*éjà vu struck me like a pickax to the heart.

The midmorning tea party looked exactly as it had the first time I'd joined them a few months ago. They all wore wide-brimmed hats to combat the sun and fancy gowns with long sleeves, which I now understood was to cover their plethora of scars. The only new face I saw was Charity, Crissen's mother. But it wasn't like I hadn't seen her before, so I didn't know if I'd say "new." Just, new to tea.

I glanced around at their smiling faces, even my mother's, and wondered how the ever-loving fuck they managed to put on such a fantastic front.

"Alexis!" Caroline crooned with her arms outstretched. "Katelynn, look! Our daughter has arrived!"

Oh my Hades. Cal's mom just called me her daughter.

I tried to blink back my wide-eyed shock, but she'd still seen it, which made her laugh.

Mom stood and breezed over to me with a grace I never even knew she had in her. Apparently, she'd been forced to take etiquette lessons as well. Or perhaps, the other queens

34

had just been generous in teaching her so that her beatings were less harsh? Gods, I hated that fucking bastard...

I melted as Mom pulled me into a tight embrace, far tighter than her casual air suggested. I knew just how important this moment was to her. How important it was to me.

"I love you, Mom," I whispered as tears once more filled my eyes.

"I love you too, my precious girl," she said with a misty-eyed smile. "I've missed you so much. Worried about you constantly."

I chuckled to keep from sobbing. "I've worried about you too. I'm so sorry, Mom. Sorry I didn't see you before I left last time."

"It's okay, Lex. It was a difficult time for y—"

"And I'm sorry I didn't write you. Actually, I *did* write you, I just never got a chance to send my letter."

"Lex. It's okay. I completely under—"

"And I'm sorry I've been such a shitty daughter."

"Alexis—"

"And that I accidentally got you married to a shitty second husband."

"Alexis, shut it!" she finally snapped before holding me at arm's length. A smile spread across her face once I finally fell silent. "There is nothing to forgive, sweetheart. None of this is your fault."

"Are you sure?" I asked, eyeing her suspiciously. Because *I* definitely wasn't so sure.

"Yes, sweetheart, I'm sure." She sighed and released me from her hold. "Now tell me, have the princes been treating you well?"

I smiled at the thought of them and nodded. "The princes are amazing. All of them."

I scanned the group of women, pausing momentarily on

Ashlynn as we shared a meaningful look. So much had changed since my first meeting with them. The first time, I hated the princes and the queens were insisting that I give them a chance. This time, I was in love with all of them—excluding Crissen—and hoping the queens approved of me as a match for their sons.

"Please sit down," Caroline urged, waving us over to the small circular tables positioned in the middle of the blossoming garden. A sea of petals—pink, orange, and yellow—perfumed the air and accented the background, making it feel even fancier than it already was.

"How is your husband?" Caroline asked eagerly. "How is my Calvin?"

I smiled wide and felt my eyes crinkle with warmth. "He's doing wonderful, Caroline, I promise."

Her blue eyes grew misty, and she nodded joyfully.

"*All* of the princes are wonderful," I assured them. "We are... well rested from our trip to Eristan, and we'll be journeying to Wessea first thing in the morning."

Delilah raised a brow. "You mean Western Blackwood?"

Wessea was her kingdom, once upon a time. But since the Storm King took over, no one dared call it by its proper name. She was probably subtly warning me, telling me someone was listening nearby.

I chuckled lightly. "Yes, of course. Silly me. I'm so terrible at history and geography."

Delilah chuckled too. "Understandable, dear, considering the whirlwind this journey has been for you."

"That's very true." I brought my teacup up to my lips and whispered, "I was wondering if I might ask you all a question. About your sons."

Their eyes darted around like rabbits, hopping this way and that to avoid my gaze, and making contact with each other. I had no idea what they were expecting me to ask: are your sons the bastard children of the gods? I mean, yeah, maybe I should have asked that question, but that wasn't what I was going for. Not just yet.

I took a deep breath and let it out slowly. "I'm going to take that as a *yes*." I inhaled another breath, hoping it would calm the stinging of nerves in my hands and chest. "I wonder what your thoughts are on harems. Or, reverse harems, as Ben likes to call it."

"Harems?" Bibi asked curiously. "You mean, do we enjoy being part of a harem? The answer is, undoubtedly, yes. We love each other and need each other like the air we breathe and the water we drink. We rely and depend on each other for emotional and physical strength."

I shook my head. "That's not exactly what I meant, but I'm glad to hear that you approve of them, at least."

"You mean," Francesca began, "do we approve of the king taking a harem? Because the answer is, we approve of everything our husband does."

Francesca—F equals "first wife." She was the Storm King's original companion, a barren woman who never produced a child of her own. She had a grudge against me from the moment we met, and I had no idea why. Okay, fine, I had a feeling it had something to do with my mom being added to the harem, but still.

Delilah stared at me with cunning sea green eyes. Eyes like Dan's. Eyes that could somehow ferret out the truth when others seemed to be confused. "I don't think that's what Princess Alexis meant."

"Well, do enlighten us," Francesca drawled sarcastically.

"Reverse means opposite," Bibi began, beginning to puzzle it out. "So, if a harem is a group of women for one man, then a reverse harem means..."

Ashlynn spoke up first. "You want to be with all of them."

"Out of the question!" Francesca shouted, slamming her

teacup down on her saucer, chipping a triangular chuck off the bottom.

"Oh, please, Fran," my mother said with an eye roll. "You don't even have a stake in this."

"It doesn't matter," she said, thrusting her big nose into the air. "It's unheard of and inappropriate."

"If it's okay for a king," I began, feeling myself getting a bit heated, "then why not a queen?"

"You are not a queen," Francesca hissed vehemently.

"*Yet*." My voice was calm but lethal.

Everyone's eyes widened, but every mouth stayed shut. They were either stunned silent, or they dared not speak whatever thoughts were flitting about in their heads.

I swallowed hard and forced myself to continue talking. "I promised them that I would marry them all, and with or without your blessing, I am going to fulfill that promise. I'd just prefer to have it."

"Our husband will never approve," Delilah admitted nervously.

I simply shook my head. "I don't honestly care. I care about *my guys*—your sons. And I care about our kingdoms and uniting them—the right way."

"What you're talking about," Ashlynn whispered as she leaned forward, "is treason."

I leaned closer too. "Everyone knows the king is evil. What he does to you"—I glanced at each of them in turn—"is evil. He needs to be stopped. But we need a figurehead. Someone—or some *group*—to support instead of him. I think that your sons and I could be that group. But, when that time comes..."

I paused, questioning the sanity of this whole thing. This wasn't exactly how I imagined the conversation going. I pictured me having a lot more inspirational shit floating out of my mouth beforehand. But, whatever. It was here now, so...

"Will you back us? When we make our move to secure the crown and unite the kingdoms fairly and justly, will you take our side?"

"Never," Francesca hissed.

She stood and scraped her chair across the cobblestones, preparing to storm off.

"Just one second, Fran," Caroline said, waving her back with a curl of her fingers. "It's time we cleaned out our closets."

"And what's that supposed to mean?" she huffed, standing firm right where she was.

"It means, we're telling the truth," Caroline replied. "About everything."

Well, my interest is piqued.

Francesca looked scared for the first time ever. "You wouldn't dare. You promised."

Caroline nodded. "But the time has come. Zacharias is getting more violent by the day. Who knows how much longer we'll be around to tell the secret?"

Fran glanced at me. "I don't trust her."

"She doesn't trust you either," Mom said. "But still she came here, trying to help."

All was silent for a few heartbeats. No one moved or even blinked. Tension was thick as butter in the air, practically smothering me, but I knew better than to speak.

"The rumors you may or may not have heard," Caroline began, "about the origin of our sons' birth—"

"Caroline," Francesca warned under her breath.

But Caroline didn't heed her warning. "They're true. Our sons are the product of intense pleading to the gods to save our lives."

Forget etiquette. My fucking mouth fell right open.

"We prayed for help," Delilah continued. "We knew if we didn't fall pregnant, we'd be killed. We wanted out of the situation, obviously, but we didn't just want to die."

"Right," Bibi added, "because this man had just crushed our kingdoms, killed our husbands and children, and taken us hostage. We wanted more than a silent death. We wanted revenge."

"And so, miraculously," Ashlynn said with a small smile, "the gods heard our plea and took pity on us."

"Zeus, Poseidon, Hades, Demeter, Hera, and Hestia," Caroline said, naming them one by one, "all six original gods, showed up to help us."

I held up a hand to stop them as I tried to regain the function of my tongue and lips. "You mean to tell me... the Greek gods are, in fact, *real*? And that, they're the *parents* of your children?"

"I knew she couldn't be trusted," Francesca muttered.

"Oh, because she's hesitant?" Mom retorted defensively. "Because the truth is mildly insane and a little difficult to believe?"

"Peace, Katelynn," Ashlynn cooed, patting my mother's shoulder.

Caroline waited to make sure Mom, Francesca, and I were finished before continuing. "None of the deities had any sort of sexual contact with us. They simply touched our stomachs and magically put a baby in each of our wombs. Honest to gods, immaculate conception."

Wait. Each of them? I glanced at Francesca who refused to meet my gaze. She was supposed to be barren, unable to conceive children. But there were six wives and six deities who'd appeared... that couldn't have been a coincidence.

"Zeus blessed me with Calvin," Caroline said.

Delilah smiled. "And Poseidon blessed me with Daniel."

"Hades blessed me with Robert," Rosemary added.

Bibi giggled happily. "And Demeter blessed me with Benson."

I turned to the other two, waiting with bated breath.

"Hera blessed me with Asher," Ashlynn said. "She is a rather prideful goddess, though, so rather than giving him her complete power, she limited him to the ability to shift form and nothing more."

Then I turned to Francesca.

Moment of truth. Was there going to be *another* Storm that somehow freaking got added into our fucked-up group?

Francesca sighed and a tear slid down her cheek. "Hestia is a goddess of kindness and understanding." Her voice quivered as she spoke. "I was barren, so Zacharias was not expecting any children out of me, but she knew how much I wanted a child of my own. She blessed me with a baby too—one I didn't carry in my womb, but in my arms—a girl that I named Tia in her honor. I didn't dare give her the Storm surname, but instead, gave her my own: Everleigh.

"I wasn't able to keep her, though," Francesca said in a whisper. "Zacharias would have accused me of betraying him. He would have killed her. So, I sent her away with my most trusted handmaiden. I visited them in Blackhaven a few times before my handmaid and I decided it was simply too risky for her; my Tia would be safer if she never saw me again. As much as it killed me, I said goodbye to my only child. At least that way I knew she would be safe."

Against all odds, my heart ached for her. Though, I did take a moment to thank the gods that there wouldn't be *another* addition to our bond.

Tia Everleigh, a lost princess with the power of the gods. In other words, a potential ally in helping us bring the Storm King down. I had a feeling I'd need to find her. If not for her help, then at least on behalf of Francesca. I didn't owe the old bitch any favors, but I knew in my heart it was the right thing to do. They deserved to be reunited.

"Thank you for sharing the truth with me," I said, touching each of their hands as I smiled. "But my question still remains: will you back us when the time comes?"

One by one, the *yeses* filtered in, until all that was left was Mom and Fran.

"Of course I'll support you, baby girl," Mom said, wrapping me up in her arms.

Then, there was only one.

"Before you decide," I said, pulling out of Mom's hug and turning to Francesca. "I want you to know that I'm going to find Tia, and I'm going to make sure she knows you're her mother and that you love her. I'm going to bring her back."

More tears welled in Francesca's eyes and spilled down her cheeks. "It's unsafe for her."

"Not if the Storm King is gone." I smiled, assuring her.

She shook her head. "I can't make any promises. If you amass enough followers to win, then I'll join you. But if you don't get enough allies, or if Zacharias finds out your plan, I'll have no choice but to stay at his side."

That response was actually better than I was hoping for.

"Fair enough. I'll take it."

I finally relaxed enough to take a sip of my tea, only find myself interrupted by Rochelle.

"Excuse me, Your Highnesses," she said, bowing low, "but Miss Alexis has a history lesson with Professor Samson now."

"Of course, of course!" Caroline said, smiling wide and brushing me away with her hands. "It was lovely to see you again, dear."

Mom stood and pulled me into one last hug. "I don't know if I'll see you again before you leave," she whispered. "Just know that I love you."

I swear I heard: *I don't know if I'll ever see you again*. Period.

I squeezed my eyes shut and tightened my hold on our embrace, never wanting to let her go. "I love you too, Mom. Stay strong for me. I'm going to fix all this, I swear."

"I'll be praying for your safety." She kissed my hair and let me go.

I considered making some snide remark about how the gods didn't give a fuck. But now that I knew that they sometimes listened to prayers and that the guys were actually *demigods*, not just some remnant of an age-old bloodline—like what I'd inherited—it got me thinking.

If the king didn't have powers of his own, how the hell was he so much stronger than they were? And why couldn't they kill him?

CHAPTER 6

*A*s Professor Samson droned on and on about Eristan, Rubio, Valinor, and Werewood, I damn near died of boredom.

It made me think of an old Greek myth, the one where Hermes literally bored the guy covered in eyeballs to his death. I suddenly wondered if Samson was one of Hermes's descendants.

I forced my eyes to stay ajar and fought off a yawn. I'd just been asleep for half a month, how the hell could I possibly be so listless just by listening to his dull-ass voice?

"And that's how Valinor and Werewood successfully avoided the Sohsol Apocalypse," Professor Samson declared blandly.

I glanced up at the old man and noticed he looked seriously annoyed. His lips were set in a thin line, and his wrinkled eyes were narrowed. "Did you hear a single word I said this entire lecture, Princess Alexis?"

I turned to Criss and shot him an "I'm in trouble" expression.

Apparently, the Storm King felt it'd do his newest son

some good to have the same training as me. While we had different etiquette teachers, we shared the rest of our classes. Criss had taken notes on every word the old professor uttered, a look of concentration and eagerness on his handsome face.

Crissen chuckled and lifted his notebook. "Don't worry, Professor. I took notes. I'll make sure she studies with me."

Samson shook his head and muttered, "I don't get paid enough for this shit."

That earned a giggle from me. "I'm sorry, Professor. I've just had a lot on my mind since I woke up."

He took a deep breath and nodded. "Understandably so, Your Highness. Why don't you two cut out early? It's almost lunch time, anyway."

He didn't have to tell me twice. I was up and scurrying off before Crissen even completely registered his words. The newest prince had to jog to catch up to me.

"*Hades*, you're in a hurry," he commented. "Where are you going?"

I shrugged as I held up my skirts. "I don't know. The stables? I just didn't want to stay and get sucked into another gods-awful lecture. I'm not sure I could survive it."

"Are you always this dramatic?" he asked with a grin.

"No. I just hate history. It's so freaking boring."

A twinkle lit up his hazel eyes with mirth. "History is fascinating."

"I have a feeling you and Prince Benson would get along great."

He chuckled and rubbed his buzzed head. I wondered if he used to play with his longer hair a lot when he was nervous. "What's that supposed to mean?"

I shook my head. "Just that he enjoys stuff like that too."

"Boring stuff?"

"You said it, not me," I said, smiling wide.

"You seriously hate history that much?"

I glanced at him and decided to reply with sarcasm. "No way! It's my favorite class of all, even beating out *etiquette* and *magic training*."

His face paled a bit. "Don't remind me."

I raised a brow. "About the etiquette or the magic training?"

"The training." He shook his head. "How am I supposed to practice with something I don't have?"

"I wouldn't worry about it," I assured him. "I couldn't access any of my powers for the first few weeks, and no one thought I was faking it."

"Yeah, but I *am* kind of faking this whole thing, you know? I'm never going to be able to wield the healing magic everyone thinks I have."

I shrugged. "Then all you can do is survive the training for a day. We'll be gone by tomorrow, anyway, and it won't even matter."

He scratched his buzzed hair and sighed. "I suppose that's true."

"I like your haircut, by the way," I said, being honest.

I'd never been one to salivate over long locks on men. I preferred the well-kept look with the perfectly trimmed stubble. My princes had me so deliciously spoiled.

His cheeks flushed a gentle pink as his hand skimmed over the fuzz. "Yeah? Well, thank you. I appreciate the compliment."

"No problem."

There was silence for a moment as we rounded a corner and started down a smaller hallway toward one of the side doors.

"So..." Crissen began timidly, as if he were struggling to find things to talk about. "What do you think about this quest we have to go on? Or these dignitaries showing up this evening?"

I shot Criss a knowing glance and whispered, "I think we need to complete the quest as quickly as possible and that we need to impress the dignitaries as best we can. Pretend *we're* the ones making the allies, not the Storm King, because... we kind of are."

He lowered his voice even further. "What do you mean?"

"*I mean*, it's time somebody took a stand against my beloved father-in-law. And those somebodies are us."

"What?" he hissed. "Are you crazy? Do you want to get our mothers killed?"

I jabbed him in the ribs, and he sucked in a sharp breath.

"No, you idiot," I grumbled. "But we're *all* going to end up dead if he remains on the throne for much longer. Something has to be done, and we're the ones with the power to evoke change. We just need to make a stand and give the people something to get behind, something to believe in."

He pursed his lips and furrowed his brows. "When?"

"Not, like, *now*." I shook my head, realizing he must have thought I was in a damned hurry or something. "Maybe after we find the Eye of the Sea—whatever the hell that is. I don't know. I haven't even had a chance to talk to the guys about this yet. It's something I thought about in etiquette lessons."

He snickered. "*Of course* you'd be daydreaming about overthrowing a monarch instead of learning a proper curtsey."

I scoffed. "As if you know me. Besides, I had my daydreams *and* I still learned my curtsies, thank you very fucking much."

I didn't know why, but he was a lot like Cal in that way: he had no trouble bringing out the feisty side of me. It instantly made me think of Rob and how mean he'd been, though, which then made me feel guilty as hell for being rude.

I sighed. "I'm sorry, Criss. I didn't mean to tell you off just then."

He shrugged. "I didn't think you said anything wrong."

"Yeah, but you've been taking a lot of shit from the guys lately. You don't need it from me too. So, I apologize."

He shot me a lopsided grin that highlighted his dimpled chin and cheek. "I insist, there's nothing to forgive. I was actually having fun bantering with you."

"Oh. Well, good." I smiled. At least he wasn't overly sensitive.

"As for me not knowing you, though," he continued, striding beside me as we pushed through a side door and onto the lawn, "we should probably fix that. I mean, since we're stuck together, we should get to know one another. Right?"

"Right," I agreed. "But not *just* me. You need to get to know the guys too."

Criss groaned and somehow made it sound graceful, almost as if he'd been a prince all his life. "They hate me, Alexis. Getting to know them is going to be difficult and probably painful."

I couldn't help but chuckle. "I'll try to help keep them... open minded."

"That doesn't exactly sound promising."

It really didn't, but I wasn't entirely sure of how much help I could be. The princes' relationship with Crissen—whatever that entailed—had started long before I'd ever entered the picture. The antagonism between them had been going on for years, and I doubted there would be a quick and easy fix to it.

I sighed. "I'll be your friend, Criss, but you really need to befriend them first. If I start cozying up to you, they're going to get jealous and even more pissed off. They'll take that anger out on *you*, and it'll make things a hundred times worse."

He stayed silent as I spoke. Probably because, while he might not have liked the words coming out of my mouth, he also knew they were true.

"*But*," I said, raising my brows and hopefully his spirits, "if you befriend them first, then they'll feel like you're *one of the guys*, rather than a threat. They'll want to include you, rather than murder you."

His mouth fell open just before he chuckled. "Gods, you have a way with words, huh?"

I grinned. "That's why Ben calls me Lexicon."

I hiked my skirts even further to keep from tripping in the grass. I thought about taking my shoes off, but the fact that we were heading to the stables kept them firmly on my feet. I did *not* want to step in horse shit. I'd probably puke.

Crissen's eyes lowered to my feet and calves, and he swallowed hard before turning away.

I grinned. "What? Am I showing too much ankle for you?"

"Not nearly enough," he muttered under his breath.

"What was that?"

He cleared his throat and spoke up. "Nothing. By all means, show as much ankle as you like."

I just laughed and shook my head.

When we reached the stables, no other princes were there. It wasn't a big surprise, though, considering we were early for lunch. A few stable hands bustled about forking hay, bringing food and water to the steeds, organizing riding supplies, and so on.

A young man with blond curls was saddling my horse up in preparation for our luncheon. The sight of him made my stomach clench. The last time I was there, Gemma's stable boy crush, Tristan, had prepped my horse. Now, he too was gone.

49

Or at least, I assumed he was the one she'd been meeting up with that night. He wasn't at the barn or anywhere else, so I was fairly certain my assumption had been correct.

Caramel, my beautiful palomino with a tan coat and creamy white mane, was waiting patiently for me to approach. I stepped closer, running my palm up her pretty face as she stared at me. She didn't huff or puff, just soaked up my attention like a sponge.

I turned to Crissen. "Do you have a horse?"

"Yeah, the Storm King gave me one my second day at the palace. Back when I thought he was... Before I knew the atrocious things he does."

He moved to the stall directly to Caramel's left and patted the horse as its head poked through the slats of the gate. It was a rich chestnut color with a dark mane that had been tied into a tight row of bun-like knobs down its neck. It looked more like a war horse than a pet.

"What's his name?" I asked as I continued to stroke Caramel's silken coat.

Criss shrugged. "I didn't think a gift from the king deserved a name."

My heart grew heavy and sank a bit. "He can't help his involvement with the king any more than we can, Criss. You should give the poor thing a chance."

His hazel eyes bored into mine with sadness for a long moment before he turned back to his horse and stroked its muzzle. "All right. Chance it is then."

"Wait. That's what you're going to call him?"

"Sure. Why not?"

I smiled and leaned my forehead into Caramel's. "It's perfect."

"You better be talking about my ass, or we're going to have some issues," Dan called from just outside the barn.

I spun around and grinned at him as he approached. "I was talking about his horse's name. But your ass *is* pretty amazing."

Dan chuckled and kissed me when he reached us, slipping his wide hands around my hips. "*Pretty amazing* is not the same as *perfect*, Sexy Lexi."

"Okay, fine. It's perfect."

The emotions radiating off Crissen in that moment were a chaotic mess. Surprise, confusion, intrigue, excitement, uncertainty, jealousy...

I wasn't quite sure how I felt about that last one. I knew he had a bit of a crush on me, and while he was handsome and it was fun to joke around and tease him, I really hadn't thought about him romantically like that.

"So..." Criss began, eyeing us with a carefully neutral expression, "is Calvin okay with... this?"

Dan smirked. "No, this is our little secret."

I pushed Dan's chest and fought off a grin. "Of course Cal's okay with it. He might technically be my husband, but he's not the main man in my life. I'm equally committed to each of the brothers."

Criss tucked both lips in, and his gaze narrowed slightly. "So, you're... dating all four of them?"

I glanced at Dan, unsure of whether or not I should correct him. After all, I was actually dating all *five* of them. Ultimately, I decided to tell him about Ash. He was in the bond with us; he needed to know these things.

"All *five* of them," I said, allowing that to sink in.

Criss had grown up knowing he was the bastard son of the king. He'd met the princes before. I was certain he'd known about Asher and his untimely death.

"I'm not sure I know what you mean," Crissen said, unlatching the gate and leading his horse out of the stall.

"There are only four Storms, since Prince Asher died all those years ago. Unless... you're talking about *me*?"

Oh shit. I never imagined his mind would go *there*.

"Not a chance in Hades," Dan growled, just as I said, "I think you'd *know* if we were dating."

I took a deep breath and tried again, making sure to whisper in case any of the stable hands were actually spies of the Storm King. Both of the guys inadvertently leaned closer, and the three of us formed a small circle of sorts, our heads almost touching.

"Asher is *not* dead," I informed him. "He's a part of the blood bond too."

Crissen's eyes went wide just as a voice startled us.

"What's up with the huddle?" Cal asked as he silently wedged into an opening between Dan and me. Rob and Ben were right on his heels, and our circle quickly disbanded.

"Tell you at lunch," Dan replied, glancing around the barn.

I turned to look too and caught a servant, who'd been standing eerily still, quickly jolt back into action, shoveling a giant heap of hay into a cart.

We were being watched.

CHAPTER 7

SHER

MUSIC PUMPED HARD FROM EVERY CORNER OF THE ROOM.

Shadows surged and lights flashed, and between the bursts of illumination and darkness, I saw people drinking and dancing and kissing and grinding. If this was a party, it was better than any stuffy event I'd ever attended back in Blackwood.

I'd long ago lost track of Ares and Dion, but considering I only had a small hole in my shell to peer out of, it wasn't all that surprising. A number of people had wandered over to stare at my egg in wonder, gaping and poking and laughing in disbelief. Apparently, wherever the fuck we were, chimeras were a rarity there too.

This had gone on for hours, partying for a while, then prodding me in their free time. By the time the atmosphere had emptied out and mellowed down a bit, fewer and fewer people wandered over my way.

That's when I realized I'd damn near missed an excellent opportunity to bust the fuck out of here. I shook the sleepies out of my baby chimera eyes and told myself to stay focused. The next unsuspecting victim to poke my shell was going to be the asshole to break me out.

A half hour or so later, after my eyes were growing heavy once more, one of the guests reached a finger out and poked me.

"Holy shit," the guy sniggered. "You think it's actually alive in there?"

He was kind of ugly with a big nose and shaggy, curly hair. His pale skin was flushed a bright pink—probably from dancing. I couldn't imagine it'd be from anything as exciting as sex.

His female companion grinned and took her own turn poking me. "Ares said it's real."

She, on the other hand, was beautiful. Why'd the ugly guys always seem to get the hot girls?

Wait. Alexis was the hottest woman I'd ever laid eyes on. Did that mean I was actually ugly? Fuck...

"You believe him?" the guy asked her mockingly.

"Of course, I do. He's the fucking God of War. Why would he lie?"

The guy shrugged. "To spark tension and animosity amongst the guests?"

The girl rolled her eyes and turned away. "Whatever, dude."

And there it was: the tension and animosity. But he was still a cocky idiot who was dead fucking wrong about the status of my authenticity. I was most definitely real, although I had no doubt Ares was totally getting off on the bickering and arguing my presence had caused.

The guy reached out and tapped my shell again, as if

testing its legitimacy one last time before giving up the argument.

I figured that was as good a time as any to make my move.

As soon as his finger pushed me even slightly off balance, I ran into the inside of my shell and put my full, pathetic baby chimera weight into the shove. It tipped, further and further, the guy's eyes growing wider and wider as he realized the severity of what he'd done, and soon, I crashed to the floor. The egg split in two and my yolk oozed out onto the floor.

As quickly as I could, I called on my shifting magic and swirled myself into a cockroach, a swift little bug that could scurry away in lightning speed.

In a panic, the dude grabbed both halves of my shell and mashed it back together, setting it inconspicuously back on its stand. Sweat beaded along his brow, and his skin had paled. He glanced around nervously from side to side, making sure no one had seen what he'd done; then he took the girl's hand and tugged her away.

"You're right, babe. I think it was real."

"See?" she boasted with a smug grin, content to let him lead her away now that she'd won the argument. Apparently, she hadn't seen what he'd done. I, for one, wasn't going to stick around to see if anyone else saw.

I scurried under one of the leather sofas as fast as my many legs could carry me, which, gods almighty, was FAST. I was finally a creature that deserved Alexis's cute little nickname of "Speedy."

Gods, I missed her already. Had she and my brothers realized what I'd done? Were they pissed? Worried? Honestly, I hoped they were still passed out and that I could somehow find a way back before they even had a chance to be troubled.

I peered out from underneath the sofa and tried to find my bearings. Shit looked a lot different from so far beneath it all. Human legs were now taller than trees. The ground rumbled incessantly, like an earthquake—from footfalls, but also from the bass of the music.

When a path opened up between the sofa and the stairs, I made a run for it. I darted like the motherfucking wind, weaving between shoes until reaching the wall and scurrying sideways along the stairs. When I hit the top, I paused, hiding around the corner. The music was softer up here, and aside from a small line for the bathroom, it was pretty much empty.

I scampered along the wall and slipped into a bedroom.

I had to be strategic about my next move. I needed someone to kill me in order for me to return to human form and snoop around. There were so many people, I doubted anyone would pay me any mind. But I also needed to make sure that whoever killed me didn't stick around to watch me shift. It'd have to be a subconscious killing, sort of. At least, on their part. I could slip under a shoe easily, but then I'd die then and there, so it couldn't happen right in the middle of the hallway. It'd have to be somewhere sort of private and yet also in the way.

I crawled back out into the hallway and reassessed the bathroom line. I could sneak in there, hide behind the toilet until the person was finished, then just as they were about to leave, dart under their shoe. They'd be all grossed out for a second, but then carry on with their lives as if nothing ever happened. That'd give me a hot second to turn back into a man and lock the door shut while I figured out a plan. After all, I was going to be naked at the end of all this. If I'd been smarter, I'd have picked a slightly larger animal, like a squirrel or some shit, so that I could drag a pair of shorts or something in with me. But the likelihood of someone unknowingly squishing a fucking squirrel was much lower than a roach, so nakedness or not, I'd probably picked the right creature.

I waited until a *man* went in—I'm not a fucking sicko—and I followed my plan to a T. I waited in the shadows behind the toilet until it was time to move.

When he was finished peeing, he turned to the sink and washed his hands. He shut the faucet off, grabbed a paper towel, dried his hands, and threw it in the trash. He turned and grabbed the knob, and... I blazed over there like the terrifying little bastard I was. I swear my little legs kicked up a foot of dust behind me as I ran. I looked up, watching as his foot got closer and closer to the floor. I had about half a second to squeeze myself between there, or it'd be too late. Buzzing faster than a fucking hurricane, I jumped, diving to the spot where I knew they'd connect with a loud, squishy *splat*.

"What the—?"

The guy lifted his shoe, curling his lips in disgust as my nasty cockroach guts strung between his shoe and my dying carcass on the floor.

"Fucking nasty," he whispered to himself before shaking his head and exiting the room.

Poof! I called on my magic and shifted faster than I ever had before. I grabbed the knob and slammed the door shut, locking it quickly before anyone else could slip in.

I took a few huge gulps of air and looked at myself in the mirror. My feathery brown hair was even more disheveled than usual, and my cheeks were flushed slightly from all the running and panicking I'd been doing lately. My amber eyes were wide as adrenaline pumped through my veins.

I needed to think of something fast, and with such limited options, I guess there really was only one way out. I grabbed the roll of paper towels and wrapped it around my lower body. It was like a tight but flimsy skirt at first, but in order to make sure my junk stayed put, I also wrapped it around each individual leg. If I took too long of a stride, that shit was going to rip right down the middle, so I'd have to be careful.

With one last deep inhale, I unlocked the door and strolled out. For the time being, the line to the bathroom was empty. The whole hallway was empty. If I could make it into a bedroom, then I could probably find a pair of pants at least so I stopped looking so fucking conspicuous.

I shuffled forward, careful not to tear the material, when a voice suddenly stopped me.

"Hey, man, what the fuck?"

I swallowed hard and glanced over my shoulder.

Shit.

It was Dion.

CHAPTER 8

LEXIS

WHEN WE REACHED THE PICNIC GROUNDS IN THE MIDDLE OF
the forest, we tied our horses to a few nearby branches. I
scanned the woods, catching glimpses of some of the old,
crumbling statues of the gods, but nothing more.

Satisfied that we were alone, I turned away and strolled
over to the stone picnic table.

Cal and Ben spread out a checkered cloth and started
passing out food, while I wedged between them. Rob and
Dan sat on the other side, arguing about tattoos, while
Crissen just stood there awkwardly.

I felt so damn bad for him. Where did he fit in? Even *I*
didn't know, so how could *he*?

I pointed to an open seat beside Dan. Nodding, he silently
lowered himself onto the stone bench. Rob rolled his gray
eyes, while Dan merely ignored him.

When all the food had been passed out—mostly breads,

pastries, and fruits—and our goblets had been filled with wine, I took a deep gulp and told them about what I'd heard.

"Your mothers told me something interesting during tea today."

Ben grinned as he stole a roll off Rob's plate. "Oh yeah? And what's that?"

"That you're not brothers."

Fucking gods, I needed to work on my tact.

"Excuse me?" Cal asked, glancing from me to his *brothers*.

"I mean, you're brothers, but not by blood."

"Lexi," Dan said, folding his hands under his chin, "what the hell are you trying to say?"

I sucked down another gulp of wine, praying it'd give me liquid confidence. Where was that fae café when I needed it?

"They told me the truth of your heritage," I began, as Rob graciously refilled my glass. "And—"

"Zacharias isn't our father?" Ben asked. I wasn't sure it was even a question. We'd figured as much in previous conversations; it had just never been confirmed.

I shook my head. "Nope. You five are direct products of the gods. So, you all have different mothers and different... fathers—well, actually, some of you have two mothers. And if you still consider yourselves related on those terms, then you technically have a sister."

"*What?*" Rob shouted, springing from his seat with clenched fists.

My eyes widened, but all I could do was shrug.

Ben shook his head, as if trying to flip the puzzle pieces in his brain to a new angle. "Start from the beginning, please. What *exactly* did they say?"

I grabbed a roll from my plate and took a bite as I thought. "Your mothers didn't want the Storm King to kill them. They needed to stay alive in order to get revenge for what he did to them and their kingdoms. So they prayed to the gods for help."

Every single face went suddenly solemn and sad.

I chewed on my roll, but I couldn't even taste it. I swallowed and set the rest of it down on my plate. "The six original Olympians answered their call—Zeus, Poseidon, Hades, Hera, Demeter, and Hestia."

"And the sister?" Rob asked, clearly not getting off track.

"Francesca and Hestia made Tia, a girl who Fran's handmaiden quickly whisked away, never to be seen again. The Storm King would have killed her or used her like he's doing to me."

"I've always hated Francesca," Rob declared, crossing his arms and finally sitting back down. "This Tia girl doesn't count as a sister."

Ben's brows furrowed, and his lips twitched. It was like he'd tried to smile, but just couldn't. "Do we still count as brothers?" he asked, looking around the group. "Technically, we're not even related..."

"We're brothers," Dan decided immediately. "Blood isn't the only thing that binds people."

"And even if it were," I added, "you're bound by that too. Just not in the way it usually means."

Rob scoffed. "By that logic, even *Crissen* would technically be our brother."

I nodded. "Yes, that's true."

He merely shook his head. "No. Criss and Tia are not my siblings. These guys, though? The ones who've been with me my whole life, suffering beside me, loving me and caring for me? They're my true brothers. I don't give a fuck who our parents are or aren't."

This time Ben really did smile. "Agreed. There's no scientific evidence in the world that can convince me we're not truly brothers."

Cal smiled. "Storm brothers, forever and always."

"Forever and always," Dan agreed with a crooked smile.

I glanced at Crissen who looked even more forlorn than usual. No matter what he did, he just kept slipping further and further from the group. It hurt me way too much to see him like that. Maybe it was because I could literally feel his emotions on the air, soaking into my skin. Or maybe it was just human decency knocking me in the head, but either way, I couldn't let him get brushed aside like that.

"Listen, you guys," I began, unsure of how the hell to even proceed. "Criss is as much of a brother as any. He might not have grown up in the palace, but he's certainly paid his dues. He's been used and manipulated. His mother has been abused and tortured. He's been sucked into this blood bond against his own free will. He's kept us alive multiple times. And he's still here, trying to help even as you shut him out. We need to give him more of a chance."

My little speech was met with silence. Rob looked irritated, like he was fighting the urge to tell me off. Cal and Ben looked thoughtful, as if they were seriously considering my words. And Dan just looked regretful, like maybe he was sorry for treating him negatively before.

"And Tia," I said, trying to cut through the uncomfortable silence, "could make a strong ally in our war against the king."

"*War*?" Cal asked, immediately sucked back into the present conversation. "Who said anything about war?"

"I did." I said the words with a confidence that surprised even me. "I decided in etiquette class that we should start secretly amassing allies, and once our numbers are high enough, make a public stand against the king."

Cal's features were severe. "That's treason, Peach."

"Okay." My tone had an almost visible shrug in it. "If that's what it takes, then that's what it takes. We can't let him sit on the throne anymore. He's a psychotic terrorist. He's got to go."

"Why don't we focus on taking him out secretly and silently? Then just ascend to the throne without bringing the people into it?" Cal asked.

I sighed, already feeling a bit defeated. There was wisdom in his words. "You think we can? I mean, we can try it. But it can't hurt to gain some supporters in the meantime."

Ben scratched his chin. "Statistically, the likelihood of succeeding in such a way is minimal. Alexis is on a more successful track. Garnering allies is probably going to be our strongest option."

Cal glowered. "We have to at least try to solve this issue without mass violence."

"We already have, *Calvin*," Rob protested. "We've tried a few times, and every single one of those times ended in us nearly dying."

"Right," Cal agreed. "So what are the odds that normal, everyday peasants with no military training would be able to defeat him if we, children of the gods, can't defeat him?"

Why the fuck could they *not* defeat him?

"Look," I decided, forgoing my roll in favor of a bunch of red grapes. "We should still be making friends and allies, because one way or another, no matter what, we're going to be sitting on the throne as soon as possible. We need to know who our supporters are. Plus, if it does end up coming to war, we'll know for sure who we can count on to help."

"Lexi's right," Dan chipped in. "We should be prepared *just in case*."

Crissen raised a hand. "I agree."

Rob glared at him. "No one asked you, dipshit."

"Rob—" I protested on a sigh, but he cut me off.

"I'm gonna take a walk."

He grabbed a roll from his plate and an entire bottle of wine, then stormed away.

I knew better than to chase after him. When I needed space, they were respectful enough to give it to me. Clearly, he needed his space now, and I respected him enough to give it to him too.

Still, I couldn't help but feel guilty. I didn't want any of them to feel like I was taking Crissen's side over theirs—and if the slight tinge of betrayal on the air was anything to go by, then that's exactly how Rob felt. The thing was, I didn't want it to be *his* side or *theirs* with *me* in the middle. I wanted it to be *our* side, all of us on the same team.

"I'm sorry, Criss," Ben said, extending his hand across the stone table. "We've been dicks to you, and it's not right."

Criss cocked his head slightly, and a small smile crept onto his lips, a dimple forming in each cheek. He took Ben's hand and shook it, timidly at first, then with a bit more conviction.

"Thank you, Benson," he replied. "I appreciate that."

"Call me Ben," the Sand Prince replied with a warm smile.

Dan followed suit, holding out his own hand. "Sorry, Criss. Rob and I can be a bit... asshole-ish. I formally apologize for both of us. And you can call me Dan."

Criss shook his hand too. "Thanks, Dan."

And finally, Cal. He didn't seem to have any reservations, so him going last was clearly not due to any hesitation on his part. "Welcome to the group, Crissen."

He smiled and took Cal's hand. "Thanks, Calvin. Just call me Criss."

"All right, and you can call me Cal. Calvin is what our *father* calls me—and Alexis, when she's mad."

I chuckled and threw a grape at his head.

"That's enough of your sass, Calvin," I teased.

"See what I mean?" he asked Criss.

Criss chuckled and finally grabbed something to eat off his plate. I hadn't realized until that moment that'd he'd been too uncomfortable to even touch his food. It made me feel terrible, but also hopeful that we were finally making some progress.

"So, Asher is alive?" Criss asked, taking a polite bite of his roll. Honestly, I'd swear he was raised as a prince rather than a blacksmith. His manners and mannerisms reminded me so much of Cal.

"He was my pet sloth for six years," I informed him, taking a sip of my wine. "But I had no idea it was him."

"He kept trying to die." Dan chuckled, tossing a grape into the air and catching it in his mouth. "But she kept saving him. It's hilarious in hindsight."

"Death is the price of his magic," Ben explained. "He can turn into any animal, but in order to turn back to human form, his animal form has to die. Otherwise, he's stuck."

"Wait, so..." Criss's brows furrowed as a small smile lit up his face. "You kept a suicidal sloth as a pet for six years?"

I nodded, acknowledging how pathetic it sounded.

"Gods, that's kinda crazy." Criss took another bite of his roll and smiled as he chewed. "So where is he now?" When our smiles all fell, he swallowed quickly and backpedaled. "I'm sorry, did I ask something wrong? We don't have to talk about it if you don't want."

He glanced away, and I could tell he was mentally kicking himself for screwing up that moment of bonding. I could feel his regret on the air.

"It's okay, Criss," I said, drawing his gaze. "We don't know where he is."

"But he's alive," Ben said, "because he's a part of the bond. We'd feel it if he were dying."

Absently, Criss rubbed his chest, no doubt recalling the

last time we'd all survived a near-death experience. "Would we, though?"

My gaze narrowed, and my heart pumped faster. "Why wouldn't we?"

Criss shrugged. "I've felt the pain of the bond three times. Twice when you were at the Lunaley, and once when you were fighting the king. How many times did Ash die on that journey? Did any of you feel it?"

No one said a godsdamned word.

My heart was officially lodged in my throat, beating my windpipe like a criminal.

"If Ash's price for magic is death," Criss continued hesitantly, "then... I have a few theories."

Ben nodded to him. "Go on."

"*One*, Ash can never truly die, because death is an integral part of his rebirth and regeneration."

Ben put his fingers on his lips as his eyes narrowed in thought. "Okay, continue."

"*Two*, we'll never feel the pain of his death because that pain is strictly attached to him and his magic. Him dying is not the same as the close calls we've all had. It's different. A different sort of magic."

Cal sighed and scrubbed a hand across his face. "Is there a 'three'?"

I could tell he hoped there wasn't.

Criss nodded. "*Three*, because of the bond, or perhaps because of your genuine demigod statuses, the seven of us can never die. You five are immortal, and because of the bond, Alexis and I get to share in that power."

Well, that was... difficult to wrap my head around. Ash would survive no matter what, but we couldn't feel if he was hurt?

"The Storm King ordered us to get a chimera egg," Cal said, pulling the conversation back to Crissen's original question. "We did as he demanded, but when we found out chimeras emit an anti-magic poison, we knew we couldn't give it to him."

"Ash wanted to turn into an egg and spy on the king," Ben continued. "We told him no, that it was too risky."

"But, of course, he did it anyway," Dan said, shaking his head. "That little shit never did like listening to what he was told."

"And we have no idea where the Storm King took the egg," I finished. "All we can do is hope he finds his way back to us."

Hope and *plead* and *pray* that he's not being tortured.

Criss's brows squeezed tight with worry. "But what if he doesn't find his way back?"

I shook my head. Truth was, I'd thought a lot about that possibility since I woke up and realized Ash was gone. I just didn't know what the guys were thinking about the issue. Now that I knew Ash might be hurting, I was even more ready to take action.

"I'll personally go after him if he doesn't show up soon," I said.

All four sets of eyes locked onto mine.

"No way, Lexi," Dan argued, shaking his head.

"Not happening, Peach." Cal crossed his arms and stared at me.

"Sorry, Sailor," Ben sighed. "But they're right."

Criss smiled sadly. "I think it sounds a little too risky too. At least for you to do on your own. I mean, you have no idea where he is, right? He could be anywhere in the world."

"Or not even in *this* world," Ben pointed out. "Remember the archway?"

I nodded. The Lunaley was actually one of the first places I'd thought about searching. If I could figure out how to get inside that arch, then I had a feeling we could learn all sorts of important things.

"If Ash is in one of those archways," Ben said, "then he could be gone for years. We have no idea how time works in there."

Oh gods, he was right. My stomach plummeted straight to my toes. Once again, I lost my appetite.

Cal ran a hand through his golden hair. "Can we at least agree that no one should go looking for Ash without consulting the group? And that we should give him at least a couple months to figure it out on his own first?"

I didn't want to agree to those terms. The first part? Maybe. The second? No way. I needed Ash back *now*. I didn't want to wait months or years. I'd waited that long once before to be reunited with him, and it'd been awful.

But it wasn't like we didn't have other shit to do in the meantime. We had to find the Eye of the Sea in order to save our own people from senseless destruction. We needed to stop the war with Timberlune and Hydratica. We needed to overthrow a king…

I sighed but nodded. "We can give it a couple months. If he's not back by then, we'll have a chat and decide what to do."

Dan glanced at Crissen. "*Chats* are honesty talks. Cal can sense truths or lies—it's his second power."

"Wait, you guys have more than one power?"

Dan nodded.

Ben gave an overview of everyone's unique brand of magic. "Cal controls the sky, and his price is his strength. His second power is honesty. Dan controls the sea, and his price is his breath. His second power is charm. Rob controls spirits and the dead, and his price is pain. His second power is bravery. Alexis controls fire, and her price is—" He sighed, his tanned cheeks flushing a gentle pink.

"—desire. Her second power is empathy. And I control the sands and vegetation. My price is the loss of all five of my senses, and my second power is my word—it's magically binding."

That was a lot of information for anyone to take in, but I could tell Criss's curiosity was focused on *me*.

"Um," he began, sounding extremely hesitant, "desire? Like, greed?"

"No," Dan corrected him with a smirk. "Like *sexual* desire. Lust. Horniness. Sex and orgies. It's a blast."

"Daniel!" I shrieked indignantly. I mean, sure, he was right, but still. He didn't need to be so blunt about it.

"*Ooh!*" Cal taunted. "You just officially got the full name treatment."

Dan flipped him the bird and pulled me into his lap. "I'm sure Sexy Lexi didn't mean it."

Ben reached over and stole a roll off Dan's plate this time. "I'm sure she *did*."

Dan stuck his tongue out at his brother, and I giggled. "I see my childish tendencies are rubbing off on you."

"I'll give you something to rub off," Dan teased, nestling his nose into my neck and kissing above my pulse.

I wiggled from his grasp and sat back down in front of my plate, blushing like a schoolgirl for some stupid reason.

Thankfully Cal changed the subject. "So, any ideas on what this Eye of the Sea actually is?"

"A literal eye?" Dan suggested. "From a siren or some other aquatic creature?"

"Or metaphorical," Ben countered. "Perhaps it's not an eye at all, but rather a seer, an orb, or an important artifact?"

My smile drooped. "So, it's another wild goose chase."

Cal smiled softly. "Probably. But if it's anything like last time, then we'll understand more about what we need to do when we arrive in Hydratica."

Criss's eyes widened, and he quickly swallowed his bite of bread. "You're not seriously considering going there?"

Cal shrugged. "What choice do we have?"

"But we're at war with them right now," Criss protested. "Going into their kingdom would be suicide."

"Yes," Cal agreed. "But *not* going would be genocide, considering the king will kill hundreds of innocent citizens if we fail."

Criss sighed and rubbed the top of his buzzed head. "I guess you're right."

Dan gave our newest member a sympathetic smile. "You don't ever get used to it. The brutality and cruelty. It never gets easier."

I put my hand on Dan's shoulder. "That's why we're going to stop him."

Criss nodded solemnly. Pain radiated off him in waves, and I could tell he was still raw and hurting from his mother's torture.

Cal let out a sigh. "Lunchtime is over. Why don't you guys go on ahead? I'm going to find Rob."

My brows furrowed as I stood. "Are you sure you don't want help looking for him?"

"Nah," Cal said. "He wouldn't have gone far. Besides, the king will take it out on our mothers if we're late. May as well save as many of them as we can."

"All right," I conceded. "I guess we'll see you at dinner then."

I didn't want to leave either of them behind. And I especially didn't want to leave knowing Rob was upset. But I didn't know what else to do. That bad feeling, that sense of wrongness, kept creeping deeper and deeper into my chest and mind, eventually manifesting into two separate fears—one, fear for Rob in the woods; and two, fear that this dinner was going to go terribly amiss.

"It'll be okay, Sailor," Ben assured me, putting his arm around my shoulders. "They'll catch up in no time."

By the time we'd saddled up and the palace was back into sight, Cal and Rob had caught up to us and galloped by, leaving us in a literal plume of dust.

I chuckled and relaxed a bit as half the weight of my worries lifted right off my chest. At least one of my bad feelings had proven faulty.

Now, I just had to hope dinner turned out the same.

$\mathcal{M}$agic training passed by in the blink of an eye.

It was good to see Taron and Tamara again, to banter with them while they raked my ass through the coals—not as bad as they did Crissen, but still. By the time training was finished, I was a sweaty mess, but I felt good. I'd gotten much stronger since the last time we'd practiced. My stamina had built, my reflexes were sharper, and the power I packed behind each punch had grown exceptionally.

I was getting closer, step by step, to defeating that sadistic bastard once and for all.

Kill the king.

Rory, the magic user who'd given me his powers upon death, had clearly left an impact on me. His infamous last words tended to circle around my head in an infinite loop, urging me to finish what he could not.

I will, Rory. I'll kill the king.

After I'd bathed, scrubbing off the sweat and soreness from training, I dressed in an elegant purple gown with black lace crawling overtop and waited for Rochelle to do something with my hair.

"Beautiful choice of gown, Your Highness," she commented as she brushed my wavy brown locks into shining perfection.

"Thank you."

"Are you prepared to face the foreign dignitaries?" she asked, as if talking about such things were no big deal.

"Of course, I am," I bit out, angered at myself for not sounding kinder.

After that, she remained silent, moving from my hair onto my makeup while avoiding eye contact of any sort.

I hated how I felt about her. Mostly because I didn't *want* to hate her. It'd just sort of... happened. I knew it was wrong. I knew there was an explanation for it, and it wasn't a good one, and yet, I couldn't stop the antagonistic feelings from surfacing anyway. I hated her because she wasn't Gemma, and I hated me for hating her for no good reason. The hate just circled around and around like a cyclone, pissing me off more and more by the second.

It was so fucking complicated.

A half hour or so later, she sighed. "Finished."

As she moved to set the makeup aside, I grabbed her wrist and squeezed. I had to actually concentrate on loosening my grip as I took a deep breath and exhaled slowly.

"I'm sorry."

Rochelle looked nervous as hell. She glanced from her wrist to my face with doe-like terror. "Whatever for, Your Highness?"

Her voice shook, and more guilt flooded me.

Good. I deserved it.

"For treating you so poorly. I feel I owe you an explanation."

She shook her head quickly. "You do not owe me anything, Highness."

I rolled my eyes, and a small grin touched my lips. "I do. See, my handmaid before you was my best friend, and... she died. So..." I swallowed hard and fought the burning in my throat that signaled the incoming of tears. "It's not you, or anything you've done. It's me and my grief. I shouldn't be so gods-awful rude, but I just can't help it. I'm going to try harder, though. I just thought you deserved to know."

She slipped her wrist from my grasp, then took my hand in hers. "Thank you, Your Highness. I appreciate that more than you know. And I'm so sorry about your friend. I actually met Gemma a few times. She was an absolute delight."

My smile widened and tears swam in my vision. "She really was."

And for the first time since I met her, I felt like Rochelle and I were actually starting to bond.

She quickly grabbed a kerchief and dabbed at my eyes.

"Please don't cry. Your beautiful makeup will melt off, and we spent so much time on it."

I laughed and blinked a few times to ward off the tears. I even fanned my hands at my face, helping to dry them up. "There. All better."

She smiled and stepped back, folding her hands in front of her. "Anything else you need from me this evening, Your Highness?"

I shook my head. "No. Please just tell the princes that I'm ready for dinner."

She curtseyed and left my room, leaving the entryway ajar as she strolled down the hall.

I heard a knock and the soft click of a door opening.

"Yes?" a male voice said.

"Princess Alexis is ready, Your Highness."

"Thank you kindly, Rochelle." Cal. Of course she'd go straight to my husband first.

A moment later, Cal was leaning in my doorway, his mountainous form taking up every inch of available space.

His breath hitched as his blue eyes scanned my body. "You look... gorgeous, Peach."

I smiled and stood. "Thank you, you look pretty handsome yourself."

He glanced down and studied his simple black suit. "Thanks."

"I look handsome too," Dan called from out in the hallway, making me chuckle.

"I'm sure you do," I called back.

"What am I? Chopped liver?" Ben asked.

I rolled my eyes and grinned, striding past Cal to peek out into the hall. "You look extremely handsome as well, Ben."

Then my eyes locked on Rob, brooding and beautiful, seeming even more pained than usual. His plush lips were pursed, and his thick arms were crossed in front of him as he leaned against his bedroom door.

Gods he was alluring.

I didn't hesitate, just let that magnetism pull me down the hall and over to him. The scent of spice and cologne filled my lungs, making me dizzy with longing. He looked hesitant as I ran my hands up his chest and neck, but by the time my fingers raked through his dark hair, he was ready for me. He wrapped his arms around my waist and pulled me into his room right before our lips touched—away from prying eyes.

Not that either of us cared if the guys saw us, because we didn't. It was the Storm King and his nasty spies that we had to be careful of.

I parted my lips against his, and his tongue immediately slipped into my mouth, caressing mine with a gentleness I

ELLE MIDDAUGH

wasn't used to from him. It was strange, and it worried me, so I did the only thing I could think of—I bit his bottom lip.

The next thing I knew, he spun me around and shoved my back against his bedroom wall. His chest pressed hard into my breasts, his mouth hot and heavy on mine, and his tongue driving me mad with need. *This*. This was the Rob I knew and loved.

"I'm so sorry," I whispered against his lips. "I didn't mean to upset you earlier."

"Shut up and kiss me, Jewels."

I did, pouring all my love, fear, worry, and passion into the dance of our tongues.

"We're going to have to talk about this eventually," I pressed, before kissing him again.

"*Eventually* isn't *now* or anytime soon," he argued. His palms skimmed my body as we drank each other in.

"Yeah, well," Cal butted in from out in the hallway, breaking us from our moment, "it's dinnertime, and if we're late..."

He didn't have to finish that sentence. We all knew the consequences of anything and everything we did—pain and torture and guilt. *Always*.

Sighing heavily, Rob released me and we exited his room without touching.

No one said anything about our moment. No one teased us or cracked any jokes. Perhaps everyone knew there was something up with our Spirit Prince and no one wanted to upset him any further, at least until we got to the bottom of whatever the hell the problem was. Obviously, it had something to do with Crissen, but *what*, I couldn't say.

By the time our group reached the bottom of the stairs, the Storm King was there, not waiting for us in the dining room like he normally would have been. He stood in the hall, surrounded by three foreign dignitaries, smiling like a normal fucking person instead of the deranged bastard he was.

His sly eyes slid onto us, and a fire lit behind their blue depths. "Ah, there they are now! My sons and the lovely princess."

Cal had to drag me down the hall because I was pretty sure my feet weren't moving.

The foreigners turned around, eyeing us curiously with sparkling eyes and cunning smiles.

The first was a man with salt-and-pepper hair, deep brown eyes, and smooth brown skin. He was dressed in a pair of black harem pants and an elaborate red and gold vest with no shirt underneath. I didn't recognize his face, but I had no doubt he was from Eristan.

Next was a woman with long black hair and tanned skin that was covered in tribal tattoos. She had a smooth cork of wood protruding from her bottom lip and both of her earlobes. Everywhere else, she was pierced with golden circlets. Her dress was long and metallic, formfitting but protective, and she carried a spear. She looked like a total badass.

And finally, another woman, tall, thin, and blonde with yellow eyes that slanted up at the sides and crackled like fire. There was a wildness to her vibe and expression that I couldn't quite put my finger on, even more so than the tribal woman. And she was dressed in tight black leather—a top that could pass for a bra, a tight skirt that barely reached midthigh, and knee-high boots that probably took her twenty minutes to lace up.

The Storm King stepped in front of them and gestured to us one by one. "Prince Calvin and his lovely wife, Princess Alexis, Lord and Lady of Nightshade Castle in Northern Blackwood."

Cal bowed, dragging me down with him, then quickly sidestepped us out of the way.

"Prince Daniel," the Storm King continued, "Lord of Ebony Chateau in Western Blackwood. Akiko, I believe you've met."

The tribal lady nodded, but her expression remained stoic and unreadable.

Dan bowed to them all with a charming grin, one that incidentally drew a responding smile from the wild leather lady.

On instinct, I made to take a step closer to Dan, but Cal held me back.

"Not now, Peach," he whispered, and a thunderous frown rolled across my features like a sky storm.

"Prince Benson, Lord of Obsidian Palace in Eastern Blackwood. Rasheem, you remember my youngest son?"

Rasheem smiled, and his eyes lit with warmth. "Youngest by, what, a week?" he teased with a chuckle, then nodded his agreement. "Of course, I remember Prince Benson. Our own King Solomon has taken quite a liking to him."

I nearly scoffed. Oh, Solomon liked him all right. Liked him enough to unite him with his daughter, Princess Camilla. But fuck that. It wasn't going to happen, war or not. I'd make sure of it.

"Prince Robert," the Storm King said, continuing his introductions. "Lord of Onyx Fortress in Southern Blackwood."

The wild leather lady spoke up. "My cousin's father is from Southern Blackwood."

Rob raised a brow. "Oh yeah? I was under the impression that cats didn't usually mate with inferior species."

"They don't," she replied curtly. "But fire is addictive, Prince Robert."

"Ah, so your uncle was a demon?"

"Uncle-*in-law*, yes."

He grinned. "Always have to make the distinction."

I couldn't imagine anything about a demon being addictive, at least, not based off the one's I'd met. But to each his own, I supposed.

The Storm King cleared his throat and gestured to his newest son. "And finally, Prince Crissen, Lord of the Lunaley."

I almost choked. "*The Lunaley?*"

When the hell had that happened?

The king's hard blue eyes landed on mine with malice. "Yes, Princess Alexis, the Lunaley. Part of the Treaty O' Ley being back in effect means that the fae and harpies have each given up their claim to the land in order to keep the peace. Blackwood has once again resumed government and ownership." He took a moment to chuckle at my expense. "Honestly, has Professor Samson taught you nothing during your time here?"

The dignitaries all laughed politely at his little joke, while *I* fumed.

He knew I couldn't have heard about Crissen's new title —I was in Eristan when the newest Storm had been crowned and then forcefully kept in a coma up until now. Clearly, he just wanted to make me look stupid. The fucking prick.

Then the king got back to business. "Children, please allow me to introduce you to our guests. This is Rasheem of Eristan, advisor to King Solomon."

Rasheem bowed with a genuine smile.

"Akiko of Rubio, captain of Queen Kiami's army." She nodded at us as the king continued. "Rubio is an island chain that swings all the way between the coasts of Western Blackwood and Eastern Hydratica."

In other words, a very important ally.

"And Princess Veda of Valinor, youngest of Queen Veronica's seven children."

She didn't curtsey or bow. I raised a brow, intrigued by her defiance. But she just stood there and crossed her arms. "Valinorians bow to no one," she said in a guttural accent.

I pursed my lips. "I thought it was Rubians who refused to bow?"

"Valinor will not bow, either," she insisted with a sneer in my direction.

The Storm King's eyes narrowed for a moment, but he recovered quickly, ignoring our mini conversation completely. "Prince Rafe from Werewood will be joining us shortly, as well."

Dan and Rob groaned, drawing a smile from me as the Storm King led us all into the dining room.

"Who's he?" I asked Cal.

Cal smirked good humoredly and shook his head. "Trouble."

The long table was set for eleven, and instead of seating ourselves beside the king at the head, Cal led us to the other side and took the opposite end, positioning me to his right. Rob and Dan each flanked the king, while Ben and Crissen sat in the very middle, across the table from one another.

Akiko sank silently between Rob and Ben, and Veda squeezed between Dan and Crissen, looking rather smug. Her self-satisfied smirk was enough to set my teeth on edge. Rasheem sat to Cal's left, directly across from me, which meant that whenever Rafe decided to show up, he'd be stuck sitting by one of us.

I reluctantly tore my steely gaze off Veda and glanced curiously at Cal. This was a seating arrangement I'd never seen before. I had to wonder if it'd been rehearsed.

"It's a power play," Cal whispered to me as he leaned in

STORM CHASER

and handed me my napkin. Then he took my hand and placed a gentle kiss on my skin. "Stop worrying about Dan."

I chuckled airily. For all intents and purposes, we looked like newlyweds still hopelessly in love, sharing in a private joke.

"Please," I whispered back, rolling my eyes. "I'm not worried in the slightest."

Cal's grin remained. "Lie."

It was seriously hard to resist sticking my tongue out at him. "Fuck you, Cal."

"Maybe later, babe."

Rasheem, who sat on Cal's left, folded his hands under his chin and smiled at us. "Congratulations on your union, you two. I see it was a perfect match."

I smiled, feeling my cheeks flush slightly, but from further down across the table, I saw Dan's jaw tick. Rob's and Ben's expressions were not any happier.

"Thank you, advisor," Cal replied politely for the both of us, squeezing my hand before letting my fingers go. Clearly, he'd picked up on his brothers' tension as well.

A line of servants entered carrying trays of food—meats, beans, steamed vegetables, breads, cheeses, and gravies. Once they deposited the food, they quickly scurried off, and after the Storm King took the first bite, the rest of us commenced.

Apparently, we didn't fear tainted food in the presence of potential allies. Surely, even Zacharias wasn't *that* stupid.

"Any plans for children on the horizon?" Rasheem asked me pleasantly, pulling a roll apart and taking a bite.

But it was the Storm King who answered. "Absolutely, advisor. They can hardly wait. *I*, for one, am incredibly anxious to see the Storm dynasty thrive."

"No doubt you are, Your Majesty," Rasheem replied easily.

"What about your other sons?" Veda asked, staring pointedly at Dan.

"Yes, Majesty," Rasheem agreed excitedly, "what about them?"

I knew he'd be trying to play matchmaker between Ben and Camilla, which was just fucking... *great*.

The Storm King leaned back in his tall chair and smiled. "I am open to propositions, but I cannot guarantee that I'll accept. We're here to talk war, after all, not happily ever afters."

Pshh. As if anyone who married a Blackwood royal would get a happily ever after.

Not that I had any intentions of letting a single foreign finger touch any of my Storms. Not even Crissen, who technically wasn't mine, but who was still stuck with us anyway, thanks to the blood bond. That poor guy was either going to have to integrate himself into the group or get used to a loving relationship with his hand. Our friendly, omnipotent lightning bolt would make sure of *that*.

I broke open a roll and dunked it in gravy. Here's to hoping I didn't ruin yet another gown.

"Well, I have a proposal," Rasheem said. "I propose a union between Princess Camilla and Prince Benson. And if not Benson, then Prince Robert would do nicely as well."

No surprise there. I shoved the roll into my mouth and rolled my eyes.

"And I propose one between myself and Prince Daniel," Veda announced.

No surprise there either, though I was a bit taken aback by her straightforwardness.

The Storm King smiled humorously. "Any other proposals?"

"Well, since we're on the topic," Akiko began staring seriously at the king. "Queen Kiami has a daughter that will be coming of age soon—Nalini. It would make strategic sense to unite her with Prince Daniel, considering he rules the Ebony

Coast." She shot a dismissive glance at Veda. "The cat shifter can stake her claim on a different heir. Prince Robert, perhaps. Since they already share citizens, it would be prudent to assume they could share rulership as well."

The Storm King nodded approvingly. He seemed to appreciate her no-nonsense air.

I didn't appreciate it in the slightest. Brows furrowed, I tore off another chunk of bread and chewed it with gritted teeth.

Princess Veda, however, was already set in her decision. "I will not choose a different heir. I suggest finding Princess Nalini a new suitor, instead. Perhaps the recently crowned Prince Crissen?" She turned to where he sat on her right side. "He's handsome and strong, and he seems to have a gentle spirit. He would make a fine husband for your princess."

Criss, who'd paused halfway to bringing a bite of steak up to his mouth, looked utterly terrified at the prospect of being auctioned off to a girl he'd never met. It might've made me chuckle if the feeling hadn't hit so close to home for me as well. Before marrying Cal, the very thought of the word marriage would've sent my blood running cold.

Before Akiko and Veda could argue further, the doors of the dining room burst open and another man strolled in. He was broad, bearded, and stacked with muscle. He wore a tattered cutoff shirt and formfitting pants.

"Is no one going to propose to me?" he asked with a wide, sarcastic smile. "I'm incredibly available."

His eyes scanned the table, and when his gaze landed on mine, he instantly started walking toward me.

"Don't even think about it, Rafe," Rob growled, gripping the table with white knuckles.

The newcomer's eyes practically sparkled with mischief as he took the seat beside me. "Oh, I'm thinking about it."

"She's taken," Ben threatened from between Rob and Rafe.

The man turned around in his chair and hung an elbow over the seat's back. "By *you*?"

"By *me*," Cal warned, keeping his voice even yet lethal.

Rafe spun back around and shook his shaggy head. "That's a shame, that is." Then he eyed Veda from across the table. "I don't suppose you're single and ready to mingle?"

A half smile tugged at her lips. "I might reconsider on your behalf."

Rafe waggled his brows devilishly.

"Since when do cats and dogs get along?" Rob wondered aloud.

The Storm King sighed, drawing everyone's attention once more. "Prince Rafe, I trust your journey here was a smooth one?"

"What gave it away?" Rafe asked with a grin. "The torn shirt?"

The Storm King cocked a brow. "I was under the impression that werewolves always dressed in rags."

Rafe chuckled. "I'm surprised you don't already have allies. You're so fucking tactful."

That he was.

I took another bite of my roll along with a cube of cheese and tried to hide a grin.

Cal leaned over and whispered, "Don't get any ideas. We're not adding him to the group."

I cut him a glare and hissed back, "I'm allowed to think someone is funny without also wanting to fuck them, *Calvin Storm*."

Cal raised a brow but grinned. "Why are you so feisty all of a sudden?"

I raised a brow right back. "Because you're being a presumptuous, bossy asshole right now."

"I have half a mind to show you just how bossy I can be."

The Storm King sighed loudly. "Something to share with the group, you two?"

"No, Father," Cal replied.

I smirked. "Calvin and I were just wondering if any of these kingdoms have needs beyond the *sexual* that might be filled by something other than a dick. Perhaps aid of some sort? Or coin?"

I shrugged nonchalantly, but I felt like a total badass for saying that shit out loud.

The Storm King glared daggers at me.

Well, good, you ugly bastard. That's what you get for making me look like a dumbass earlier.

Rasheem cleared his throat but didn't say a word.

Prince Rafe chuckled and grabbed a random goblet from the table, chugging its contents until the whole thing was empty. "I like this girl. Are you sure she's taken?"

"Quite," Cal insisted.

Rafe grinned devilishly. "Well, Werewood has a need that no dick can fill..."

"If you say a need for pussy..." Rob growled, allowing the vulgar threat to hang in the air.

But Rafe merely chuckled. "Get your head out of the gutter, Storm. I was talking about alcohol—beer, specifically, but I suppose any kind will do in a pinch."

I raised a brow. "Werewood would accept *beer* in exchange for an alliance with Blackwood?"

"Amongst other things..." Rafe shrugged. "I mean, why the hell not? Drinking and fighting are what werewolves do best. Why not kill two birds with one stone—no offense to the half-harpy in the room—and do them both at the same time?"

"We'll consider it," the Storm King said with a sneer.

Rafe shot him a scathing look. "I wasn't talking to you, Your Royal Dickheadedness. I was talking to *her*."

The Storm King's glare intensified until dark slits were all that was left of his eyes. "You would make a deal with an ex-peasant over a king?"

Rafe graced him with a lopsided smile before nodding. "I would."

"*Get out*," the king shouted, pointing stiffly at the door. "There will be no alliance of any sort with you or your band of mutts. Go beg for bones somewhere else."

Rafe chuckled, grabbing yet another goblet and downing it before standing up and strolling toward the door. "If I recall correctly, Your Majesty, it's *you* who's begging for allies, not *me*. But even mutts have standards."

With that, he sauntered off, slamming one of the heavy double doors as he went.

The Storm King ground his teeth and rubbed his temples. "Anyone else have any requests?"

Veda spoke up. "Valinor could use some help with our volcano situation."

King Zacharias raised a brow. "And what would you propose we do? It's a godsdamned *volcano*. We can't just knock it down or plug it up."

Veda's already stoic expression hardened; then she pointed at me. "She controls fire. Send her to Valinor and let her see what she can do."

"Out of the question," the Storm King said, leaning over the table. "*She* is the future of the Storm dynasty. She will not become a sacrificial offering to Valinor's torrid volcano. At least, not until she bears an heir."

I smiled mockingly. *Yes, as soon as I pop out a kid, by all means, toss me in!*

"Any other requests?" the king growled.

"Metal," Akiko said, speaking up. "Gold, iron, silver, steel, whatever you have."

The king's eyes narrowed. "How much?"

"All of it," she said with zero emotion.

"No." The Storm King leaned back in his chair and tapped his fingertips together. "I'll give Rubio twenty-five percent of any metal ore Blackwood mines."

She shook her head. "Not ore. Finished, smelted metal. And not twenty-five percent. Seventy-five."

He glowered in her general direction. "Twenty-five percent of our finished metal and that's final."

She shrugged. "Then we do not have a deal."

"How about this?" he growled, standing from his chair to hover menacingly above his guests. "You join Blackwood in the war against Timberlune and Hydratica, or I will rain down every ounce of artillery I have on all of your kingdoms until not even a crow is left flying!"

Veda stood and met his gaze across the table. "You will not threaten Valinor. My time here is finished."

"Then your kingdom will be the first to go," he whispered darkly.

She paused, considering his words carefully, before her jaw ticked. "If you reconsider my offer to wed Prince Daniel, or our request for Princess Alexis's help, then send Queen Valla a letter. If not..." she squared her shoulders, "then you'll have another war on your hands."

As she marched off, the Storm King pinned Akiko and Rasheem with an intense stare. "Choose your next words very carefully."

Akiko stood. "I will need to consult with Queen Narina. She will send a letter with her reply."

"Tell her to be quick about it," the king threatened. "I'm an impatient man."

She nodded her understanding, then left.

The Storm King sighed and turned to Rasheem. "And Eristan?"

Rasheem smiled, but no mirth touched his eyes. "Blackwood has already done much for King Solomon. His only request is a betrothal between his daughter, Princess Camilla, and one of your sons."

"Done," the Storm King said, pushing away from the table and stomping toward the door. "She can wed Prince Crissen, Lord of the Lunaley."

Crissen's eyes went wide, but he somehow managed to keep from gaping. Even still, I could feel his panic from across the table.

Rasheem hesitated. "Majesty, I should have been more specific. King Solomon requests either Prince Benson or Prince Robert to be wed to his daughter."

The king looked utterly irate. His eyes practically glowed with the fire burning in their depths, and his fisted knuckles were white as bone. "I will consider his request."

Rasheem nodded, bowed deeply, then strode out the door.

Then Zacharias turned his fiery glare on us. "Get out of my sight."

He didn't have to tell us twice.

We were gone faster than a lightning bolt could strike.

CHAPTER 10

"**A**re there any special temples located nearby?" I asked the guys, pushing through a side door into the cool night air. The sky was an inky black with hardly any stars and only a sliver of a moon, and a crisp breeze blew through the trees, colder than I was used to. Winter was getting closer.

I turned around in time to see Cal and Ben sharing a curious glance.

"There's the temple of Hera located not too far away," Cal replied, clearly intrigued but not wanting to be brash and ask me outright.

"And are there any priests available after dark?"

"Priests?" Cal asked, allowing the full force of his curiosity to show.

"I'm getting married tonight," I said matter-of-factly. "You heard the Eristani dignitary. They want Ben or Rob for their precious 'desert flower'. And the Valinor chick wants Dan. The Storm King is desperate for allies. He will agree to the terms, and our bond will be destroyed. I can't allow that to happen. I love you *all*, and I won't risk losing any of you."

Cal was silent for a moment. "Not even to save your country and win a war?"

I gave him a flat look. "You know the answer to that, Cal. Did I give you up in order to prevent war with Timberlune? No. There's no point winning a battle on the back of a lie. If we win, it better be because we were honest and true and smart and strong. Not because we deceived someone into helping us."

Fingers slipped into mine. I glanced down and followed the tanned arm up to Ben's gorgeous face. Love and adoration shone bright in his warm brown eyes as he gazed at me. "I'd be honored to marry you, Sailor."

Then Rob strode up to my right and nudged my shoulder with his crossed arms. "I suppose I could marry you. If you insist."

I chuckled and smacked his burly arm. "Of course, I insist."

Then I turned to Dan who looked pale, even in the moonlight. "Are you okay?"

He nodded.

"If you don't want to do it," I said, backpedaling quickly, "then I'd never make you. I just thought—"

"No, I want to. I'm good."

Cal cocked his head. "That's a half truth, Dan. What's going on?"

My stomach instantly plummeted to the ground beneath my feet, and I felt sick. My flirtatious Sea Prince... didn't want to marry me? Blood pounded through my veins like miners through a cave, and all of a sudden, I felt dizzy. He didn't want me?

My throat was tight and hot, and tears threatened to spill from my eyes. "I'm so sorry. I must've read this situation all wrong."

"No, Lexi, it's not like that," Dan protested, bridging the gap between us in a couple swift strides.

I couldn't help it; when his arms wrapped around me, I silently cried into his warm chest.

"I want to marry you, baby girl," he muttered into my dark hair as he squeezed me tightly. "I'm just scared. Remember how I told you I was afraid of being a shitty boyfriend?"

I sniffed and nodded but didn't dare risk talking. My vocal cords might snap under the strain.

"The same thing goes for being a shitty husband," he said, stroking my hair as he spoke. "I don't want to suck at this, and because of that, I feel like I'm not ready. How the hell am I supposed to prepare for something as serious as this?"

"He's telling the truth, Peach," Cal confirmed from somewhere beyond us.

It was a damn good thing I could feel the love and worry radiating off Dan's skin, or I might've been tempted to not believe him, no matter what Cal said.

"Is this because of Sofia?" I asked, pulling away as I asked the question. I couldn't bear to be hugging him when he answered, just in case he said yes.

Still, he reached out and took my hands. "Am I hesitant about marrying you because I'm still in love with her?"

I nodded, allowing my eyelids to drop closed and the tears to stream freely.

"No. I love *you*, Alexis. I swear it." He pulled me back into his arms and hugged me tightly. "My relationship with Sofia —specifically the way it ended—really fucked me up, though. It's the reason I'm hesitant or doubtful about a lot of things, but you have my whole heart. I promise you that."

"Truth," I heard Cal declare, and I took a deep breath, allowing it to wash away the pain of feeling unwanted.

"I'm sorry," I said, sniffling and wiping my eyes. "I shouldn't have just assumed you'd be okay with it."

"It's fine, Lexi. I *am* okay with it."

I shook my head. "But you're not. You need some more time, and that's totally okay. I'll marry Ben and Rob tonight and wait for you until you're ready."

"No, I'm marrying you tonight too, no matter how scared I am, because I fucking love you."

Rob came over and put one arm around Dan and one arm around me, hugging us both fiercely. Ben did the same, from the other side, and the four of us clung to each other, drawing strength and courage from one another.

We stayed like that for a while, allowing love to lift us above and beyond anything that would get in our way. It was an incredible feeling, almost spiritual and definitely intoxicating. The tears from a moment ago fled like a shadow from the sun, and all I could feel was the warmth and strength of our bond and commitment. I was happier than the crescent moon smiling up in the sky.

"So, about that priest..." Ben said, teasing, yet encouraging Cal to answer the original question.

We all laughed, and the four of us broke apart, turning to Cal and Criss who were smiling proudly, as if they were pleased with us for banding together and figuring this out on our own.

The Sky Prince blew out a breath and ran his hand through his blond hair. "There's one in Blackhaven. But that's quite a walk."

"Is there one here at the palace?" I asked.

"Yes," Cal replied, "but he's one of the Storm King's lackeys. He's eating coin right out of the king's hands."

I shrugged. "I don't care if he runs and tells the king what I've done. Hell, that's half the point. I want the king to know that these men are mine. That they're not playing pieces he can use and abuse."

Cal grinned and slowly shook his head. "All right, then. Let's round him up. I'm assuming you want the ceremony to be intimate and held at the temple of Hera?"

I smiled and nodded, pulling Ben, Rob, and Dan in closer to me. "If that's the closest one, yes."

"Well, if you're using the palace priest," Criss said, drawing our attention, "why not just use the palace temple? It's a hell of a lot closer than the temple of Hera, and that way we won't be freezing our asses off in the cold tonight. Plus, it's a lot closer to your beds for the honeymoon."

Rob cocked an arrogant brow. "You sound like you're invited to the ceremony."

Criss's brow furrowed. "Am I not? I thought since—"

"Of course you're invited to the ceremony," I interrupted, jabbing Rob in the ribs.

"Yeah, well," Rob conceded in a growl, "just as long as he's not invited to the *consummation*."

But I refused to let our newest Storm be excluded anymore.

I ran my palms up Rob's chest and smiled. "I don't see why he can't... watch."

Dan groaned and bit his bottom lip. Clearly, he was up for a little show.

"That wouldn't bother you?" Cal asked me tentatively.

I shook my head. "There's a difference between exhibitionism and *forced* exhibitionism. Just like there's a difference between sex and forced sex. Or labor and forced labor. *Force*, being the keyword. As long as we're not forced to do it, and he's not forced to watch, then I don't have a problem with it whatsoever."

"What do you say, Criss?" Dan asked, grinning cheekily. "You up for a little voyeurism?"

To my surprise, neither Rob nor Criss argued. Honestly, I kind of figured Rob would be adamantly against it and that Criss would be too shy to agree. These guys never ceased to amaze me.

"Then it's settled," Cal declared. "I'll be a voyeur tonight too, since it's not my wedding this time. Are we holding the ceremony here or at the Temple of Hera?"

I pursed my lips. "The temple. I don't want another marriage in that fortress of pain. Besides, I can control fire. I'll make sure the temple stays nice and toasty for us."

Their gazes darkened as they realized just how true that statement was. After all, if I used my fire, there was going to be a flood of horniness and desire to follow.

"All right," Cal said with a knowing grin. "I'll find a servant and send for the priest."

AN HOUR OR SO LATER, WE STOOD BEFORE THE TEMPLE OF Hera.

It was a long, white, open-air structure that was lined on three sides with columns. The fourth side was a solid stone wall with an altar at the back, a smooth statue of Hera carved into the wall above it. She was decently intact too, with only a small chunk of her nose and her left hand missing.

Rob, Ben, and Dan each stood to the left of the altar with their hands folded in front of them, while I stood on the right clutching a bouquet of roses. The priest stood on a stool behind the altar, and Cal and Criss sat on a stone bench before us smiling like crazy. It was strange how contagious happiness could be. Our joy infected them, even though there were merely watching, and their smiles made us smile even wider.

I glanced down at the lacy white gown I wore, which was

mostly transparent and breezy as fuck. When Cal went to find the servant and the priest, he'd apparently taken a detour, grabbing me a white dress from the palace seamstress. She'd insisted that the gown wasn't finished, that the lace hadn't yet been attached to the silken underlayer, but Cal didn't seem to give a shit. Seeing how I looked in it, I now understood why—I was hot as Hades, like a fallen angel about to burn for her sins, and I'd never felt so sexy.

The Storm King's priest, a tall and thin man with a nose too large for his face, looked pissed to have been dragged out into the woods in the middle of the night to perform a ceremony that would no doubt get him in trouble, but as long as the marriage went through, that's all that mattered to me.

The priest sighed. "Is there any amongst you who would oppose this unorthodox union?"

"Nope," Cal said easily.

"Definitely not," Criss agreed.

"Of course not," the dickbag muttered, rolling his beady little eyes before opening a booklet of some sort. "Let us begin. Do you, Alexis, take these *princes* to be your lawfully wedded *husbands*—in addition to your current husband, Prince Calvin?—come hell or high water, as long as you *all* shall live?"

Apparently, like the Storm King before him, this priest would be cutting straight to the chase with none of the flowery poetics. Whatever. The sooner we were officially married, the better.

"I do."

The priest then turned to my grooms. "Bear with me on this next part. It's going to take a minute. Prince Robert, do you take Princess Alexis as your lawfully wedded wife, come hell or high water, as long as you both shall live?"

"I do," Rob said with a sexy smirk that made my girlish heart flutter.

ELLE MIDDAUGH

Oh my gods, this was really happening! *Again.*

"Do you, Prince Benson, take Princess Alexis as your lawfully wedded wife, come hell or high water, as long as you both shall live?"

Ben grinned, eyeing me with so much loving warmth that I could feel it in the air around us. "I do."

"And finally, do you, Prince Daniel, take Princess Alexis to be your lawfully wedded wife, come hell or high water, as long as you both shall live?"

There was a moment of silence, but thankfully not hesitation, while Dan simply stared at me with an appreciative lopsided smile. "I do."

The priest began scribbling in his notebook. "Do you have the rings?"

The guys and I shared a wide-eyed glance. Um, no, of course we didn't have rings. This whole thing was rather impromptu, to be honest, and besides, I only had so much room on my ring finger, and Cal's diamond took up a *lot* of it.

Cal stood from the bench and fished around in his suit pocket. "You're all lucky I came so prepared." He handed us each golden bands, which we quickly slipped onto the proper fingers.

"Well, then," the priest muttered. "By the power vested in me by his majesty the king and the gods above, I hereby declare you all officially married. You may now... uh, take turns kissing the bride."

I rushed forward, kissing them each in turn, feeling the strength of our bond increase as we filled it with love.

The priest scribbled in his notebook one last time before turning to leave, but Crissen stopped him. "The seal? It's not certified until the priest imprints his official seal onto the document."

"Nice catch," Cal commented, clearly impressed, as he and Criss shared a fist bump.

Our priestly friend stopped dead in his tracks, glowering at Criss as he turned around. "Oh yes, of course, how could I have forgotten?"

One heated blob of wax and one press of a ring later, and the seal was complete.

"Oh and we'll, of course, be needing *our* copy of the document," Criss added. "Complete with your seal, if you don't mind. It'd be far too easy to lose your document before it got to the king, making it seem as if it never happened. We can't risk that, now can we?"

My three grooms and I all grinned at Criss's efficiency. Thank the gods we'd allowed him to come. He might be the only reason our wedding became official.

The priest glared at him once more, but said nothing, simply removed another page and began scribbling. When he was finished writing, he again dripped wax on the document and pressed his ring into it. "There. *Your* copy."

"Much obliged," Criss said with the bow of his head.

The priest bowed back. "The gratification is all mine, Your Highnesses. I shall inform His Majesty at once of your treach—I mean, *your union.*"

And with that, he was gone.

We waited a while before any of us spoke. Cal touched the air, checking to be sure the priest had truly left. When he nodded, we all exhaled a sigh of relief—Dan loudest of all.

"Holy shit, I can't believe I just did that." His smile was huge despite the near-terror in his voice.

"And how do you feel about it?" I asked, unsure I actually wanted to know.

But he picked me up and swirled me around. "I feel elated. Light and carefree. It's amazing."

When he set me down, I turned to Ben. "Can you believe it? We're married!"

He ran one hand through my hair and slid the other around my waist, dipping me so low my hair brushed the temple floor. Then he planted a suggestive kiss on my lips and grinned. "I *can* believe it, Sailor, and I'm so damned glad it's true."

After he released me, I turned to Rob. "When I first met you, I never imagined I'd ever be married to you."

He smirked and crossed his arms. "And now?"

I uncrossed them and wrapped them around me. "Now, I can't imagine living life without you by my side. *Any* of you. I love you all so much."

We shared a giant group hug with me in the middle—even Criss joined in on the glorious moment. And, though I knew he wasn't an equal member of the group just yet, I still felt contented to have him there.

If only Asher could have been a part of it too...

"So," Dan said, rubbing his hands together anxiously, a devilish look in his sea green eyes. "Who's ready for the honeymoon?"

CHAPTER 11

*S*uddenly, flaky brown vines, thicker than my thighs, slithered all around us.

I turned to Ben, watching in awe as he worked his magic over the vegetation. At his command, the vines twisted, braiding themselves into a barrier of sorts that stood nearly four feet tall and surrounded the temple like a fence.

A few moments later, he stumbled and dropped to his knees, swiping at his eyes as if he couldn't see properly.

"Anyone have some water?" he shouted, making me flinch. I knew it wasn't out of anger, but rather his inability to hear properly—the price of his magic was losing his five senses—but still, it was loud.

"On it," Dan replied, closing his eyes and holding his breath. Soon, water funneled over from a nearby stream and poured into Ben's awaiting mouth.

When the Sand Prince had drunk enough, he shook his head, finally coming back to his senses. "Thanks, man."

"No probs."

Then Ben turned to me. "All right, Sailor, light it up."

I grinned and rolled my eyes.

"Time for the literal *and* sexual heat, huh?" I teased, which earned me a sexy wink from Ben. Gods, I lived for those winks.

"*Fire.*"

As soon as the word left my lips, peachy-pink flames curled out of my palms, swaying happily on an invisible breeze. I aimed a palm at the vines on my left. "*Fire.*" Flames shot across the temple and crashed into the dry, peeling vines, instantly lighting them on fire. Then I turned to the vines on my right. "*Fire.*" And the process repeated. I did that a few more times until the flames wrapped around us in a perfect circle, enveloping us in heat.

A heat I felt on the *inside* too.

I yearned to be touched—to feel hands scraping up my arms and legs. To be teased—to feel lips and tongues and fingers tantalizing my skin. To be fucked—in every delicious way imaginable by as many of these sexy men as possible.

"There's our girl," Dan said, voice low and evocative. He eyed me like a naughty demon, my flames dancing wildly in his eyes.

Ben approached me first, taking my face in one of his wide palms. His thumb gently parted my lips, so I snaked out my tongue to taste him. *Mmm.* Like salt and smoke and spice and seduction. His lips parted as I moaned, so I kept going, sucking his thumb into my mouth and swirling my tongue around it as if it were his cock instead.

It made the burn of my desire blaze hotter.

From the corner of my eye, I saw Cal and Criss take seats on separate stone benches, the latter shifting his gaze between us and the floor. I could tell he was nervous, but also that he wanted this. I could practically taste his arousal on the air, and it fanned my lust flames even higher.

Ben popped his thumb from my mouth, and suddenly Rob was there, kissing me with wild abandon.

Dan's hands slid up my sides and brushed across my breasts, making my nipples harden. I was pretty sure they'd popped right through the lacy fabric of my gown, making them easy targets for tweaking and arousing—thank the fucking gods.

Then Rob was gone and Ben was back, filling my vision with nothing but him, tan and shirtless in front of a back-drop of night and fire and floating embers. I watched in torturous awe as he slowly dropped to his knees and lifted the hem of my gown. His fingers grazed up the heated flesh of my thighs, lifting my dress inch by inch, making me quiver with anticipation. His gaze never once left mine until my pussy was bared before him. Then and only then did his eyes dip lower, darkening with arousal as they took in my swollen lips and clit.

Dan took over where Ben left off, sliding the dress the rest of the way up my body, making damn sure to brush my aching nipples as he went. Then he threw it on the altar before Hera's statue.

Like, surprise, bitch! An offering for you! I almost chuckled.

A second later, Rob was sucking one of my nipples and pinching the other, Ben was eating my pussy like the last juicy fruit in the desert, and Dan was tongue-fucking my mouth with a scorching-hot passion. Cal panted on the bench as he stroked his cock, and Criss watched intently with a hooded gaze, apparently not yet ready to pull his dick out and play. Even still, it was hot as hell, and it was all way too fucking much. I came faster than I'd ever come in my entire life, screaming as my body bucked and exploded with pleasure.

When I finally finished writhing, the guys backed away in preparation for the solo rounds.

"Atta boy, Ben," Rob commended him, before lowering me onto the stone floor and taking his place between my legs. He was already butt naked. Apparently, *he* was going first. "You ready for some pain, baby girl?"

I was currently numb with pleasure, so a little pain sounded absolutely fantastic.

I nodded, and he railed into me like a battering ram, forgoing any foreplay or gentleness whatsoever. Considering my cunt was wet as a monsoon, I supposed there really was no need for it. He pushed in as far as he could go, filling me to the breaking point, before pulling out and fucking me even harder.

Leaning forward, I arched my chest into him and scraped my nails down his back. Even without his dick getting instantly harder, I knew he liked to receive pain more than he liked giving it. Pain was part of his power, part of who he was.

"Harder," he begged as he wrapped his arms around my waist and thrust into me.

I scratched him again, digging my nails as deep as they could go, probably drawing blood as I went, which was undoubtedly exactly what he wanted.

His movements grew frantic then, and as I bit down on the flesh of his neck, he came apart inside of me. His growls and groans filled the air, echoing off the columns and tress before being swallowed up by the crackling flames all around us.

Panting, Rob backed away and smiled at me. "Best. Orgasm. Ever."

Dan took Rob's place between my legs, sliding the head of his cock up and down my slit. "We'll see about that."

"You think you're going to have a better one?" I teased.

He grinned deviously in return. "No, *you* are."

I gasped as Dan finally sank inside me, slow and steady,

teasing every nerve ending in my body as he went. Fuck, it was hot.

He grabbed my hips, lifting them up so he could drive into me from a different angle. My mouth fell open, and I thought my eyes rolled into the back of my fucking head. Dear gods, whatever he was doing was hitting *all* the right spots.

"You like that, Sexy Lexi?" he teased with a smirk.

"Yes," I moaned, and he slid in and out a little faster. The head of his dick rubbed and stroked some elusive place inside of me, one that somehow made me insane with need. "Don't stop," I begged him.

"I won't if you won't."

I reached up and threated my fingers in his sandy brown hair, pulling it tightly as I squirmed in his grasp. "Gods, Dan, I'm gonna come soon."

"Me too." He gritted his teeth as he carefully thrust in and out of me, never breaking his rhythm.

"*Me too*," Cal groaned from the bench, his dick straining hard against his hand.

Fuck, it was hot.

As long as Dan didn't change a godsdamned thing he was doing, then I would be gone in about three... two... one.

I cried out as I came hard, squeezing him tightly as my pussy throbbed. Then Dan came too, pumping into me much faster than he had been a second ago. And Cal growled from the sidelines, moaning as he spurted waves of milky cum onto the floor near his feet.

Hades, Zeus, and Hera, my body was limp after that. I sprawled out on my back across the cold stone tiles, trying to catch my breath.

I still had one to go.

Ben approached me once more, stroking his dick as he shook his head. "Those are some hard acts to follow."

"I'm sure you'll manage," I teased.

He grinned in return. "Guess we'll see."

He climbed up onto the altar and laid down on my discarded dress, resting his hands behind his head. His dick was literally the tallest point on his body in that position, and just the sight of it, all thick and veiny, made my mouth water.

"I want you to fuck me, Sailor. *Now*."

At his command, I immediately scampered over and crawled on top of him, running my hand up and down his hardened shaft, reveling in the sticky fluid already coating his head.

His hand came down hard on my ass before gently caressing my stinging flesh with his palm. "I said *fuck*, you naughty girl, not *tease*."

"Yes, sir," I whispered, positioning him at my slit before swallowing him up with my lower lips.

He groaned as I rolled my hips, so I kept it up, gyrating those babies in the slowest, most seductive motion I could. I ran my fingers up the sweaty plane of my stomach, over my swollen breasts and into my hair, tangling it sensually above my head. His gaze darkened as his eyelids became hooded, and I knew he was enjoying his show.

Leaving one hand in my hair, I lowered the other and pinched my nipple, tweaking the little nub until it was rock-hard.

His lips parted as he watched me, and I felt him swell even further inside me.

Swallowing hard, he turned left and glanced at Crissen, surprising the hell out of me. "Give him a show, Sailor."

I paused. "What?"

Ben grinned, but it looked like more of a grimace. He must've been getting close.

"Fuck *me*, but watch *him* while you do it. See if you can get us both off."

Holy motherfucking gods that sounded hot.

I glanced at Criss over on the bench; he also looked pained as he stroked his cock. At least he wasn't feeling shy anymore.

"Okay..." I grinded my hips once more, watching Criss's lips part as his eyes drifted south to where my skin met Ben's, then north to where my breasts bounced as I moved.

Using both hands, I rolled my nipples, arching my back as the sensations jolted through my body like tiny zips of lightning. Criss pumped his dick harder as he watched me, and as I watched him pleasuring himself, I got even more aroused. It was a delicious cycle.

I rocked my hips back and forth, panting as the pressure of another orgasm started to build. My brows furrowed, and my lips parted. Criss gritted his teeth and jacked his cock faster. Ben thrust up into me, pushing me that last little bit before I careened off the edge of ecstasy.

I cried out as I came, pulsing in pleasure as Criss shot hot cum all over the temple floor.

"Yes," Ben growled, coming barely a moment after the two of us, bucking beneath me until he was completely and thoroughly spent.

We remained at the temple for a little while longer, smiling and catching our breath. I could hardly believe what we'd just done—and not just the fantastic sex, but the marriages too. Our hearts and souls were slowly tangling tighter together, and I loved every bit of it.

"I need a bath," I admitted, fanning the sweat on my face.

Dan chuckled. "I think we all do. Luckily, there's a river nearby."

He held his breath and funneled some water over to douse the flames surrounding the temple. Ben recoiled his viney barrier, then drank some of Dan's water to counter the price of his magic. When everything was back to normal, we bathed in the freezing cold stream before making our way back to Blackwood Palace.

We might've celebrated a small victory that night, but we had even bigger battles ahead of us. Starting tomorrow, with the quest to find the Eye of the Sea.

CHAPTER 12

*B*efore dawn the next morning, we all gathered at the front steps of the palace, where our bags were already packed and waiting for us.

And so was a note:

YOU'LL PAY FOR WHAT YOU'VE DONE.

WONDER WHO THAT COULD'VE BEEN FROM?

I rolled my eyes and grinned, pleased that I'd pissed the sadistic bastard off one last time before I left the palace. Gods, I hated him. But then my smile fell. He said *you'll* pay for that, as in *me*, but I still had a bad feeling he would take it out on the queens.

Hold on, ladies, just a little bit longer. I swear, I'll kill the king.

Dan took a moment to speak with a nearby servant, explaining that we'd be traveling to Ebony Chateau on horseback and that our luggage should follow us via carriage. Since Hydratica was only a ship's ride across the sea from there, I had a feeling Dan's kingdom was going to be our base of sorts while we completed this next insufferable task.

Our next stop was the stables, where I was once again reunited with Caramel. Just thinking about her sweet-treat moniker had my heart dripping into a puddle of misery.

Sweets... it's what Asher used to call me. The Shifter Prince. The idiot who'd turned into a chimera egg and handed himself over to the Storm King.

I closed my eyes against the sudden urge to cry.

Gods, I loved him. I loved them *all*, but it was maddening to have even one of them away from me. Who knew where he was? If he was safe? If he'd be able to find his way back to me? To *us*?

An arm slipped around my shoulders and pulled me into a gentle embrace. When I opened my eyes, I saw Ben's handsome face looming above mine.

"It's all right, Sailor. He'll be okay."

I nodded immediately, knowing he needed to hear those words just as much as I did. Ash was his brother, but also his best friend. Losing him for real was not an option for either of us.

"Saddle up," Crissen gently prodded us, taking the lead on his chestnut stallion, Chance. "The sooner we find that Eye of the Sea, the better."

I glanced at Cal who quirked a brow. *He* was usually the one in charge, but I could tell he was interested in seeing what Crissen could do. If the newest prince was any good at it, then that might give Cal a nice little break from having to be the responsible one all the time.

As Ben and I climbed into our saddles, Rob and his horse stomped over to Crissen. "Let's make one thing clear, jackass. The Storm King might've *said* you were in charge of this mission, but you are *not* in charge. You shouldn't even *be* on this mission. You're a fucking liability."

Crissen didn't deny it, which made me feel bad for him all over again. Hadn't we gotten past all this last night? Didn't the honeymoon mean anything to them?

Criss's jaw ticked. "Just because you'd prefer me to hang back and act as your backup lifeline doesn't mean I'm not qualified to lead this mission, asshole."

To my utter relief and surprise, Rob chuckled. Apparently, Crissen biting back was acceptable in his eyes? Perhaps it was a sign of bravery, which would have appealed to Rob's second power.

"All right," Rob conceded arrogantly. "Let's see what you can do."

Criss's lips tugged upward at the corners, as if he were fighting a victorious grin. "All right, then."

Dan raised his hand, and his horse stomped his hooves into the ground. "Can I make a request?"

"Sure," Criss said, leaning in the saddle as he turned to him.

Dan smiled wide, and sexy little dimples tucked into each of his cheeks. "All I ask is that we make *one* stop first."

"RAVENWOOD TAVERN?" CAL ASKED, READING THE SIGN ALOUD in disbelief. "You're going to get wasted first?"

Rob shrugged and dismounted immediately. "Sounds good to me."

Dan chuckled and dismounted too. "No, dickhead, we're going to get breakfast. I'm fucking starving."

We entered the Ravenwood Tavern, pleased to find it mostly empty. From what I remembered of Blackleaf, the bar traffic was highest in the evening around dinnertime, not for breakfast, and I had a feeling this place would be the same.

The six of us walked over and grabbed a table in the farthest corner we could find.

We'd barely gotten seated before an old woman approached us, and if it weren't for the apron over her shirt, I wouldn't have even realized she was the waitress. I'd have assumed she was just an old lady there for breakfast.

"What can I get you?" she asked, eyeing us carefully. It was clear we were richer than most, but just how rich hadn't registered on her radar just yet.

"What are your breakfast options?" Dan asked, smiling pleasantly.

The old woman blushed and buried her head in a menu. "Scrambled eggs and vegetables, scrambled eggs and meat, scrambled eggs and mushrooms, scrambled—"

"I'm getting the feeling that scrambled eggs are your specialty?"

She blushed again, the sagging skin of her cheeks turning bright pink. "Basically."

Dan smiled wider, and I got the sudden urge to lick his adorable little dimples. Thankfully, I refrained. I didn't need to stake my territory against an eighty-year-old woman, now did I?

"All in favor of ordering a giant-ass skillet of scrambled eggs and meat?" Dan asked us.

Everyone mumbled this or that, which Dan took to mean compliance.

"That's what we'll have, please."

"Alrighty," the waitress said, tucking the menu under her armpit. "Give me about fifteen minutes. I'll have to gather another basket of eggs from the coop."

She turned to walk away, then paused. "Oh, and would you like anything to drink before I get your order going?"

"Coffee?" Dan asked us.

Bleh.

"I kind of hate coffee," I admitted.

Crissen held up a hand. "Me too."

"Fuck you," Rob grumbled in his general direction. "But if Jewels doesn't like coffee, then we can also order tea."

"Coffee and tea," Dan informed her, even though she could no doubt already hear what we'd all said.

"Coming right up, young man."

When she turned around and shuffled into the kitchen, I leaned over and licked Dan's face. It was fresh and clean and tasted like Elysium.

He chuckled and licked me back, grinning like crazy. "What the fuck was that about?"

I snuggled into his side. "Your dimples are absolutely adorable. I needed to lick them."

His eyebrows shot up, and an amused smirk captivated his lips. "Well, my dick is even more adorable, so please, feel free to lick that too."

I knew he was totally joking. I'd offered to give him head before. He was just so hell-bent on "giving" pleasure instead of "taking" it that he hadn't let me get anywhere close.

My eyes darkened at the challenge, my eyelids becoming hooded. "Is that right?"

I grabbed my fork off the table and dropped it on the floor.

"Oops. I seem to have dropped my fork. Let me just shimmy down here and pick it up real quick."

The smile completely dropped off Dan's face, and he gave me a challenging glare. "You wouldn't..."

I furrowed my brows. "Oh, but I would. In fact, I'd love to."

"That's *taking*," he warned me with a frown.

"Taking what I want from you? That sounds an awful lot like 'giving' me what I want, doesn't it?"

The other guys exchanged dirty and curious glances. "Is she going to do what I think she's going to?" Cal asked.

And I finally dipped beneath the table.

I got to work on Dan's pants, undoing the buttons and sliding the material down his legs, and all the while everyone just kept up the conversation as if nothing shady was about to happen.

"Here's your coffee and tea," the waitress announced above my head.

"Thank you, ma'am," I heard Dan say as I gripped his thighs. His leg started bouncing, and a devilish grin crept onto my face. He was excited. Maybe a little nervous because he was extremely out of his element, but still excited.

I grabbed his shaft and stroked him slowly, testing his actions, feeling the vibe. I sure as hell didn't want to do something that he truly didn't want me to. I wasn't a monster; I was just a horny girl in love with five different men. It made sense in my mind anyway.

Instead of tensing up, he relaxed back into his chair a bit, almost as if he were giving me more room. I nodded to myself. He wanted this, no matter what he might've said. I thought it might've been the exhibitionism that turned him on so bad. He definitely liked it last night.

"I got one of the other waitresses to gather the eggs," the old lady drawled, making this whole thing even naughtier. "I thought I'd take my fifteen-minute break and chat with you fine folks for a bit."

"Absolutely," Rob said quickly. I could practically see the evil grin on his face. He wanted to make Dan sweat; he wanted to make him get off in front of a little old lady, and I had to admit, I wanted that too.

So, without wasting another moment, I licked my lips and slid the tip of his dick into my mouth.

He groaned but hid it under a cough. It got a number of chuckles out of the guys.

"So," she said, and I heard her flick a match and light up a cigarette. The smoky scent didn't take long to perforate the air. "You fellas from the palace?"

"Whatever gave you that idea?" Cal asked, while I sucked Dan's hardened cock.

"You're dressed for it. You nobles or something?"

Ben chuckled. "Something like that."

"What business do you have here in the citadel?" she asked after exhaling a deep puff of smoke.

I bobbed my head slowly, up and down, over Dan's shaft as he squirmed in the chair.

"Just passing through," Crissen said. "On our way to Ebony Château."

"Ebony Château!" she gasped, accidentally sending herself into a coughing fit. The deep rumbling of her lungs suggested she'd been a smoker since she was a fucking *child*.

"I've always wanted to see the château. I hear it's gorgeous."

"I don't know," Rob teased. "What do you think, *Dan*?"

He made a strangled sort of sound before clearing his throat. "It's, ah, it's a very... gorgeous place."

Rob fucking chuckled like a demon. "What's your favorite part, bro? Dan's been there before, you see," he informed the waitress. "Many, many times, right, Dan?"

"Mm-hm," Dan muttered, and I could practically see his hooded eyes closing as the sensations wrecked him.

"Well?" Rob prodded. "What's the best part?"

"All of it," he replied, his voice sounding strained.

I took that as my cue to suck a little harder, bob my head a little faster. I grabbed the base of his shaft and pumped with that too.

He gasped and once more cleared his throat as a cover up.

"Um, the waves are my favorite part. I mean, the ocean. I love how... fucking wet it is... and how the waves crash over and over and over..."

"Is that what the ocean is like?" Ben asked, and I thought I heard a bit of a husky whisper in his voice as well. "It's... wet and rhythmic? Tantalizing."

"So tantalizing," Dan agreed. "Relaxing and exciting and intense all at once. It's incredible."

"I'll just bet it is," Rob added.

The old lady sighed. "I'd love to see the ocean one day. It sounds amazing."

"Oh, it's *absolutely* amazing," Dan assured everyone. "Everyone should see the ocean at least once in their life. Except, not this ocean. Um, I mean, no. What I said before. Everyone should..."

I ran my tongue in swirls around him, making sure to touch each inch of skin before swirling back down and taking as much as I could into my mouth.

"Fuck..." he hissed. "I have a headache. I'm just going to lay my head down for a moment, if you don't mind."

"Yeah, I'll bet your head aches," Rob teased.

"I have a headache too, for what it's worth," Cal mumbled.

I giggled at his words, sending sexy vibrations thrumming through Dan's erection.

He sucked in another hiss of air, and I could feel his legs trembling beneath my palms. He was getting close, and I was getting more aroused by the second.

"What's the food like over there?" the waitress asked, taking another drag on her cigarette. I knew, because I could hear the dried-out weed sparking as it caught.

"You like seafood?" Cal asked her.

"No idea. What's it like?"

"It's like normal meat," Ben began, "but softer and with a

slightly different scent. If you cook it properly, it's amazing; otherwise it's... well... fishy."

"Don't forget some of it's kind of rubbery," Rob added. "Like mussels and scallops and shit."

"Maybe a mushroom-like texture?" Ben asked.

"Yeah, I'd agree with that," Cal said.

Suddenly, Dan's fingers threaded through my hair, pulling tightly. Salty cum shot out into my mouth and filled my cheeks, making me panic for a moment. Swallow or spit? With my gag reflex, I'd better spit or I'd probably end up vomiting.

I collected it all in my mouth like a good girl, then when he finally let my head go, I popped my lips off and drizzled the mess on the floor. Was it my finest hour? No. Did I regret it one little bit? Also, no.

"Maybe I'll skip the seafood," the waitress said. "Not that I'll ever get to go there. The trip alone would cost more than I make in a year."

"Nah," Rob disagreed, setting a cup down on the table above my head. "As long as you have a good horse, you could make the journey in a couple days. And as long as you didn't need to stop, you wouldn't even have to pay for food or an inn."

I could practically see her flat look in the silence. "I'm eighty-three, young man. If you think I could make a trip like that on a horse without stopping, then you're vastly overestimating my stamina. I'm not as young as I once was."

Ew, gross. Old lady stamina. With nothing else to do, I crawled over to Rob's side of the table. He seemed to enjoy giving Dan a *hard* time. I wondered if he'd fare any better?

I touched his thighs, and they instantly jolted in surprise, smacking up into the table above.

I smothered a giggle, but the old lady wouldn't have heard it anyway, not over the other guys' laughter.

"What's the matter, Rob?" Dan teased, sounding much more relaxed than he had a moment ago. "You seem a bit jumpy."

"Nope. Not jumpy, just... ah, fuck. I don't even know."

"Restless leg syndrome," the old waitress replied. "Usually it affects me when I'm trying to lay down and go to sleep, but sometimes it hits when I least expect it."

"Yep," Rob agreed quickly. "That's what it must have been. My *legs* are restless."

I undid his buttons quickly, hoping I could get another round of teasing in before the old biddy went off her lunch break. As I unleashed his cock, the old woman said, "So why would a bunch of nobles be heading to Western Blackwood, anyway? Hopefully it doesn't have anything to do with the war."

"Well, you see—" Crissen said, just as Cal quickly added, "We're forbidden to speak of such things."

Ben chuckled, the deep reverberation of his voice giving me goose bumps. It was a damn sexy laugh. "We're actually just visiting some relatives. I hear the war hasn't even begun. Honestly, I don't think it's anything to worry about. Most kingdoms talk big talk, but no one can walk the walk that Blackwood does."

I wasn't sure if his words were true, or if he was simply trying to ease the old lady's mind, but either way, I hoped he was right.

I licked my swollen lips once more and took Rob's head into my mouth.

He groaned and slammed his face down on the table. "I think I have a headache now."

"How's yours, Dan?" Cal asked.

"Much better now, thank you."

"You guys get headaches a lot?" the old lady asked.

"Not a lot," Cal admitted. "But when we do, they are... intense."

"Is it a stress-related thing? Because of the nature of your jobs?"

"Um," Ben said, trying to explain as best he could. "It's kind of because of our job. I mean, it started out being job related, but now it's just..."

"The aches in our heads are pretty much nonstop now a days," Dan continued. "We just never catch a break. It's a personal problem, though, one we should take care of *way* more often."

There was silence for a moment while I did my thing. Rob's quadriceps tightened beneath my grasp, and his cock swelled even thicker.

"You boys are a little weird," the old lady admitted.

"We get that a lot too," Cal said, fabricating a total lie.

No one ever called the princes weird.

"And now that I think of it," the old lady continued, "wasn't there a young lady with you guys when you first came in?"

"Uh..." Cal hesitated.

"Yes, of course," Crissen finished. "She had to use the ladies' room, though. Powder her nose, or whatever the hell ladies do in there."

The old lady took another drag of her cigarette. "Pretty sure they just piss and shit like you boys do."

Everyone broke out into laughter, except Rob, who was steadily getting tenser in my grasp.

"Well, anyway," the old lady said, and I could practically hear her knees creak as she stood up, "I better get back at it. Your breakfast will be ready any minute now. It was nice talking to ya. And if you feel like bringing back a memento for an old lady in the woods, I wouldn't mind having my very own piece of the ocean."

"We'll certainly consider it, ma'am," Ben agreed.

I sucked harder, pumping faster, trying to get him off before she left.

"Oh, ma'am?" Dan said, apparently on the same wavelength as me. *Let's fuck Rob over like he did me!* "Before you go, could you please tell us a bit about your other menu selections? Our lady friend was thinking about trying the meat, but she was afraid it'd be too *hard* for her."

Rob groaned, and quickly said, "Fuck this headache."

"Yeah, the menu is pretty simple," the waitress said. "And, yes, the meat actually *is* a little tough. The soft cuts usually go straight to the palace or the priests. You'll have to tell your friend to work it around in her mouth a bit before trying to swallow it."

Dan fucking laughed out loud. "Oh, I'll tell her."

On cue, I started swirling my tongue, *working it around in my mouth* as the old lady had instructed.

"Fuck," Rob groaned, and I felt him tense up everywhere. He was shooting hot cum into my mouth a moment later, his leg banging into the table a second time as he came undone.

"Ah, there it is," Dan said, making absolutely no sense to the old lady, I'm sure. "Thanks so much for your time, miss...?"

"Brenda," the old lady said. "Just call me Brenda. I'll be back in a moment with your breakfast."

"Thanks so much, Brenda."

I spit one more puddle onto the floor and wiped my mouth, preening like a peacock.

"Is it safe to come back up?" I whispered.

"*No*," Cal and Ben both answered at once. Clearly, they each wanted a turn before I resurfaced.

I giggled and popped back up above the table anyway, repositioning myself in my seat. "Don't worry, boys, we still have lunch and dinner."

Crissen stared at me in disbelief. "Did you seriously just give them both head under the table?"

I raised a brow and shrugged.

Rob punched Crissen's arm. "Don't get any cute ideas, dipshit."

Criss held up both hands in a surrendering gesture. "I wouldn't dream of it."

CHAPTER 13

SHER

I TURNED TO FACE DION, PANIC RACING THROUGH MY VEINS.

How was I going to lie my way out of this one? It was literally *his* party. He'd know damn well whether he invited me or not, and *spoiler alert*, he didn't.

The party god grinned as he strolled closer to me. "What'd you do, lose a bet or something?"

I raised a single brow. Was it possible he seriously thought I was a random party guest? "Something like that."

His lips tugged even wider as he assessed me. "Want a pair of jeans or something?"

Jeans? "You mean, like pants?"

Dion grabbed the material of his pants and shook it. "Yeah, man, jeans. Denim. They might end up being a little baggy on you, but it'll be a fuck of a lot better than the paper towel thing you got goin' on."

I glanced down and chuckled. "Yes, I suppose you're right."

He waved a hand over his curly-haired head and led me down the carpeted hallway. "So, who invited you anyway? Affie? Seff?"

"Uh," I hesitated. "Affie."

Whoever the fuck that was.

Dion grinned and opened a door off to the right. "You look like her type. She always goes for the pretty boys. Is she the one who set up—" He gestured to my near nakedness. "—this punishment?"

I chuckled. "Easier to rip off later, right?"

I glanced up, half-assed expecting a lightning bolt to shoot down and zap me in the mouth, but it never came. Apparently, our bond was only magically enforced for the physical. The better of the two, if I was being honest.

Dion laughed and entered the room, digging through a chest of drawers before withdrawing a washed-out, light blue pair of *jeans*. He also opened another drawer and tossed me a pair of boxers.

"You want a shirt too?"

I ran a hand through my hair. "If you don't mind?"

He wandered over to a closet, sifting through shirts of various lengths, textures, and colors. He settled on a dusty blue one with short sleeves and white lettering, throwing it on the top of my ever-growing pile.

"Get dressed. I'll wait for you outside. I got a beer pong tournament goin' on in ten minutes, and Ares disappeared, so I need a replacement."

I pointed all five fingers of my right hand at my chest. "*Me?*"

"Yeah, *you.* Whoever you are."

"Adam," I said, reverting back to the name I always used when trying to hide my true identity.

He grinned and nodded. "Well, Adam, hurry the fuck up. We can't be late, or we forfeit, and I refuse to lose to Heracles and Perseus like that."

I'd never met the pair in my life, but I'd grown up hearing stories about them and the rest of the gods. The logical side of my nature told me to back the fuck out, that playing drinking games with the gods was a terrible idea. The competitive side of my nature, however, agreed with Dion: we couldn't just lose by default. Whatever this beer pong was, we needed to win.

"All right," I conceded. "Just give me a minute."

As soon as he shut the door, I scrambled into my borrowed clothes. The jeans fit great, hugging me in the ass and thighs while simultaneously leaving room for my dick. The shirt was soft as fuck, accentuating my pecs, biceps, and neck. I couldn't wait to see the look on Alexis's face when she saw me in *this*. She was going to jump me on sight.

Smirking, I slipped from the room and found Dion leaning against the wall, his arms and legs crossed casually.

"The clothes fit, I see."

"Yeah," I said, looking down to assess myself once more. "Thanks for letting me borrow them."

"No probs, man." He waved an arm over his head. "Let's get this competition started."

I followed him down the stairs, through the dance room with the flashing lights where my egg once sat, and into a dining area of sorts.

The floor was a shiny marble, and a diamond chandelier hung from the vaulted ceiling above. Instead of a long table with multiple chairs, though, there were four shorter tables with no chairs. On their tops, at opposite ends, sat two two-dimensional pyramids of... cups. Or so I assumed. They looked like no cups I'd ever seen, and yet I was fairly certain they were filled with beverages. Beer, by the smell of it.

Beyond each table end stood a pair of competitors holding tiny white balls. I had no idea what the hell this game was about, but I was definitely curious.

Dion led us over to the first table, which had the only empty spot. Every other one was filled, meaning there were sixteen of us playing in all.

"Rules," Dion began, pointing past everyone's heads to a giant, glowing canvas with moving letters; it had to have been magical, "are on the wall."

I tried to read them, but none of it made any fucking sense—bouncing, swatting, rollbacks, reracks? *Fingering?* Dear gods, what kind of a game was this? I had a bad feeling I was going to end up getting zapped by a lightning bolt for real this time.

"Brackets," Dion continued, pointing to another glowing picture that had everyone's names written on it, even mine, "are beside the rules. The tourney lasts as long as it has to. Winners earn bragging rights, and they split the pot. Buy in was a grand, if you recall, so the amount is fairly substantial. If there are no other questions or concerns, we're going to get this party started."

His words were met with a few whoops and shouts of excitement, and soon there were little white balls flying through the air everywhere. I watched as Dion and one of our competitors took their positions, careful not to allow their wrists to pass the table's edge. They stared each other in the eye, and on a silent count of three, they tossed their balls at each other's cup pyramids.

I raised a brow. Interesting.

Both balls landed in cups full of beer. I waited to see what would happen, but nothing did.

The guy's partner removed the ball from the beer cup and shook it dry. Uncertain, I stepped forward and did the same. We did the strange silent count off and let our balls fly. Both of us missed. My ball hit the rim of a cup and shot off to the side, bouncing across the marble floor before disappearing beneath someone else's table.

My eyes went wide. Now what? Was I supposed to go after it? Was I in trouble? There was something about *bouncing* in the rules, but I didn't know what.

Dion simply pulled another white ball from his pocket and handed it to me. "You better warm up fast, pretty boy. I can't have you missing cups all night."

I nodded. Okay, so getting the balls into the cups was the main idea. I could handle that.

"Who's your partner?" one of the guys across the table from us asked.

"Adam," Dion replied as they silently counted off and made their shots. "Ares bailed."

This time Dion's ball went in, but the other guy's didn't.

"Fuck," the guy shouted.

Dion fist pumped in the air, then turned to me. "All right, Adam, you're up. Don't miss this time."

I chuckled. "Great. No pressure."

I waited for the other guy to count off with me, but this time, he didn't. I guessed I was on my own. I took a deep breath, pulled back, and let the ball fly. Again, it hit the rim of a cup and bounced off.

Dion pursed his lips in my general direction. "Are you one of those guys who can't play sober? Do I need to get you shithoused a-sap?"

I had no idea what the hell he'd just said. *Shit housed? A sap?* Like, what was he going to do, cover me in tree sap and shit on me? This game was so fucked up. I knew I should've backed out when I had the chance.

Dion sighed. "Herc, go grab the tequila."

Herc rolled his baby blue eyes and crossed his arms. "Make Percy do it."

"I can't do it," Percy countered. "It's my damn turn."

Herc, which must've been short for Heracles, growled before stomping off.

Percy—or, Perseus, I assumed—took his spot behind the table and shot... sinking his little white ball right into one of our cups. "Drink motherfucker!"

Dion grabbed the cup, removed the ball, and chugged until it was completely empty. Then he set the cup aside, belching loudly, and took his own shot... which, again, sank directly into a cup.

As Perseus grumbled and drank, Heracles returned with a tall, thin glass bottle full of something golden. He cracked open the lid and handed it to me.

I took it uncertainly as an extremely potent odor filled the air, singeing my nostrils and damn near making my eyes water.

"Drink," Dion ordered. "It's your turn next, and I need you on point."

What the fuck was I gonna do? Tell him no?

I cocked my head and tipped the bottle to my lips. The golden shit burned like hell going down, and when I exhaled, it felt like I was blowing flames.

As Herc lined his shot up, Dion gestured to my bottle again. "Again. You clearly need as much help as you can get."

I eyed the nasty shit with curiosity. It was going to help me play better?

As Herc sank his shot into another of our cups, I narrowed my eyes and took a few huge gulps of the liquid fire. If I wanted to kick our opponents' asses, then I needed to not suck. If this fire water would help me to not suck, then so be it.

Heat from the burning drink filled my belly and coursed through my veins, making me a tiny bit lightheaded.

Dion pointed at the cup, which held Herc's ball. "That's

your cup, bro. But listen, 'liquor before beer in the clear'. So, before you drink that, you gotta drink a bit more tequila, okay? Just a few more gulps. It'll hit you soon, and we'll be good to go."

I nodded my partial understanding. More gold stuff equaled a more skillful Asher. *Adam.* Fuck. I gulped down a bit more of the tequila and wiped my mouth on the back of my hand, handing the bottle back to Herc. When my hands were free, I grabbed the cup of beer and chugged it. I kinda felt like puking, but the more I swallowed, the further down it all went, so I was eventually all right.

Herc nodded approvingly. "So, who invited you anyway? You a friend of Dion's?"

I opened my mouth to lie, but Dion cut me off. "I never met this man in my life. But Affie invited him."

Herc raised a brow. "Aphrodite invited you?"

My mouth fell open.

"Of course, she did," Dion defended. "Can't you tell? He's so *pretty*. Seff usually goes for the bad boys."

Herc scoffed. "Persephone went for the *ultimate* bad boy, D. Doesn't get much worse than the king of the underworld."

Holy shit, I can't believe they actually thought I was invited by Aphrodite or Persephone.

I glanced at Herc and Percy, then over to Dion. After studying them for a moment, I scanned the rest of the room, moving from face to divinely perfect face. The sheer amount of the power in the room would have been enough to strangle me if I'd been paying a damn bit of attention.

I swallowed hard. I needed to win this tournament as fast as possible then get the fuck back to Blackwood before anyone realized I didn't belong there.

Or worse, before Ares returned.

CHAPTER 14

LEXIS

I<small>T WAS THE MIDDLE OF THE NIGHT BY THE TIME WE'D REACHED</small> Ebony Chateau.

Exhaustion weighed so heavily on all of us that we'd crashed to sleep in seconds flat, as a group, huddled in Dan's massive four-poster bed—with Criss on the very end, farthest away from me.

By morning, I was still out cold. I hadn't even noticed the sun rising over the watery horizon and climbing up above the cirrus clouds. I hadn't felt the sweltering temperature increase or heard the loud cawing of the gulls.

In fact, it was almost lunchtime when Cal, Criss, and Ben finally decided to rouse the rest of us.

"*Wake up,*" Ben sang in his deep bass voice, instantly drawing a smile from my lips.

Rob groaned from my left and threw a pillow at him, while Dan moaned from my right and buried his head under the comforter. Apparently these two guys were *not* morning people.

I was neither an early bird nor a night owl, but rather something in between. A robin, maybe, just pecking at the ground whenever I got around to it.

"*You better have tea and sweets*," I sang back before cracking my eyes open and sitting up.

Gods love them, Ben was already holding a silver platter full of pastries and muffins, and Cal had a white and gold teapot in one hand and a matching teacup in the other.

"You guys are amazing," I said with a sigh as I took a cream cheese tart and a cup of tea.

"Way to make the rest of us look bad, dickheads," Rob grumbled, feeling around the bed for another pillow to throw at them. He was damned lucky that first pillow hadn't toppled over Ben's tray of goodies, or there would have been hell to pay.

Dan tossed the covers off his head and sat up too. "Did you at least bring coffee?"

Criss held up a pot of the potent black stuff. "Got ya covered."

"Thank the gods," he muttered before stumbling from bed and pouring a cup.

As we ate and sipped at our blessed caffeine, Cal strode to the front of the group, his arms carefully tucked behind his back. His blond hair was brushed off to the side so that a few strands dropped down into his clear blue eyes. He had a look of "business" smeared across his face, and I had a feeling we were about to get a lecture.

"We need to send some letters," Cal began. "Starting with Timberlune. We need to explain to the king and queen what happened and see if we can get them to call off the war."

I took a deep breath and shook my head. "Cal, they already said there'd be no second chances."

"We have to at least try, Peach. If you never ask, the answer is always no. But if you do..."

"Then it's still going to be no," Dan finished flatly.

"Fuck you, Dan," Cal retorted without blinking.

Dan just chuckled and rubbed at the sleepies in his eyes.

I smiled at their banter and looked back up at Cal. "Maybe if we tried Bria? She was able to help us once before."

"That's an excellent idea," Cal agreed. "And then after *that* letter, we need to send one to Eristan. King Solomon will surely back us after all we've done for him."

"Will he, though?" Rob asked, sounding skeptical. "You heard his dignitary at dinner. I have a feeling he's not gonna back *shit* now that Ben and I are officially married to Alexis."

My stomach sank. I knew that would probably happen, but still, it freaking sucked.

"What about Hydratica?" Dan suggested as he leaned over and poured Rob a cup of coffee. "We could go directly to the twins."

I remembered them mentioning that the Hydratican princes were twins back when we were in Eristan. Camilla had been interested in courting one or the other; either would do, apparently. She just wanted a powerful union, and she didn't really care where it came from. I didn't know the twins' names, though.

"And say what, exactly?" Crissen asked, his tone curious.

Dan shrugged as he set the coffee pot down and brought his own cup to his lips. "I guess, see if we can strike some sort of a deal or a treaty. A ceasefire, if you will."

Ben rubbed his chin, which had grown some sexy stubble during our journey, and contemplated Dan's words. "It would at least be beneficial to know their stake in this war."

Rob scoffed and ran both hands through his dark hair. "We already know their stake. They've wanted to wipe Sohsol off the map since the apocalypse."

"You mean 'Southern Blackwood,'" Cal corrected sarcastically.

Rob rolled his eyes and flipped him off. "Whatever. *My people* are the ones they're after. There's not going to be a ceasefire until one side or the other is decimated."

All heat drained from my body, and a thin layer of cold sweat broke out across my skin. *Decimated*? Like, totally and utterly destroyed? It was one thing to talk about war and strategy. It was another thing entirely to realize countless people were about to die.

"We still have to try," I decided. "If there's even a chance of saving our people, then we have to take it."

Rob's hardened expression softened, and he gave me a fleeting smile before turning back toward Cal. "Fine. Send the letters. I don't think it's going to help, but Jewels is right —it can't hurt to *try*."

Cal nodded. "We'll also want to send letters to Valinor, Rubio, and Werewood for that exact same reason. We already know they have needs—help with a volcano, precious metals, and beer of all things. I'll get started writing them straightaway. In the meantime, we'll wait for their replies before we make any sort of move. We can't risk messing this up before we even start."

"How long is this going to take, do you think?" I asked, downing a few unladylike gulps of my tea. Madam Annette would have tsked her tongue off.

Cal's lips pursed off to the side. "A couple hours to write the letters, a couple days for them to get there. A few days for the recipients to contemplate and compose a response. Then, a couple more days for the letters to get back. All in all, I'd say... three days to a couple weeks, depending on the country and their distance from us. Why?"

"Well, I just thought that if we have a bit of time to spare while we wait on the letters, maybe we could go ahead and resume the old dates?"

Cal didn't hesitate for a second. "Of course we can, Peach. I didn't realize you were feeling upset about all this."

I shook my head. "I'm not upset. I understand this shit is important—way more important than a silly date. But we're human, or at least partially human, and I think we need to nurture our human connections even in the midst of chaos. It'll help keep us sane."

"Sailor's right," Ben agreed. "It'd be nice to reduce at least some of the stress by having one carefree day to ourselves to just... live."

"Then it's settled," Dan declared, raising his coffee cup. "The dates resume as soon as possible."

Rob stood, bridged the gap between us in one giant step, and grabbed my hand. "I call first date. Starting right now."

"No fair!" Dan shouted.

"Second date!" Cal and Ben yelled at the exact same time.

"Damn it!" Dan growled.

Rob chuckled. "Sorry, bro. Should've been faster."

"So, who's second and who's third?" Cal asked Ben, since they'd technically tied.

I grinned. "Why don't you two go together? I owe you both, anyway." Then I winked.

Cal's blue eyes darkened and fell closed, while Ben bit his bottom lip.

"Sounds good to me," Ben decided.

Dan groaned. "I can't believe I'm fourth. *Fourth*. How am I supposed to wait that long?"

"Uh," Criss said, drawing our gazes. "Can I be fifth?"

"Fuck no," Rob growled from my side, his hand tightening possessively around mine.

But Dan apparently disagreed. "Yes. As long as I'm not last, then yes."

Rob shot the Sea Prince a deadly glare. "You'd let him fuck our girl just so you don't have to be last?"

"Whoa!" Criss shouted, putting both hands in the air. "I never said... *that*. I just said I wanted to go on a date too."

"Alexis's dates always end in sex," Dan informed him.

"Unless the Storm King fucks it up," Cal muttered.

Ben shook his head. "I've been on a date with her that didn't end in sex."

"So have I," Rob admitted.

"Really?" Dan asked, a smug grin sliding onto his face. "Guess I'm the only lucky one, then."

Everyone glowered at him, even me—though my glare was more challenging than deadly.

"All right, asshole," I said. "When we get to your date, not only will you be *last*, but it will *not* be ending in sex."

"What?" he protested indignantly.

But Rob was totally onboard with the idea. "Done!"

"Agreed!" Cal and Ben said, *again* at the same time. I had no idea why they were on such a similar wavelength that day, but it was kind of amusing.

Criss's eyebrows rose in pleasant surprise. "So, I can go on a date? And I get to be *fourth*?"

Rob pointed sternly at him. "Don't make me change my mind."

Criss snapped his mouth shut and tried to hide a grin; he failed rather miserably. It made me grin in return.

Rob and I stripped out of our bed clothes and got dressed. Everyone else joined in, too, getting ready for the day ahead. There was a lot of bare skin and flashing body parts. There were a lot of stolen glances and heated stares. Just as I was beginning to wonder if we were going to make it out of there without a full-blown orgy, Rob grabbed my hand and led me toward the door. Clearly, he was eager to get our date started, but before we could get through the arch, Cal stopped us.

"Oh, Peach, one more thing."

I glanced over my shoulder, waiting patiently.

"I'm going to start composing the letters while you're gone," he said, buttoning up a pair of pants. "You don't have a problem with me writing Bria, do you?"

A tender smile lit my face, flooding me with warmth and affection. How freaking considerate was this man? Making sure I was okay with him corresponding with his ex.

I shook my head. "No, I don't mind. But thank you for asking. That actually means a lot to me."

Cal smiled and nodded in return.

Not allowing any other distractions to come up, Rob quickly tugged me out the door.

We jogged down the chateau steps, and before we even got outside, the sound of the surf rose up and filled my ears, washing me in tranquility and contentment. It was hard to believe that a *sound* had that kind of power, but the ocean most definitely did. I smiled and breathed deep, taking in the salty sea air as if it were an expensive perfume I needed to savor.

"This place is amazing," I said, when we finally made it onto the beach

Dan's castle had been built at the top of a small cliff, over-looking a crystal-clear, aquamarine cove below. As such, his city was two-tiered—half of the houses, shops, and buildings were up above, lining the precarious edge of the clifftop, and the other half were down below, lining the sandy shore. Steps had been carved into the cliffside at various points, allowing the citizens to get from one section to the other easily—if extreme cardio could be considered "easy." I, for one, was already dreading the journey back to the chateau. All those stairs could go suck a big one.

Rob shook his head. "Yeah, it's nice. But it's fucking hot as Hades."

I glanced at the men and women around us. Some of them were lying in the sand, others were walking down the sandstone streets. Most men were shirtless and wearing only shorts, and most women wore dresses with petite skirts, exposing most of their legs. *All* of their legs, actually; the only thing the skirts really covered were their ass cheeks.

"Well, *you* could always just take your shirt off," I suggested, raising my brows enticingly. I'd be kidding *no one* if I said I didn't enjoy looking at Rob's tattooed body sans clothing. "*Me* on the other hand, I'd love to go shopping to buy a short dress like that."

I pointed to a woman across the street who had a toddler in each hand beside her. Her dress was white, sleeveless, and breezy at the bottom. She even had a matching pair of sandals to go with it.

Rob smirked. "You wouldn't last ten seconds in a dress like that."

I nudged his arm with my shoulder, but it was like smacking into a rock, his muscles were so hard. "What's that supposed to mean?"

"*It means*, I'd have you out of that fucking thing in an instant. I'd hate to get arrested for indecent exposure in my brother's kingdom."

I couldn't help but laugh. "Dan wouldn't care. He'd just want to join us."

Rob chuckled too. "That's true."

"I'm serious, though. I want one of those gowns. They look so cool and comfy."

Sighing, Rob squeezed my fingers before veering toward the nearest shop. "Come on then. I'll buy you one."

My smile spread wide. "Are you serious?"

He shot me a flat look. "Do I look like I'm kidding?"

"You never look like you're kidding, grumpy ass."

"Don't insult the person offering to buy you something. That's just rude."

I giggled and skipped along beside him as we entered the shop. I was expecting it to be cool in there for some weird reason, so I was sadly mistaken when the sultry air practically suffocated me. At least it smelled nice. Gentle perfumes and colognes mingled sweetly with the salt in the air and the fresh scent of cloth. Gowns and dresses of all lengths and colors dotted the space, drawing my eye in a hundred different directions, but the ones with the short skirts were what finally kicked my feet into motion.

I stopped in front of them, touching the butter-soft material with my fingertips as I searched for the perfect one.

I turned to Rob. "Want to do another trust building exercise?"

He raised a brow, mildly intrigued. "You want me to choose your dress for you, don't you?"

I grinned and nodded. "I'll have to *trust* that you'll choose well."

"And what about me?"

"You'll have to *trust* you can keep from ripping it off me."

His gray eyes darkened as they filled with heat. "Fine."

To my surprise, he flicked past the sexy black and red dresses and went straight for the ivory-colored one.

I pursed my lips. "Did you pick that simply because I liked that girl's white dress?"

It'd be practical if he had, but a little disappointing, if only because he hadn't put much thought into it.

"Not at all," he said. "Where I come from, Southern Blackwood, it's always freezing cold and snowing. We mostly dress in white, gray, and blue—hues of our environment. I wanted you to wear something that reminded me of home—a home I hope you can see one day."

I immediately grabbed the white dress off the rack and hugged it to my chest. "I love you, Robert Storm. You chose well."

He cupped each side of my face and pulled me in for a tender kiss. "I love you too, Jewels."

My heart fluttered, torn between arousal and adoration. I glanced from one gray eye to the other. "I'd love to see your kingdom one day."

"*Our* kingdom, babe. We're married now, remember? You're the official Lady of Onyx Fortress."

Again, my heart fluttered, tickling my insides like a feather. *Lady of Onyx Fortress* had a definite ring to it. But *married to Rob Storm* sounded even better. "Then I can't wait to see *our* kingdom someday soon. I'm sure it's absolutely beautiful."

"It is, but not nearly as beautiful as you."

The pattering of my heart increased, and my body temperature rose. Rob wasn't one to dish out compliments freely, so when he did, the impact was lethal. I felt like melting into a puddle at his feet, or jumping his bones on the floor between racks of clothes—whichever happened first.

Getting married must've turned him into a bit of a romantic, and I was totally there for it.

He released my face and took my hand once more, leading me up to a desk where a prim, middle-aged woman sat behind it. Her hair was clipped into a loose twist, and she had a tiny set of spectacles on the bridge of her nose.

Rob handed her an absurd number of jewels, then gestured to my right where a cylindrical curtain hung like a waterfall on a metal frame. "Get changed. I have someplace I want to show you."

"You actually know your way around this place?"

His brow quirked. "Ebony City or this store?"

"Both, I guess." After all, he seemed to know exactly where

the desk had been as well as where the changing area should be.

Rob chuckled. "It's my brother's kingdom, Jewels. I've spent so much time here, it's like a second home. A third home? I don't fucking know. It's like home, though."

I giggled and did my best to maneuver in the tiny space, shimmying out of my old gown and sliding into the breezy new dress. It looked good on me, from what I could tell. I was afraid the white of my skin would clash with the white of the dress, but my life had changed since my days of being a jewel miner. I now saw the sun on a daily basis, and I'd just spent an extended stay in the desert, so it was safe to say I'd had my first tan in over six years. My breasts filled the halter top perfectly, creating a fantastic amount of plump cleavage, and my hips looked curvy as fuck beneath the breezy skirt.

"There," I exclaimed with a smile as I withdrew the curtain.

Rob's eyes went wide and immediately locked onto my tits before darting down to the amount of leg I was showing. "Holy fucking gods, this was a bad idea."

But the clerk shook her head and tapped her lip. I didn't know why she wasn't speaking aloud. Maybe she had some sort of a speech issue? Then her eyes lit up and she held up a finger. She hurried to a different section of the store and returned with a beautiful metal clip. Seashells and pearls decorated its surface, giving it a pale pinkish hue. She disappeared behind my back, twisted my hair into what felt like a knot, then secured it with the clip. When she moved to stand before me again, she smiled and nodded, apparently pleased with her work.

Rob glanced at her and nodded his approval. I guessed he liked the updo too.

"Thank you," I said to her, and she bowed to me in return.

Rob took my hand and led me back out into the fresh

seaside air. This time, I felt much cooler and even a bit freer. I spun in a circle as the wind tickled my legs and watched in awe as my skirts spun around me like the petals of a flower.

"Fucking Hades, Jewels, you're flashing me your underwear. Do you know how hard it is to *not* rip them off you, right now?"

I stopped spinning and ran my hands up his muscular, tattooed chest. "You're a big, strong prince. I'm sure you can resist."

Mirroring my motions perfectly, he ran his hands up my chest too, squeezing my breasts tightly in front of anyone and everyone. "I'm not so sure about that."

Heat pooled in my core, and my lady bits flared to life once more.

"Is the place you want to show me... secluded?" I asked, my voice coming out all husky and low.

A devilish smile captured his features, and he nodded. "Ready to go?"

Fuck yeah, I was.

I bit my bottom lip. "*So* ready."

CHAPTER 15

"So, where *are* we going?" I asked Rob as we walked. The further we got from Ebony City, the curiouser I became.

"You'll see" was all he said. There was a tiny smile on his handsome face, making his lips look even more lush than usual. Gods, I wanted to lick them.

What the fuck was up with me wanting to lick the guys lately?

The path before us was nothing but sand with blades of grass poking up in random spaces. Out here, there were more trees and no other people—trees with jagged green leaves and ringed trunks; trees with long, weepy branches and moss hanging from their limbs. The shade they provided was just enough to make the humidity bearable.

As the foreign forestry grew a bit thicker, I noticed a wrought iron gate tucked quietly into the trees on the left. Beyond it was a small pond with a fountain in the middle, raining down droplets that probably half evaporated before they could even touch the water beneath. Surrounding the fountain were countless, pristine white gravestones. Though, "stones" was a crude word for what they were. They were more like statues, carved with the skill of the gods themselves. They depicted all sorts of things, but mostly angels and saints and temples.

He'd taken me to a graveyard. Why I was surprised, I had no idea. Rob was the *Spirit Prince* for fuck's sake.

"You're really romantic, you know that?" I teased, nudging him with my shoulder once more.

"You said you wanted to walk. This is my favorite place in Western Blackwood."

I snuggled into his side as we crossed under the gate's high metal arch. Paths meandered in all directions, some distinct, some vague, all disappearing off into the trees, leading to some unknown destination. We continued straight, walking in comfortable silence until the forestry thinned out once more and a panoramic vista of the ocean beyond captured our view.

The gravestones there were smaller and much older, eroded into illegibility, but still beautiful and mystical. Vines crawled along the spongy ground and climbed over the stones, decorating them with a natural and ancient sort of elegance.

"I can see why this is your favorite place," I said quietly, smiling as the salty air blew through my hair and tousled the moss dangling from the trees.

He squeezed my hand tighter and stopped walking.

"There's actually something I'd like to try... if you're up for it?"

I raised a brow. "And what's that?"

He shook his head and grinned, biting his bottom lip enticingly as he did so. "You have to agree first."

I smirked. "Fine. I agree. Now tell me."

But *again*, he shook his head. "I'd rather just show you."

He held out his arms, and all at once the world went dark.

Spinning stars and explosions of dusky colors consumed me as the astral plane filled my vision. I'd only ever seen this place once before, back in Eristan, but it was as gorgeous as ever, like a midnight sky in another galaxy. The darkness was somehow brilliant, as if lit by a moon that didn't exist. It was fascinating.

The dark lights eventually calmed to a halt in front of a semitransparent liquid mirror. It was tall but not very wide, almost like a doorway in the middle of nowhere. On one side, I saw the reflection of myself. On the other, I saw an astral version of Rob.

He held out his hand, and his fingers pushed through the mirror, coming out on my side.

What the ever-loving fuck?

"Are you...?" I wasn't even sure how to vocalize the absurd question flitting about in my brain. "Are you taking me to the astral plane? Is that even possible? Can humans cross over without dying?"

He wiggled his fingers, encouraging me to take hold. "You'll be fine, Jewels. Trust me."

Taking a deep breath, I gathered every ounce of courage I possessed. Then I took his hand... and stepped through.

THE ASTRAL PLANE WAS BREATHTAKING.

It was this nighttime world full of peaceful spirits in corporeal form just going about their business with gentle smiles on their faces. Stars filled the sky above, and black roads and sidewalks crisscrossed the ground at our feet. Tall houses emerged from where the gravestones used to be, almost as if the graveyard were a neighborhood of sorts.

"Come on," Rob said. "We don't have much time."

A moment later, lights blurred all around me as we sped

somewhere different. I have no idea how we moved. It was sort of like floating at the speed of light or something. When we stopped, we stood before an old three-story manor with nothing but a field of wildflowers surrounding it. In the astral glow, the manor seemed to be light gray with black-as-coal trimmings around the windows and door.

"What is this place?" I asked, turning to Rob.

"It's my home," he replied with a smile. "In case I ever actually die, I wanted to be prepared."

"Does that mean you have a grave somewhere already?"

"Yep." He pointed beyond the wildflowers to where a few other manors stood. "I convinced Dan, Cal, and Ben to get gravestones near me too."

"Wait." My mind was whirring a mile a minute. "So, you won't go to the underworld when you die?"

He chuckled. "Jewels, this is the underworld. The Astral plane is that tiny space between the human world and the underworld beyond. You were on the astral plane for like ten seconds when you started out, but as soon as you took my hand, you crossed over into the underworld."

I gasped and covered my mouth. "Oh my gods, is Hades going to like, freak out that I'm here?"

"Nah. He's a king. He's got more important shit to do than micromanage every soul that passes in and out. I've never seen him once, in all my years of coming here. It's kind of weird to think he's actually my father..."

He shook his head and rolled his eyes.

"Anyway," he continued. "We're wasting time. I don't know how much longer I can keep us both here."

"It's draining your power?"

He nodded.

"You're feeling pain and coldness right now?"

"A bit," he admitted. "We should still have enough time, though."

"Enough time for what?" I asked, quirking a brow.

He sighed and shook his head. "How quickly you forget."

Lights flashed, and we once more jumped through time and space. The next second we were standing in, what I presumed to be, Rob's underworld bedroom. It was dusky inside, so I couldn't tell if the silken sheets were crimson, plum, or navy, but we were definitely staring at a massive four-poster bed.

"*Oooh*," I said, dragging the vowel out as realization dawned on me. "*That's* what we're doing."

Holy shit! We're going to have sex in the motherfucking underworld*!*

"A little light?" he asked innocently as he pointed to the candles lined all around the room.

I narrowed my eyes and pursed my lips to keep from smiling. "You planned this, didn't you?"

"Of course I planned it. I set the *scene;* now you set the *mood.*"

The mood. *Right.* Unquenchable horniness dropping in three... two... one...

"Fire."

As I said the word, flames rose to life in my palms. Down here in the underworld, they were electric blue instead of their usual shade of peach. They still danced like flowers in a summer breeze, though. Cheeky bastards.

I walked around, lighting each candle one by one, feeling the lust building step by step, until the last wick was ablaze. But when it came time to extinguish my flames, Rob grabbed my wrists and halted me.

"Don't," he murmured. "Hold it."

Hold it? Did he know how hard that was going to be for me?

We stood there, staring into each other's eyes as the lust burned stronger, gaining strength as it swirled wildly through my veins. My breathing quickened, and my skin crawled with heat. I gazed lower, yearning to slide my tongue across his pillowy bottom lip. I leaned forward and prepared to do just that, but again he halted me.

"Wait."

I practically growled. The sound made his cock jump, and my eyes immediately snapped to the huge tent pole rising in his pants. The sight of it calmed my growl into a sultry purr. I wanted to reach out and touch him, to stroke him, to feel him harden within my grasp... but my fucking hands were on fire and my wrists were caught in his grasp.

Frustration filled me once more, and I thought about extinguishing the flames—Rob's orders be damned.

He moved both my wrists into one of his big hands and took my chin with the other, lifting my face back up. "Not yet, babe. Almost."

I moaned, feeling the desirous tension stretching through my entire body like a band. My nipples hardened into tiny pebbles beneath my ivory dress, just begging to be pinched, and my panties pooled with the wetness of excitement. The alluring scent of my arousal filled the air, driving me insane with need. The temperature increased even further and a thin layer of sweat beaded at my hairline.

I couldn't stand it much longer.

My breathing came in jagged waves, my body all but screaming for release. He released my chin and held out his hand, hovering barely an inch away from my breast, taunting me.

"What do you want, Jewels?"

I want you to fucking touch me already!

I didn't say that, though. I just pushed my breasts into his awaiting palm and moaned like a whore when his thumb and forefinger clamped around my nipple.

"It's affecting me too," he groaned. "I want to fuck you so bad right now."

I clenched my fists tight, extinguishing my flames, and pushed him backward onto the bed. I slowly pulled my dress up my body, releasing my lust-heavy breasts before throwing the soft material on his bedroom floor.

His breath hitched, and his erection bulged even further.

Then I turned around, dipping my thumbs into each side of my panties, and slowly dragged the lacy material down my legs, giving him a full view of my ass and pussy as I did so.

"Fucking Hades," he growled, tearing his pants off from where he lay. "Come here."

He didn't have to tell me twice.

I snaked up his freezing cold body, making sure to brush every heated inch of my skin across his. If he was that cold already, I had no idea how much longer he'd be able to hold his magic.

He flipped me over and raked his fingers up my legs until he clenched my hips tightly. "I'm going to fuck you so hard it hurts, so I want you to be ready."

Pushing my knees apart, he bent down and kissed my inner thighs. As his lips slowly teased closer to my clit, two of his fingers slid past my slit and curled inside. He stroked me rhythmically, making my entire body buzz with anticipation and need. When his tongue finally snaked out and devoured me, the sensations were intense. He stroked me from the inside, licked me from the outside, and continued the pattern over and over at just the right tempo.

I swear the guys must've been taking notes and sharing insider tips on how to get me off the fastest. It seemed like each new orgasm was just a little faster than the last, more tailored to my liking, more powerful.

Before I could even shout out a curse word or two, I was coming apart in his hands—and his mouth. My body bucked and spasmed as the pleasure drew out for what seemed like an eternity. When I finally came down from my euphoric high, my mind and body were blissfully numb, and I had a love-drunk smile plastered onto my face.

Rob eventually withdrew his fingers and tongue and chuckled darkly. "*Now* you're ready."

He thrust into me with no further warning, spearing me to the core. I gritted my teeth and hissed against the pain as a subsequent wave of pleasure rolled in after. He pulled out most of the way, then railed me again. This time I couldn't hold back my cry as the ache slowly bled into desire.

"That's right, baby," he growled in praise. "Show me how much it hurts."

He rammed into me again and again, punishing and plea-suring my body all at the same time. It was almost too much to handle. I reached out and clawed at his chest, digging my nails in deep so that he could have a taste of his own medi-cine, but I knew he fucking loved it.

He gritted his teeth and shouted as the underworld snapped from his grasp, and we were once more thrust into the real world.

Sunlight assaulted my eyes, but the sweet crash of the surf caressed my ears. I glanced left and saw my dress crumpled in the sand. Then I turned right, surprised to find the grave-yard back in sight.

"Don't stop, Jewels," Rob begged from up above me, digging his fingers into my hips, and I realized he hadn't yet come. The shout from a moment ago must've been due to him losing his hold on his magic, not his orgasm.

I pushed him over, and we barrel-rolled across the sandy grass until I was the one on top.

I raked my nails up his chest until my hands were wrapped firmly around his throat. From the way he started panting and moaning, I knew he'd be coming soon. Adding a bit more pressure, I leaned into him and rocked my hips. Less than a minute later, he was losing his mind.

"Oh my fuck," he groaned as his orgasm hit and squeezed my hips even tighter.

The sight of him losing control underneath me, the sound of his shouts as they ripped through the air, the feel of his cock as he exploded inside... it was enough to send me spiraling into another pulsing orgasm.

I let go of his neck as his thumb found my clit, and I rode his body until we were *both* finally sated.

When it was finished, he pulled me down on top of his chest. "That was incredible. *You* are incredible."

I kissed him gently on the lips, pleased to feel the burn of my magic had subsided, as had the chill of his. We complimented each other so perfectly.

"*You're* the incredible one. I can't believe I got to have sex in the underworld. How badass is that?"

"Totally badass," he agreed with an eye roll. "And not at all creepy."

"It's not!" I protested. "It was nothing short of beautiful and not eerie in the slightest. Those assholes who called you a freak and made fun of you when you were younger have no idea what they're missing. I'm kind of glad they did too; now I can selfishly hoard you all for myself."

He chuckled and kissed me once more. "Hoard away, babe. I'm all yours."

Gods, I fucking loved him.

One date with him—one date with any of them—was never going to be enough.

CHAPTER 16

*T*he next day came in the blink of an eye.

It was early morning, and while Dan went to assess how his kingdom had fared in his absence, the rest of us were enjoying the beach. I'd tried to tag along with him, to see him in his element, but the others insisted it would be a "date" and therefore it was a no-go.

Ben and Criss were constructing a giant-ass sand castle that looked better than Blackwood Palace, while Cal, Rob, and I relaxed in the sunshine. I had on the same tiny white dress Rob had purchased for me the day before; the guys were relaxing in lightweight beach shorts.

Well, not *all* the guys were "relaxing." Cal's feet were wiggling, and his fingers were jittering. I could tell he had something on his mind. I propped myself on an elbow and faced him.

"What's up, Cal?" I asked, shading my eyes from the sun.

He immediately sat up. "You know how I said we'd do nothing until the return letters came in?"

I sighed but smiled. "Yes."

"Well, I think we should at least plan what our responses will be no matter what their reply is."

Rob sat up on my left and glared at his brother. "You mean to tell me, you want us to *guess* what they're going to say and then plan a hundred different responses just in case one of them is correct?"

Cal nodded eagerly.

"You're fucked in the head, bro," Rob muttered before lying back down in the sand.

I lifted my hair, allowing the ocean breeze to cool the dampness at the nape of my neck. "You know who might be interested in doing that? Ben and Criss. They're both intellectually oriented. I'm sure they could help you come up with a thousand potential responses, not just a hundred."

"Intellectual?" Cal asked. "I thought Crissen was more leadership oriented, like me."

"He's that too," I assured him. Then I stood and dusted the sand off my legs and ass. "You know what? Maybe we'll just let Criss tackle that question on his own? He's more than capable, and besides, you, me, and Ben have a date we need to get to."

"*Yes*, get him the fuck out of here," Rob grumbled, which earned him a spray of sand from Cal's foot.

As he spit and sputtered, Cal yelled at the castle-builders. "Ben! Criss! Come here for a minute!"

Ben put the finishing touches on a rampart before following Criss over to us. "What's up?"

"Cal's being a fuckhead again!" Rob shouted with a mischievous smirk.

"Robert, I swear to the gods," Cal started, but Ben put his arm out and halted him.

"Seriously," Ben said, trying again. "What's up?"

"You and I have a date with Alexis," Cal told his brother. Then he turned to Criss. "And while we're gone, I was wondering if you wouldn't mind helping me with something?"

"Sure," Criss said, tucking his hands into his navy-and-white-striped shorts' pockets. "What do you need?"

"I need you to help me do some thinking. We sent out three letters with the intention of either stopping the war or getting aid for it. When the return letters filter in, I want to be ready. I want to plan our course of action in advance, that way we're able to act quickly as soon as we know what their responses are."

Criss nodded thoughtfully. "You want me to brainstorm possible outcomes and plot potential courses of action."

"Exactly," Cal said with a relieved smile. "As many as you can think of."

"All right. I'll do that while I finish building the sandcastle. I'm better when I'm working with my hands."

At that, he glanced over at me and his cheeks flushed slightly. Was he ashamed of his humble upbringing as a smith? Or was he embarrassed about imagining using those hands on me? I had a feeling it was the latter, so I pulled my lips in and carefully stared down at the sand. I didn't want *anyone* getting the wrong impression—whatever that might've been.

"Great," Cal replied. "I'll catch back up with you after this date, and we can figure some shit out."

Criss grinned and nodded, retreating back toward the sandcastles. "Enjoy yourselves."

"Oh, we will," Ben assured him with a platonic wink. "Don't fuck up those ramparts."

Criss chuckled. "You're the one who collapsed the last one."

"Yeah, well, we don't need any more mishaps, now do we?" Ben retorted sarcastically.

Criss merely rolled his hazel eyes and wandered off.

I turned back to Cal and Ben and clapped my hands together. "So, what do you guys want to do today?"

"Whatever you want," Ben replied smoothly in that deep bass voice.

"There's surfing, which is challenging yet awesome," Cal began. "There are theatres with plays to see. There are hundreds of little shops to peruse and buy things. There are art classes where you drink wine while you paint."

"Done!" I shouted, jumping up and down in the sand. "I want a new dress, so I'm not stuck wearing this white one all the time. Do you know how hard it is to keep white clean? Then I want to drink wine and paint."

Ben chuckled. "Yeah, if we're drinking it'd probably be best to *paint*. I think surfing might be a bad call."

"So would theatre," Cal added. "Wouldn't want to get thrown out."

I rolled my eyes and raised a brow at him. "First of all, you're a prince. No one would dare throw you out. Second, you're Calvin Storm; nothing about you is rowdy or disrespectful."

"It was me," Rob called from where he lay in the sand. "I was the drunk asshole at the theatre. And I didn't get thrown out. I got escorted out by our friendly neighborhood Sky Prince. In my defense, the performers were terrible."

"Stay out of this *Spirit Prince*," Cal chided. "This isn't your date."

Rob just rolled over in the sand so the sun could tan his chiseled back.

Cal took that as our sign to go. He grabbed my hand, and Ben offered me his elbow. When the three of us were linked, we were on our way to the painting shop.

"Thicker! Longer strokes!" the art instructor called out in a dramatic and whimsical voice.

I stared at my eggplant and giggled soundlessly as I took another sip of wine. *Thicker. Longer.*

There was a basket of fruits and vegetables set up in the middle of the room and ten of us in a circle around it. We were to paint the image as we saw it. Some people were in view of an orange, while others saw grapes. Me? All I could see was an eggplant, a cucumber, and a banana. One-track mind, right here.

I washed the purple out of my brush and patted it dry on an old stained cloth. Thank the gods the art instructor had given us all smocks to wear—I'd have hated to get my newest short-skirt dress all messy. It was a floral mixture of turquoise, chartreuse, and royal blue. Very beachy, the seamstress had assured me. I dipped my brush in green and proceeded to outline a thick, long cock—I mean, *cucumber*—just as she'd said. And when I was finished with that, I painted a thick, long banana.

Cal leaned over and whispered, "Very artistic, Peach."

Ben leaned in from my other side. "Maybe *that* should be our team tattoo? Suggestive fruits and vegetables."

I giggled again and added some brown spots to the yellow peel. "And what would *my* fruit be?"

Cal gestured to his work of art.

I couldn't help but grin. A strawberry half and a spread open *peach*. Because, of course. I had to admit, I could see the resemblance to labia. Then I turned to Ben's painting. Two cantaloupe halves with two blueberries in the center and half of a papaya underneath. Different fruit, same sexual image. Apparently my boys had one-track minds as well.

"I'll consider it," I told them, sipping at my wine. After all, it was still better than tits and dicks.

"Time's up, my little starving artists!" the instructor called. "Show me your masterpieces!"

All ten of us swiveled our artwork around to the center of the circle. I was met with some interesting images. Some looked like paintings right out of a book. Others, like a child had finger-painted them. But only the three of us had gone the erotic route. Their wide eyes and open mouths suggested just how surprised they were to see *a bit more* than just an eggplant, a peach, and a cantaloupe.

"You can either take your art with you," the instructor said, "or leave it here for me to display in tonight's art show. Have a gods blessed day!"

"Let's leave them," I told the boys before finishing off the rest of my wine. "I have a feeling we'll win *for sure*."

"*Right*," Ben agreed sarcastically.

Cal chuckled. "Well, I'm not carting a strawberry-vagina around all day, so we may as well."

Leaving our smocks and suggestive paintings behind, we exited the shop and strolled down the street once more. I was a little tipsy from all the wine, so I kept swaying between the two of them like a happy little flower.

"What do you want to do next?" I asked.

"The theatre?" Ben teased.

"No." Cal's reply was stern, making me giggle.

Suddenly, Dan appeared up ahead, his arms almost over-flowing with beautiful white flowers.

"Aww," I cooed as my shitty grin spread wide. "Are those for me? You're so damn romantic."

Cal glowered at him. "You're ruining our date."

"Yeah, man," Ben agreed. "You can't outdo us when it's not even your turn."

"Fuck you, guys," Dan huffed, turning to shove the stack of blooms into a cart that a servant was pushing behind him. "These are *orkyda blossoms*."

Why did that name ring a bell?

"They're all over Ebony City," Dan continued.

Then it dawned on me. Orkyda blossoms were the flowers the Storm King had planted across the kingdom. The ones that were supposedly explosive when combined with alicorn dust and dragon fire.

"I need them all removed immediately. Will you guys help me? I already have Rob and Criss scouring the clifftops." He pointed up to the second tier of the city.

"Of course we will," I replied immediately. Cal and Ben didn't hesitate to agree either. I fucking loved that about them. Instead of getting pissy about our date being cut short, they knew Dan's need, and his citizens' need, was far greater than their own.

Then a thought came to me. "Wouldn't it be faster and more thorough to just make an announcement and have the citizens pull out any plants they find?"

Dan sighed. "Yes, but I was really hoping to avoid starting a mass panic. They're already on edge as it is with the war looming close."

I nodded. He was right. No need to worry them unnecessarily.

"Can we each have a servant and a cart?" Cal asked, jumping into leadership mode.

"Absolutely." Dan turned to his servant and gave him a few orders. "Dump the cart in the chateau courtyard. We'll burn all the blooms tonight. Tell the other servants to do the same. And while you're up there, send a few more servants out with carts."

"Yes, Your Highness." The man bowed before rushing away.

When the servant was out of sight, Dan scrubbed both hands across his face. "This is a fucking nightmare."

"It's all right, bro," Ben assured him, placing his hand on Dan's shoulder. "We'll get it taken care of."

"Mind if we split up?" Cal asked, and I wasn't sure if he was talking to me or Dan. "We can cover more ground that way. As long as you think it's safe?"

"Of course it's safe," Dan replied. "I've busted my ass this past decade to make sure Ebony City is one of the safest places to live in all of Blackwood. That's partially why I'm so pissed off about these fucking flowers."

Cal turned to me. "Are you okay with being on your own? Or would you like one of us to go with you?"

I put a hand on my hip, swaying a bit where I stood. "I have the power of *fire* at my command, Sky Prince. I'll be fine."

He looked skeptical.

"Besides," I continued, "Taron, Tamara, and Camilla trained me well. I know how to kick some serious ass if need be."

"Which there *won't* be a need for," Dan assured us.

Still, Cal looked torn between letting me go on my own and wanting to babysit the fuck out of me.

I crossed my arms, concentrating very hard on not tipping over. "I can do this, *Calvin*. Give me some gods-damned credit."

Finally, he sighed. "Fine."

A few minutes later, Dan's servant returned, along with two extra helpers, all with carts in tow. One was a girl, who promptly got assigned to me. Whatever. I had no doubt she was just as strong as any boy servant I would have got. Us girls needed to stick together anyway and keep sticking it to the man.

After that, we were off, scouring the city for any and every hint of orkyda blossom we could find. My servant— whose name was Reesa—and I took the eastern edge of the city where the sand mixed with grass and actual trees grew. We filled cart after cart, searching for blossoms long after the sun began to dip on the horizon, bathing the city in its golden shadow, long after the gold turned to dusk, and the luminescent moon rose high into the midnight sky.

"We should get back to the chateau, Your Highness," Reesa suggested, glancing warily from the dim-lit shops on our left to the shadowed tree trunks on our right.

I sighed. "I suppose you're right. We'll have to finish uprooting the rest of the little bastards tomorrow."

There were a terrifying number of orkydas scattered about; the Storm King had been nothing short of thorough. If every city in every quadrant had this many blooms, then we were probably fucked.

A breeze rolled in from the forest, gently lifting a few tendrils of my dark hair, sending my nerves buzzing with energy.

What the...?

It was like lightning crackling through my veins, vibrating every cell, warming my skin.

I turned back toward the forest and scanned the trees. Though I saw nothing, I had a niggling suspicion that magic was nearby. From whom or from what, I had no idea. But I was determined to find out.

"Reesa, you go on ahead. Dump the cart in the courtyard. Tell the princes I'm in the woods across from—" I read the name of the nearest shop. "—Bargador's Books."

Books! It'd been so long since I read a good book. I was going to have to sneak in there some time before our visit here was over.

Her expression turned fearful. "Your Highness, traveling the woods alone in the dark is unsuitable for a princess."

I wasn't a damsel in distress; I could do shit on my own.

But I wasn't a total idiot either, which is why I wanted her to fetch the princes.

"I'll be fine," I argued. "Just deliver my message, then rest. You've had a long and tiresome day. And tomorrow we'll be at it again."

She nodded solemnly and scurried off with the cart bouncing softly behind her.

The magic I'd sensed didn't feel... bad. Powerful, yes, but not evil. I wasn't frightened of it; I was merely curious. How I inherently *knew* any of that shit from a simple breeze was anyone's guess, but still, I was sure that I did.

With one final glance behind me, I made my way into the woods and toward the buzzing energy.

CHAPTER 17

*T*iptoeing carefully through the woods, I came upon a moonlit glade.

The grass of the clearing looked a dusty blue shade in the pallid starlight, but the creature standing in middle was bright white and practically glittering. It stood on four strong legs with golden hooves, and on its majestic head sat a single, spiraling gold horn.

"Oh my gods," I whispered to myself. I'd never seen anything like it.

At the faint sound of my voice, the creature's head snapped in my direction, and it ruffled it's feathers.

Feathers?

I looked closer, stunned to find the horse-like creature also had two massive wings tucked into its side. It shook its silky white mane and cracked its longhaired tail, snorting at me.

"Holy shit," Ben muttered, appearing out of nowhere on my left. "It's an alicorn."

I gasped and spun around, surprised to find that *all* the guys were already there.

"How the hell?" I questioned in a whisper, clutching at my chest as my heart hammered.

Ben cocked his head toward Cal, whose whole body sagged as he reached into his shorts pocket and withdrew a velvety pouch. He worked the drawstring open with limp fingers and shakily brought a dark ball of chocolate up to his mouth.

One of his special energy treats. I knew he relied on them when he used his power over the sky, which cost him his strength. I'd tried the little morsels myself a couple times, and they were delicious.

I suddenly had a sneaking suspicion that Cal had *flown* them all there.

"I'm sorry," Rob rasped in a harsh whisper, "but did you just say *alicorn*?"

Ben turned to him and nodded.

"So, the Storm King was right?" Criss marveled with a gaping expression. "They're not extinct after all."

"They're beautiful," Dan added quietly.

"They really are," I agreed, turning my gaze back to the glittering creature. "What do you think it's doing here?"

Ben shot me a grim expression before turning back to study the glade. "There doesn't seem to be any chains, wires, or fences."

"It still seems trapped though," Rob argued. "Otherwise, it would have run off when we all appeared. It definitely sensed us."

Ben nodded his agreement. "I'm sure it caught our scent on the air. Let's move a little closer and see what happens."

We inched forward, slowly at first, but with more ease and determination as we drew nearer to the magnificent beast. It watched us with steady eyes, unstartled, but wary just the same. When we got too close, it trotted to the opposite side of the little meadow and continued staring at us.

ELLE MIDDAUGH

There was a circle of charred grass surrounding the glade, right at the edge of the tree line—it must've simply looked like a shadow from further away—and atop the burnt grass, were tiny chunks of what appeared to be white paper.

Ben knelt down, picked up one of the white scraps and rubbed it between his thumb and forefinger. Then he brought it to his nose and sniffed. After that, he broke off a piece of charred grass and studied it, too.

He turned to us, gesturing to the white stuff. "These are torn orkyda petals." Then he held out the blackened grass. "What are the odds these scorch marks are from dragon fire?"

"Probably 100 percent," I muttered.

"That's what I'm afraid of," he admitted. "I have a feeling that if the alicorn were to attempt crossing that barrier, it would combust. It must've sensed danger in the air or something, that's why it instinctually knew not to cross the threshold."

"So let's dig it out," Dan suggested. "Get rid of the dragon fire and the petals. Give the damn thing at least a three foot berth and—"

"And what?" Cal interrupted. "Let it free? The Storm King will just capture it again and hold it hostage in another location we don't find right away. It could be trapped for months before we find it again."

"Or," I argued on behalf of the beast, "it can escape and live its life in peace, free from the Storm King and all of humanity that would use its magical dust for evil."

"Assuming it didn't get caught," Cal stressed, eyeing me sternly. "Which isn't a solid assumption, considering it's one of the last of its kind and it *still* got caught."

I glared at him. "It still deserves a chance. What would you propose? Rescuing it from one cage and putting it in another? That's not a rescue; it's a transfer. We're better than him. Let's prove it."

Cal stared at me for a long moment. They all did. But soon they all came to the same conclusion: that I was right.

"Fine," Cal admitted. "We'll free the alicorn. But if it gets caught another time and we have to free it again, then we're going to do things my way—transferring it *for a time*, yes, but not permanently. Once we find a safe and suitable place to relocate it, we'll most definitely do so."

"Fine," I agreed. "But for now, let's let the poor thing try to make it on its own."

Dan and Criss immediately got to work, using nearby rocks to dig out chunks of soil where the grass was charred. Once all signs of orkyda blossom and dragon fire were gone, we backed away and waited silently behind some trees.

The alicorn snorted and stomped its golden hooves. When we didn't move closer—or at all, really—it trotted over to the gap we'd dug in the barrier. It sniffed, as if testing the air for some sort of magical current. The next second, it lurched forward, crossing the threshold in an instant before spreading its wings and flying into the midnight sky. The fact that it could fly away now that the barrier had been removed, proved to me that someone had placed the creature there intentionally and probably by force.

My heart swelled as I watched it until it disappeared into the night. The Storm King had no doubt already collected dust from it, so the threat of explosions was still very real. But we'd saved an innocent creature's life. That had to count for something.

"We did the right thing," Dan decided, placing his dirty hands on his hips.

Ben nodded. "Now, I'm just wondering where the dragons are."

And, of course, he was totally right. If alicorns were still alive, then we had no choice but to believe dragons were as well.

"We'll find them," I assured my Sand Prince with a confident smile. "One way or another."

"I hope you're right, Sailor."

Rob chuckled. "If lightning bolts are anything like dragon fire, then we should put Criss in charge of finding them."

Cal turned to Rob and raised a brow. "What's that supposed to mean?"

It was difficult to tell in the moonlight, but it seemed as if Criss's cheeks had flushed.

"Ask the ladies' man, over there," Rob replied, jabbing a thumb toward Criss, who at that point, I was *certain* was blushing.

"I'm *not* a ladies' man," he assured us bashfully.

For some reason, my stomach twisted into a knot. "What happened, Rob?"

"Poor bastard was just trying to finish his sandcastle," Rob began with a shit-eating grin, "kept getting interrupted by hot girls. Every time one of them got brave enough to touch his arm or his leg—*bam*!—they got zapped away by a bolt of fucking lightning. It was hilarious."

I turned to Criss and did my best to keep my jealousy in check. This was stupid. He wasn't even one of my guys. Not yet, anyway. So, why was I feeling so possessive of him? "Is this true?"

His mouth opened and closed a few times before any words fell out. "Yes? I wasn't flirting or anything. I wasn't checking anybody out. I didn't ask for them to approach me. It just sort of... happened."

I looked at him—*for real*—for the first time in... well, *ever*.

His buzzed light brown hair lent him an edge of daring. Beneath that, he had beautiful hazel eyes—a swirling mixture of green, blue, brown, and gold—and a set of dimples cute enough to keep my lick-happy tongue busy for days.

He wore a pale blue dress shirt that was only half buttoned up, allowing some of his chest hair to show, and his sleeves were rolled up to the elbow, showcasing his biceps. Actually, the whole thing was tight enough to showcase every rippling muscle in his body.

At his hips, everything narrowed beneath his shirt into what I recalled seeing was a serious "V." The lines of his abdominals were cut deep, drawing my gaze down to the outline of his dick as it rested underneath his khaki shorts.

I swallowed hard, wondering what it'd be like to let him touch me. To slip his tongue into my mouth, run his hands up my sides, and sink his cock between my thighs. Heat rose to life within me, and my gaze darkened.

I was surprised to find that I *wanted* him. That my imaginings weren't just born of curiosity; that they were also filled with excitement and longing. The revelation was confusing, though. I didn't know if it was okay for me to want him or to be feeling any of those things.

All of this happened within seconds, so before anyone could somehow read my mind or pick up on my mood, I quickly changed the subject. "I'm tired."

Cal nodded. "It's been a long day."

"And it'll be another long one tomorrow," Dan promised us. "Hopefully it'll be the last day we're stuck yanking orkydas from the ground, though. We have other shit to worry about."

"I wonder if any letters will come back early?" Ben pondered aloud, which set Cal off.

"Criss," he began, sounding excited at the prospect of politics and business. "What'd you come up with today?"

Criss, who hadn't been nearly as *un*observant as the rest, fought hard to drag his gaze away from mine. I had a feeling he knew exactly what I'd been imagining, and that he'd been imagining it too. In some fucked-up world, on some alternate plane, we were probably mind fucking each other. "A lot of things," he replied, before glancing back at me.

I couldn't help it, my lips parted as I once again thought about kissing him right there in front of everyone. It was a feral urge, one that was hard to deny, but I managed. Barely.

Criss swallowed hard and concentrated on not looking at me.

I wasn't sure whether to be thankful or pissed off.

Cal and Criss walked back through the woods toward the chateau as they discussed our various options. Dan and Rob exchanged a bored eye roll but followed after them. Ben and I, on the other hand, exchanged a smile.

"You want to grab a drink?" he asked me, tucking his hands into his shorts' pockets. "I know it's late, but there's a pretty sweet beachside bar at the cove if you're interested."

I glanced up at the moon, trying to gauge what time it might've been. The sun hadn't set *that* long ago. And honestly? A drink sounded wonderful. I turned back to Ben and grinned. "I suppose it *is* still your date..."

He bit his bottom lip almost shyly. "I'm sure Cal won't mind if we go without him."

I laughed. "Cal's the one who left without *us*!"

This time Ben laughed, throwing an arm around my shoulders and pulling me close as we brought up the end of the line. When everyone else veered up the cliffside stairs toward the chateau, Ben and I carried on straight, walking until the sandstone streets became a boardwalk and the boardwalk became a sandy beach.

Ahead, lights, which were suspended in the air by nothing at all, twinkled like stars. In fact, they *looked* like stars—stars that had fallen from the sky and decided they had nothing better to do than illuminate a local outdoor bar.

"Faerie lights," Ben whispered in my ear, giving me goosies. "Rumor has it, the owner traded a fae something terribly valuable in exchange for them."

"What did he trade?"

Ben shrugged. "No one knows."

I narrowed my eyes in suspicion. I wasn't sure if he was telling the truth or teasing me.

Ben pulled out a tall chair and gestured for me to sit at the bar; then he hopped onto the stool right beside mine. With a wave of his hand, he flagged down the bartender.

Music swam through the air like an eel, curling back and forth between the customers who were either drinking or dancing or both. My foot tapped to the alluring beat, and my hips and shoulders swayed.

"What can I get ya?" the bartender asked us, focusing way more on me than Ben. He was young and handsome with dark hair and shadowed stubble, but he wasn't one of my Storms, so the attraction wasn't there.

Ben smirked, eyeing the poor bartender with sympathy as he pined over me. "Ladies first."

"I'll take something fruity," I decided. "And strong."

The man smiled, a blush touching his cheeks before he turned to Ben and his smile faded. "And you?"

"A whiskey on the rocks."

The bartender nodded. "Coming right up."

"Hold on," I said, stopping him before he could rush off. "Are you the owner of this place?"

"Sure am," he replied with a nod.

I leaned forward and pointed to a faerie light before crossing my arms. "How'd you get those?"

He chuckled as he grabbed a glass and wiped it out with a white towel. "Ah, the faerie story has been making its rounds again, I see."

I glanced at Ben then back at the tender. "So it's not true?"

"No, it is. It's just sometimes the tale is popular and other times it fades out."

I waited patiently, not to be deterred.

He cleared his throat. "I traded a fae for them. He was a travelling type, stopped by before setting sail. I had a few nautical trinkets decorating the place, but one of the pearls in particular took his interest. He asked for the pearl in exchange for the lights, and since the pearl was a worthless decoration to me, I accepted."

I nodded my agreement. As an ex-jewel miner, I was a little biased. Pearls were worse than rocks, nothing precious about them. "So, you didn't have to trade something terribly valuable after all."

The tender chuckled and set the dry glass down on a shelf behind him. "I wouldn't say that. It was nothing to *me*, but to the fae, it was valuable. He said it'd fetch a pretty price in Hydratica, but I couldn't care less. The very next day another pearl washed in, and I replaced it."

He pointed to a wooden sign hanging above the bar. It read: The Salted Pearl. In the top right corner, a dip had been carved in the wood to allow a small sphere to sit. Inside the dip was a champagne-colored pearl.

I grinned and cocked my head. "I'm curious, what did the original pearl look like?"

"It was about the same size as that one. A strange color, though. Pale like a pearl, but with hints of lavender, or lilac, or maybe even periwinkle." He nodded to himself. "It was pretty, but surely not worth more than a few extra coins. I was lucky to get the faerie lights in exchange."

"You certainly were," I agreed.

He smiled and backed away. "I'll be back with your drinks in just a moment."

When he left, I turned to Ben who was staring at me in

curiosity. I leaned closer to him. "What are the odds of that pearl being the Eye of the Sea?"

Ben's eyes went wide. "What?"

"Think about it. Why else would a common pearl be valuable enough to trade for magical faerie lights? No one else in Blackwood has these, at least, not that I've seen. They must be rare, and why would a fae trade something rare if not for something rare in return?"

Ben's eyes darted from side to side as he worked out my suspicions like a math equation in his brain. "If the fae did as the bar owner says, and he took the pearl to Hydratica to sell, then the Storm King is right—the Eye really is located in enemy territory."

I nodded.

"Fuck."

"Yeah," I agreed. "*Fuck*."

CHAPTER 18

*T*he next morning, we finished ridding Ebony City
of orkyda blossoms.

Reesa and I had scanned every corner of the eastern side,
and by lunchtime, we'd deposited the last few cartloads in the
courtyard.

The night before, while Ben and I were learning about the
Eye of the Sea, Dan and the others had burned the previous
day's haul. Apparently the flowers burned sickly sweet, so I
was almost glad I'd missed it. I didn't need anything putting
me off of my sweets, now did I?

Ugh. *Sweets...*

My heart squeezed and sadness tore through my chest
like jagged lines of black lightning, filling me with darkness
and fear. I'd been trying so fucking hard not to think about
him, not to *worry* about him, but Asher's handsome face
immediately invaded my mind as soon as I'd thought of the
word.

His warm smile captivated me, followed by the intensity
of his amber eyes framed in dark lashes. I'd long ago memo-

rized every detail of his features, and I yearned to trace them now, to feel his skin beneath my fingertips.

I squeezed my fist and clutched it to my chest.

I love you, Asher Storm. Come back to me. I'm dying slowly without you.

"Princess Alexis?" a voice asked, jarring me from my moment.

I realized I'd been staring at the massive pile of flowers in the courtyard and that the voice was Reesa's.

I cleared my throat and spun around. "Yes?"

"Is everything all right?"

"Yes, of course." I forced myself to smile.

"Highness, if I might press..." She fiddled with the hem of her pale blue servant gown, her skin looking incredibly tan in comparison. "Are you distressed because something bad happened last night? I've been worried sick about you."

This time my smile was genuine. It was sweet of her to worry. "Thank you for your concern, Reesa. But, no, nothing bad happened last night. The princes found me, and all was well."

Her expression was still fretful, though, so I figured I'd better give her a few more details.

"I'm just worried about someone. I haven't heard from him in a long time, and I'm afraid I might not see him again."

The poor girl's eyes widened, and her mouth dropped open. No doubt she was wondering how the ever-loving *fuck* five guys weren't already enough to satisfy me. Well, duh, Sex Princess over here! But seriously, I couldn't have her thinking there were more men—even though there were.

"He's an old friend," I assured her, which was at least a partial truth.

That seemed to pacify her, though. She curtsied and left me alone once more in the courtyard. It didn't take long for

the rest of the guys to filter in with their servants and carts—
Cal, Ben, Rob, Dan... and finally, Criss.

I was terrified to admit that my ridiculous heart skipped a
beat when I saw him. It wasn't that I didn't still feel that way
about my other Storms—because I most definitely did—it
was just, I wasn't expecting to feel it toward *that* Storm. It
was new, and dare I say it, sort of exciting.

After saying a few words to his servant, Criss strolled
over to me and clasped his hands in front of him, rubbing
them anxiously. "Today's the day."

I smiled and nodded. "Sure is."

"I've been thinking about this a lot this week, so I have
some ideas I want to run by you, if that's okay?"

"What'd you have in mind?" I crossed my arms, inadvertently pushing up my breasts, which immediately caught his
hazel gaze.

Quickly, his eyes shot back up to my face, and he cleared
his throat. "Um. Well. Pottery for one."

I raised a brow. "Pottery?"

"Yeah, well, I figured you enjoyed art since you went
painting yesterday. And I like to use my hands, so I thought
combining the two might be fun?"

I'd rather see you "use your hands" on me.

Zeus Almighty, Alexis, chill the fuck out.

"Sure," I said with a smile as heat rushed up my neck.
"That sounds great."

"Cool," he replied with a grin. "I was also thinking about
finding a bakery and sampling some chocolates?"

"I'm definitely down for that."

"Awesome." His grin widened and dimples appeared in
both cheeks. "And then I thought *you* could choose something for us to do? Afterward, we could have a picnic dinner
on the beach, away from the fray."

I reached out and touched his arm, and anxious energy

slammed into me like a heat wave. This schoolgirl crush I'd recently developed was absolutely absurd. I both hated and loved it.

Cal paused in the middle of his conversation with his servant, his eyes locked on where my hand touched the newest Storm's skin. "You treat our girl right, Criss."

"Of course I will," he promised immediately, and I withdrew my hand.

"But not *too* right," Rob stipulated sternly.

Criss took a deep breath and smiled. "Of course not."

"Yeah, and if you could cut your date short so that it's my turn sooner, that'd be great too," Dan tacked on with a grin.

Criss opened his mouth to say something then paused. "No, I can't even pretend to agree to that. Today's my day. You can have her tomorrow."

Ben chuckled. "He'll probably come interrupt everything right in the middle like he did to Cal and me."

"Hey," Dan said, crossing his arms in his own defense. "That was a kingdom-wide emergency. We all agreed it was important."

"I know," Ben admitted. "But still, you totally fucked up our date. I think Cal and I should have another one before Dan gets his turn."

"In favor," Cal said, raising his hand.

"*In favor*," Rob agreed, grinning like the fucking devil he was. He just loved stirring the pot of dissention.

"No," Dan said at once. "Fuck you, guys. We voted once already; no takebacks. Tomorrow's my day with Lexi, whether you assholes like it or not."

Criss reached out and took my hand, pulling me toward the path that led away from the chateau and into the city.

Rob pointed at our hands with a glower. "Three-foot rule."

Criss sighed. "That's not a thing."

"It is now," Rob decided. "You need me to tag along and enforce said rule?"

I watched Criss roll his hazel eyes, never once loosening his hold on my hand. "I'm a prince, *brother*. I don't need a regent." Rob shot him a deadly glare, which somehow made him chuckle. "In all seriousness, man, just relax. I promise to be a perfect gentleman with her. I just want to get to know her better."

"I regret this already," Rob muttered.

"No takebacks," Criss said with a wide smile, mimicking Dan's words from a moment ago.

"Godsdamn it," the Sea Prince muttered, shaking his head. "Using our words against us. I see how it is."

Cal chuckled. "He acts just like us already."

"Exactly." Dan waved us off before gathering a few servants to start the final orkyda bonfire. "I want this shit burned as soon as humanly possible. I don't want a single bloom left behind."

"Aye, Your Highness. But what of the ashes?"

As they discussed their fire plans, Criss and I slipped from the courtyard and made our way into Ebony City hand in hand.

It was awkward at first. Unnatural. To be touching him in such a way. And yet, it felt good. Right. Like yet another piece of the Storms of Blackwood puzzle was fitting together.

"So," he began, smiling brightly, "tell me about you. Who is Alexis Ravenel, really?"

I chuckled softly. "Just a poor jewel miner from Blackleaf who ended up at the wrong place at the wrong time. Or, the right place at the right time, if you believe in fate or whatever."

I told him the story of how I'd received my powers; then I

filled him in on everything that had happened in my life since. My mom being taken into the harem and tortured. Speedy being killed and reappearing as Asher/Adam. The Storm King hurting Gemma to manipulate me, then eventually killing her —gods, that still gutted me. I told Criss about falling in love with the guys. About our journey to Eristan and to the Lunaley —the land that he now technically ruled. He'd never seen it, so he asked for as many vivid details as possible. I recalled as much as I could, including the deadly chimeras that would have killed us if it weren't for Criss's addition to our blood bond.

It was so easy to talk to him. I just opened my mouth and the words flowed like a river, and never once did I worry that he'd judge me or make me feel ashamed. In fact, the more we talked, the more I liked him—which was dangerous fucking territory. Until he got the approval of the guys, all of this was way too far up in the air.

"What about you?" I asked, swinging our hands between us as we made our way to the bakery. "What's the real Crissen Storm like?"

He grinned and bit his bottom lip, making me yearn to bite it instead. Heat flared to life in my core, settling right between my legs. Leave it to my lady bits to make this all the more difficult.

"I grew up in Blackhaven. Never knew my father," he began. "So when I was just a young boy, the local blacksmith took pity on me and agreed to train me. Said a man needed to know a trade or he wasn't worth a single jewel."

I laughed. "I'm sure you'd be worth a hundred jewels, even if you couldn't hammer out a sword."

He glanced at me, and his smile softened. "Thanks."

"Yeah, no problem. But just one thing."

"What's that?"

I shook my head as I thought. "The Storm King is sterile

—or so the rumor goes. None of the Storm Princes are truly his kids. So, who's your *real* father?"

Criss shrugged as if he couldn't care less. "No idea. Maybe the fucking blacksmith?"

I laughed and bit my bottom lip. "Maybe."

Criss pointed in front of us, and the bakery was suddenly within sight. "Ready to sample some treats?"

"Absolutely."

I wasn't sure if I was referring to him or the chocolates.

AFTER WE'D FILLED OURSELVES TO THE BRIM WITH SWEETS, WE made a couple coffee mugs at the pottery shop—Criss's was awesome; mine sucked. He assured me mine just had more *character.* And then we were on our way to my part of the date: Bargador's Books.

"A bookstore, huh?" Criss asked as we stood outside the shop, eyeing the rows of books through the front glass.

I nodded. "Yep. I love to read."

"So do I, actually," he admitted.

I had the sudden image of him naked on a mountaintop sipping whiskey and reading a naughty romance, the book just barely covering his junk.

I shook my head. *Snap out of it, Lex.*

"What kind of books do you enjoy?" he asked, as he held open the door for me.

I stepped inside and beelined for the romance section. I grabbed the first racy cover I could find and wiggled it in his vision. "What do you think?"

His cheeks flushed a gentle pink. "Erotica. Nice."

I put a hand on my hip and pointed the book at his face. "They're not erotic. I mean, yeah, the sex scenes are steamy as fuck, but there's an actual plotline too. Sex is the perk, not the point."

He grinned and nodded his concession. "I'll have to take your word for it."

"Or maybe you'll just have to read one for yourself sometime," I challenged. "In fact, I dare you to read a passage from a novel of my choice at our picnic dinner tonight."

"What? No way."

"Oh, come on!" I practically begged. "Only *I'll* be there to hear you. There's no need to be afraid or embarrassed."

"I'm not afraid," he argued.

"Then take the dare."

He pursed his lips and narrowed his eyes at me, and fuck if it wasn't sexy as hell. Heat once again flooded through my body, and I fought the urge to fan my face.

"Fine. I accept your dare, but I offer you one in return."

I cocked my head with confidence. "All right. Hit me with it."

"I dare you to sit in my lap while I read it."

I rolled my eyes and smirked. "You think I'm afraid of a boner? Pssh! Dare accepted."

"I wasn't finished," he teased as we strolled through the aisles, scanning the books. "I dare you to sit in my lap and *not* kiss me."

My heart leapt into my throat, and my pussy swelled. Pretty sure my panties were already wet.

"All right," I began hesitantly. I wasn't so sure I wanted to take that dare, actually. But I wasn't one to back down from a challenge. "Humor me, though. What happens if I fail?"

Criss leaned in so close his nose nearly brushed mine. "We'll discuss the terms of your failure if and when the need arises."

Oh, fuck, I was so screwed. Hopefully not literally, because Rob would kill us both, but actually, I was secretly kind of hoping it *would* be literally. My body was definitely ready to take him for a test ride. And then probably a follow-up ride, just to be sure the first one wasn't a fluke. And maybe a third, because third time's the charm, right?

Shut the fuck up.

Instead of taking a healthy step back, like I should have, or bridging the gap between our lips, like I wanted to, I simply reached behind him and pulled a book off the shelf. Then I slid it between our faces. "This one. I want you to read this one to me."

He leaned back and stared at the cover. "*A Crown of Blood and Ashes*. Sounds romantic."

"Oh, it is," I assured him, waggling my brows.

He snatched it from my grasp and tucked it underneath his arm. "All right, then. Let's get it. Any more books you'd like to purchase while we're here?"

I sighed theatrically. "You know the way to a woman's heart, don't you?"

He chuckled. "Yep. *Books*. Just run my finger down their spines, spread open their... pages... and bury my face in them until dawn."

Holy shit.

That was the sexiest inuendo I'd ever heard.

This time, I really did fan my face. "It's hot in here. Are you hot?" Of course he was. "Let's get down to the beach and start that picnic. I think the ocean breeze will do us some good."

He chuckled darkly, completely aware of how his words had affected me. Then he gestured to the checkout desk.

"After you, Princess."

CHAPTER 19

*C*rissen and I loaded up on fresh breads and fruits, aged cheeses and wines, and a few salted meats and sugary treats—for good measure. We also grabbed a thick blanket to sit on and a wicker basket to hold it all.

By the time we neared the beach, the sun was cozying down beneath the horizon, preparing for sleep. There were a few bonfires blazing in the sand with different parties going on around each, a few couples making out in the shadows, and a bunch of customers hanging out at The Salted Pearl.

We bypassed all that noise, making our way through some of the natural stone archways of the cove before discovering a tiny strip of beach covered in soft white sand. It was quiet, aside from the gentle crash of the surf, and alone, aside from the countless stars shining up above.

In other words, it was perfect.

Criss set up our picnic spot while I skimmed my book in search of the perfect scene. I wanted to prove that the thing had a plot beyond the erotic, but I kind of wanted to tease him too; so I tried to find something in between. When I found the one I wanted, I placed the book's ribbon between the pages and snapped it shut.

"Found the perfect passage, did you?" Criss asked with a grin as he sat down and began dishing out food.

"I think so," I said, grinning back.

It was weird, but I suddenly felt shy, like his opinion mattered to me all of a sudden and I wanted him to like me. I mean, *the book*. I wanted him to like the book... and me. Shit.

After we each had a full plate, he pulled our handmade mugs from the basket and filled them each with wine. Both of them were striped; though, his lines were perfectly straight, and mine seemed to be drawn by a drunk toddler. His stripes were nautical perfection: navy blue and pure white. Mine were a bleeding mixture of dark teal, turquoise, aquamarine, and eggshell blue. Whatever. As long as the damned things held their fluids, that was the important part.

I popped a cube of cheese into my mouth and smiled. "I had a really nice time with you today."

He grabbed a strawberry and did the same. "Likewise. But it's not over yet. Don't rush it."

I shook my head, and longing filled my chest like a physical weight. The same could be said of our relationship, and I couldn't allow myself to rush that either. "I wouldn't dream of it."

He grabbed another strawberry and dropped it into his mouth. "Good. Because I have more questions."

Chuckling, I leaned back on an elbow and grabbed a few grapes. "Ask away, Your Highness."

"Thank you, Your Highness," he said with a mock bow. I bowed my head in return, and we both chuckled before the mood turned suddenly serious. "What's your favorite color?"

I burst out laughing, not expecting such a lighthearted question. "I don't know. Blue? Green? I used to see nothing but brown dirt and damp black rock for most of my life. It was always such a blessing to see the sky or the leaves."

"Who'd you lose your virginity to?" he asked, without missing a beat.

I rolled my eyes. Of course he'd ask a sex-related question. "A guy named John. He was okay looking, I suppose. Kind of a dickhead, honestly, but I was just so fixated on the act of having sex that I really didn't care who it came from. I didn't like him much—*definitely* didn't love him—and the sex was super subpar. After it was over, I wondered why steamy romance books existed at all."

Criss burst out laughing, so I threw a grape at his head.

"What about you, jerk face? Who'd you blow your load into after a whole minute of painful penetration?"

He laughed a bit longer then wiped some tears from his eyes. "Touché. My first time was a lot like yours. Okay-looking girl, no love involved, just wanted to know what sex felt like." He shrugged.

"What was her name?"

"Janis."

"Janis?" I asked, feeling irrationally jealous all of a sudden. "That sounds like the name of a hippopotamus. Was she big and gray and mostly hairless?"

"*Hades*, you're feisty right now." He reached out and pulled me into his lap, wrapping his hands around my waist. "Are you jealous?"

I scoffed, pushing my hands between our chests in an attempt to keep my sanity.

You can't have him, Alexis. Not until the guys agree.

"Of course I'm not," I argued. "She just sounds like a big-nosed, river-dwelling thunder-cunt, that's all."

He burst out laughing again and shook his head. "Let's not talk about her." He unwound his arms from my waist and slid them up my sides. "In fact, while we're here in this exact position, why don't I read you a book?"

My breath hitched as I realized he was hard beneath me. I was literally sitting on his boner, and though I swore it wouldn't affect me, it totally was. I found myself longing to grind into it, to tease him and experience him to the fullest. But there was sadness there too, because I knew I couldn't.

I leaned over and grabbed the book, threading my hands behind his neck as he opened it to the bookmarked page.

"I watched intently as his brows furrowed," Criss read. *"Then his jaw clenched, lined in sexy stubble. His hand slowly slid across his bare chest to where the arrow was lodged. When his fingers brushed the carbon fiber shaft, his eyes instantly snapped open. Beautiful hazel eyes, tropical blue mixed with mint green—they drew me in even as those eyes darted over to me, confused as fuck and maybe even a little panicked. He ripped the arrow from his chest."*

His gaze darted up to mine, and I was met with a set of eyes exactly as he'd just described. Hazel and beautiful. "You get off on bleeding men?"

I laughed and pushed on his chest. "Just keep reading."

Criss cocked his head and did as ordered. *"'Why am I not healing?' he asked. Concern laced his words. I stole a peek over my shoulder. The wound was still streaming blood down his perfectly carved chest. 'You were poisoned,' I said. 'I gave you an antidote that saved your life, but it's going to take some time for the toxins to completely run their course.'"*

Criss glanced up at me. "Okay. I get it. There's obviously some sort of a story going on beyond the erotic."

I rolled my eyes. *"Obviously."*

He flipped several pages ahead and bit his bottom lip. *"'Give me a reason to leave,' he whispered. His hands found my hips, and he pulled me closer to him. I shook my head. 'I don't want you to leave.' Then his mouth was on mine, our tongues tangling in a rush of frantic desire. Desperate, yet thorough. Hard, yet passionate. Our bodies curled together until there was nothing but a flimsy line of fabric between us. 'I thought about this all damn day,' he groaned into my mouth. 'What I wanted to do to you.'"*

Criss stopped reading and stared deep into my eyes. The heavy-hanging arousal in the air made the mood extremely tense. I wanted him, but I shouldn't. I was desperate for him, but I couldn't have him.

"I relate to this man so much right now," he muttered, dropping the book to run his hands up and down my spine. "I've thought about *this* all day. Getting you in my arms, in my lap, kissing you thoroughly. Passionately. Desperately."

Get off his lap, Lex, before you're getting off on his lap.

I knew I couldn't actually kiss Criss, no matter what my body was thinking. Kisses led to touching, and touching led to sex. I couldn't let that happen, not without the consent of my guys. My *husbands*. Even though Criss was undoubtedly a part of our group—a part of *us*—we'd just had to wait a little bit longer.

As he leaned in to kiss me, I leaned back and chuckled. "Not yet."

He grinned and nodded, a mix of disappointment and appreciation. "You're better than I thought you were. You just won the bet."

I smacked his chest and climbed out of his lap. "That's right, so you better pay up."

"*Hm*, what were the terms again?" he asked, feigning amnesia. "I seem to recall there being none."

"They were 'to be determined,' I believe," I said, playing along.

"*Ah*, yes," he recalled. "Well, in that case—"

Suddenly a loud howl echoed into the night. The sound was melancholic, possibly even pained. I wasn't intimidated by it, but I was definitely curious. Did the poor creature need some help?

"A wolf?" Criss asked.

Then from out of nowhere, it hit me.

Asher! Oh my gods, Ash must've been back and looking for us, and when he saw me with Criss, he must felt dejected. I was suddenly so glad we hadn't taken things further than we did.

Scrambling to my feet, I darted in the direction of the sound. Running in sand was harder than it looked, though, so I made almost no progress before I was once again out of breath.

Criss caught me quickly and jogged at my side. "What the hell are you doing?"

"I think it's Asher," I huffed as I ran. "I think he's back. He must be in wolf form."

Realization and understanding dawned on his face, but to my surprise, instead of becoming crestfallen, he became determined. "Let's find him then."

That's when I knew, beyond any shadow of a doubt, that Criss was one of us.

The closer we got to the sound, the more the truth of the scene unfolded. The howling hadn't been that of a wolf, but rather an injured seal bleeding out on the shore. A bony old man sat at the creature's side, petting it as it wailed in agony.

I paused.

Okay, so it wasn't a wolf. It could still be Asher though. All I had to do was check for a dot on his throat...

"Excuse us?" Criss asked as we drew nearer. "Is there a problem?"

The old man turned around with tears in his eyes. He had a long white beard and a head of thin hair to match. "I'm not as strong as I once was," he admitted, not exactly answering Criss's question.

When we were close enough, I scanned the poor creature's neck but found nothing in the way of a distinctive spot. My hopes sank like an anchor. It wasn't him; it wasn't Ash.

I turned to Criss and shook my head.

He nodded compassionately in return, then directed his attention back to the old man. "Is there anything we can do?"

The old man turned to stare between Crissen and me. "*She* has powers," he said matter-of-factly. "*You* don't. How could you possibly hope to save this seal?"

Criss blinked, momentarily taken aback before he regathered his wits. "I don't believe people need magic in order to help others, sir. I might not be able to fly or move mountains or shoot fire out of my palms, but if you tell me what I need to do, then I can try to help you save this creature."

The old man smiled, and a look of peace and utter contentment passed across his face.

"Perhaps you can help me after all," the old man said, holding out his hand.

Criss hesitated for a moment, then shook the old man's hand in greeting. "I'm Crissen. Nice to meet you."

"I'm Gare," he said, squeezing Criss's hand with feeble, bony fingers. "I'm so glad I met you too. Please, save the seal."

And right on cue, like a scene from a bad horror novel, the old man's gaze went blank, and he crashed to the ground at our feet, deader than dead.

CHAPTER 20

"*W*hat the fuck is happening?" Criss cried.

I thought maybe he was just being dramatic or asking a rhetorical question at first—I mean, obviously the dude had just kicked the bucket—but when I saw the golden glow of magic gathering above Gare's unmoving chest, I knew immediately what was happening.

Because the same thing had happened to me.

"Oh my gods," I gasped. "A magical dead guy is about to give you his powers!"

"*What?*" Criss shouted, scrambling backward as the magic orb of energy grew bigger and brighter over Gare's dead body.

Then, with no further warning, it shot through the air and pierced right through Crissen's chest, dropping him like a fly to the ground.

I stood gaping, surrounded by a dead guy, a dying seal, and a knocked-out, recently-turned-magical Storm. Shocked would not even begin to explain how I felt.

Was this seriously my life?

"Criss!" I hissed, kneeling down to shake him. His body

rocked, but he didn't rouse. "Criss, you have to save the seal. It was poor Gare's dying wish."

But still he didn't stir.

"Shit," I muttered aloud. Glancing at Criss's hand, I had a strange idea. Magic was typically instinctual—at least, the magic I'd experienced was. It came out when it was needed whether you coaxed it or not. Near-death situations seemed to be a magical specialty.

Well, the poor seal was definitely near death. A great deal of his blood had already drained from his body and leaked into the sand beneath him.

Criss was a solid five feet away from the creature though, so in order to make it work, I was going to have to drag one or the other. Considering the seal was injured and in pain, it made more sense to not disturb him. Grabbing Criss's hand and forearm, I started tugging. Inch by inch, we made our way closer, until finally his palm reached the seal's side.

I took a labored breath and swiped at my brow. It'd been a while since I did any heavy lifting like that. I almost missed the familiar burn in my muscles. *Almost.*

I sat down in the sand and waited, but nothing happened. A warm wind blew across the ocean, ruffling my tiny skirt and my hair. I watched as the seal's chest lifted one last time, then fell eerily still. A tear slid down my cheek, and suddenly, I felt incredibly alone.

Still, I couldn't just leave.

I had no idea how long Criss would be passed out or how he'd feel when he came to. Would he remember what happened? Would he be confused? Scared? In pain? Magic manifested in all sorts of different ways, and I had no idea what Criss's would be.

I crawled over to him and curled up next to his chest, forcing my eyes to close.

It was going to be a long night.

~

I AWOKE THE NEXT MORNING TO THE SOUND OF GULLS CAWING and Crissen groaning.

My eyes snapped open, and I watched him lean over and prop himself on an elbow, rubbing both eyes with a single hand.

"What happened?" he croaked, prying his eyelids apart with apparent difficulty.

I sat up and glanced at the bodies lying motionless in the sand beside us. "You don't remember?"

Criss blinked a few times before awareness finally crept into his eyes. "Oh my gods. *He* died." He jabbed at finger at the old guy. "And he somehow gave me his powers. What the fuck kind of powers were they anyway?"

I shook my head. "I have no idea, but it's likely to manifest in a different way than his did. My magical dead guy, Rory, used his fire powers to melt metal and craft weaponry. Me? I got cutesy peach flames that bring on insatiable waves of horniness."

I shrugged, but I could tell the explanation wasn't enough for Criss.

He rubbed his buzzed brown hair as he thought. "What was he doing here last night? What all did he say?"

I took a deep breath. "He was with the seal. Maybe he was an animal shifter?"

Criss's brows rose. "Like Asher?"

Fuck, it hurt to hear his name and not know whether he was okay or not. "Yeah, like Ash. He also said, 'I'm not as strong as I once was,'" I added.

Criss nodded. "And just before he died, he said 'save the seal.'"

"Yep."

"What if he was a healer?" Criss pondered.

I smiled sadly. "It's possible. But I tried to make you heal the seal last night, and nothing happened."

Criss frowned. "Maybe I needed to be conscious?"

He stood and put both palms on the dead seal's side. "What do I do?"

My eyes went wide as I moved to the seal's other side, staring Crissen straight in the face. "I have no idea. It took me forever to learn my own power. I do know my magic requires a vocal command unless I'm dying, though."

"So, I just say something out loud to make it happen?" he asked. But before I could answer, he said, "*Heal.*"

Just like the night before, nothing happened.

"Shit," he cursed. "I was really hoping that would work."

"Me too," I said with a sympathetic smile. "But I don't think you can *heal* dead things. It's probably too late for him now."

Criss sighed. "*If* that's even what my magic can do."

"Right."

It was definitely frustrating in the beginning stages of magic when you simply didn't know.

"Come on," I said, taking his hand in mine. "We need to get back to town and tell someone about the old man. He deserves a proper burial."

"Yeah," Criss agreed. "And I'll bet the guys are tripping balls right now. We never came back last night. We haven't been back yet this morning. They're either freaking out thinking I killed you, or worse, they're thinking I fucked you."

I laughed, and he squeezed my hand a bit tighter. His skin was warm and rough against mine, strong and protective. I liked holding it more than I cared to admit.

"Hopefully they trust me enough to know I wouldn't do that—not until I have their approval."

His hazel eyes found mine as we walked across the sand. "But do you *want* to?"

"Does it really matter?" I hedged.

"*I* think so."

Sighing, I decided to tell him the truth. May as well. He was bound to us. His inclusion in the group dynamic was imminent. It was only a matter of time before that came to fruition in the form of crazy, wild sex. Or so I hoped.

"Yes, okay? I'd very much like to fuck you." There I went my usual *grace* and *tact*. "I didn't at first, but the more I get to know you..."

I trailed off. I was saying more than I'd planned to. A simple "yes" would have sufficed. Or hell, a plain old head nod.

"The more you get to know me...?" he prodded, all but begging me to continue.

I took a deep breath. "The more I like you. The more I care about you. The more attracted I become."

He stopped walking and immediately took my face in his warm palms. Some emotion swam in his eyes, making them sparkle. I wasn't about to call it *love*, but I'd settle with something like *affection*.

"I feel exactly the same way," he said, before releasing my face and taking my hand once more.

We didn't talk for the rest of the walk into town, but it wasn't an awkward silence by any means. It was more of a contentment, a satisfaction surrounding our togetherness that didn't require words.

After reporting the old man's death and whereabouts to some of the local guards we made the grueling ascent up the cliffside steps. Not gonna lie, I had to stop at least twice to catch my breath and give my burning thighs a break. Fuck cardio, man. It could die a brutal, ugly death.

By the time we made it into the chateau and up yet

another flight of stairs, the guys were waiting for us at the top.

Bam! Without any hint of a warning, Rob's fist connected yet again with Crissen's nose, instantly drawing a river of blood.

"Fuck!" Criss shouted, cradling his face in pain.

"What the hell, Rob?" I shouted, stomping closer until I was all up in his shit. "You agreed to let him take me on a date!"

"But not to keep you out all night!" he shouted back. "Not to fuck you! We have rules, Jewels! And I thought we had loyalty and commitment!"

I pushed his chest. "We do, you moronic caveman! He didn't fuck me last night!"

"Then why didn't you come back? Why'd you spend the night with him?"

"Because he got powers from a magical dead guy!" I cried. "He was passed the fuck out on the beach, and I didn't want to just leave him there, so I stayed!"

"Is that true?" Rob demanded, shooting Crissen a glare just before his mouth fell open. "Your nose..."

I turned toward Criss too, stunned to find the blood had not only stopped flowing, but it had faded away completely. There was no evidence of the wound whatsoever. Not on his face, his hands, the floor, or anywhere.

"You were right," I said, gaping. "It's healing magic. How do you feel?"

He blinked and slowly shook his head. "Just a little tired."

"Whoa, whoa, whoa," Cal said, intervening. "Start from the beginning, please. Tell us everything."

Criss glared at Rob. "Can I get a word in edgewise before being clocked in the face for shit I didn't do this time?"

"You might not have fucked her," Rob acknowledged, "but did you kiss her?"

Criss shook his head. "She wouldn't let me."

Rob had the decency to look uncomfortable for once. He sighed and ran both hands through his dark hair. "Sorry, Jewels. I overreacted and made unfair assumptions. Can you forgive me?"

"Maybe in a few minutes," I growled, still irritated that he'd accused me of cheating.

Cal took a deep breath and let it out slowly, glancing between me and Crissen, then across every other solemn face in the room.

"We need to have a *chat*."

But there wasn't time for one.

Suddenly, a servant rushed up the stairs with a pink face and a heaving chest. Clearly the man had been running.

"Edden, what's wrong?" Dan asked. He stepped closer and grabbed the servant by his shoulders, meeting him at eye level. "Is it the war?"

Edden shook his head quickly. "No, Your Highness. At least, I don't believe so. But a Timberlune entourage has just arrived, and Princess Bria is demanding to speak to you all."

"Oh, fuck," I muttered as my heart lodged in my throat. "I guess we're about to get our reply *in person*."

Dan pinched the bridge of his nose. "Send her up, Edden. We'll be in the fourth council room."

"Uh—" I began to protest.

But Dan quickly righted his wrong. "The *third* council room."

Everyone knew I had a thing against even numbers. Thankfully, it amused them enough that they went along with it. Or maybe they just loved me enough? Either way, I was incredibly grateful. Even numbers made my damn skin crawl.

As Edden bowed and rushed back downstairs, Dan led us

into the appropriate room. It was a square space with a giant square table in the center made of foot-thick dark wood. Four chairs sat on each side—four, four, four, four, *gross*! Why not fives? Or threes? Ugh, but they'd already gone out of their way to accommodate me once, so I didn't comment and make a nuisance out of myself. I'd just have to grin and bear it.

Cal, Dan, Ben, and Rob took the far end, so Criss and I each took a side closest to them. Bria and her entourage would have the entire opposite side of the table. Hopefully she hadn't brought more than nine others, or they'd be either standing or waiting in the hall.

Cal leaned forward and looked at Criss. "Just like we talked about."

Criss nodded. When I shot him a curious glance, he freaking winked at me. My gods, the last thing I needed was another sexy winker making my panties melt.

A few moments later, Edden stepped into the room, huffing and puffing. "Her Highness... Princess... Bria."

Bria stormed in with a deadly glare on her face. A line of guards filtered in after her, flanking her everywhere except for the front.

"Bria, welcome," Dan said cordially. "Please sit."

Surprisingly, she did as asked. Two guards sat down on either of her sides, while the others stood in a line behind her.

Dan smiled. "I must admit, I'm rather surprised to see you here. I'd assumed you'd simply reply to our letter with another letter."

"I burned your letter," she said matter-of-factly. "I came against the better judgement of my advisors and guards, simply because I wanted to give you Blackwood bastards a piece of my mind."

Dan held out both hands before lacing his fingers beneath

his chin. "By all means. We're prepared to listen to whatever you have to say."

She drummed her pale pink nails on the table. "I trusted you. You made a promise to me. A promise to help save my people and my kingdom, and what did you do? Instead of helping us keep our magic, you cut it off completely. You're nothing but promise-breakers and filthy backstabbers. Our kingdom is weak and dying, and it's all your fault. Of course, I understand now that that was your exact intention. So, I've actually come to congratulate you."

Dan took a deep breath. "We did not intend for this to—"

"Congratulations, Storms!" Bria shouted over him. "You've successfully wiped Timberlune off the map! In a few weeks, we'll all be gone. But I can die peacefully knowing that Hydratica is going to tear you apart and burn you to the ground. They will avenge us."

"Bria, please," Cal began, sounding truly apologetic. "We almost died trying to secure the Lunaley for the fae. *Multiple times*. The fact that the magic is gone... it wasn't our fault. We did everything in our power to help you."

"Lies!" she spat. "Venomous lies off a forked tongue! You're snakes, all of you."

Ironically enough, I used to think that about them as well.

"Bria, they're not snakes," I assured her. "They're telling the tru—"

"Shut up, Alexis," she snapped at me. "You have the sharpest fangs of them all. I trusted you with our deepest, darkest secret, and you used it against us. You promised me a victory; you promised that once this was fixed and my people were saved, I could marry Orion and be happy. But you only filled my head with lies. You're nothing but an evil witch, and I resent ever confiding in you. I hope the Hydraticans kill you for your crimes."

I was stunned speechless. My lips set in a taught line. My

throat hot and tight. I'd never had someone spew such vile things at me. I'd never had anyone wish for my death—not even the Storm King.

"You will not come to my kingdom," Dan warned in a dark tone, "and threaten my princess."

She laughed bitterly. "Oh, that's right. I heard about the *triple marriage*. The evil whore stole all four of you." She turned to Crissen and grinned malevolently. "Are you next? I'd head for the hills if I were you. Run while you still have a chance."

"Bria, that's enough!" Cal shouted, slamming the table with balled-up fists.

She stood and pushed her chair to the side. "Yes, I believe it is."

And with that, she marched out of the room with her hoard of guards following.

Silence filled the room like a pit of knives. It was like if anyone made a sound—one word, one *breath*—they'd careen into the sharp blades below.

I swallowed hard, feeling the onset of tears approaching.

Miners don't cry, Lex. They were just words. Suck it the fuck up.

I concentrated hard on my hands in my lap, not wanting to make eye contact with any of the guys just in case a tear slipped out anyway.

"Another thing, Your Majesty," Edden said from the doorway Bria just exited.

"Yes?" Dan asked. He didn't sound very optimistic about the upcoming news, but he did seem grateful for the breech in silence.

"You received a return letter today."

I glanced up saw a mixture of expressions on the guys' faces. Confusion. Hope. Fear.

"It would have to be from Hydratica," Dan surmised. "They're the closest."

Edden nodded. "It is, Highness. It bears their seal."

"Do you have it with you?" Dan asked.

Edden stepped forward and withdrew the envelope. "Of course, Your Highness."

As soon as Dan had the letter in his hands, Edden took his leave.

Carefully, Dan broke the seal and opened the parchment.

"Read it out loud," Cal said.

Dan nodded.

SQUALLS,

It has been ages since we last saw each other, and much has changed since then. We should meet up for some pinni in Mahana to catch up. Leave as soon as you get this. We won't wait long.

Sincerely,

B & Z

DAN GLANCED UP AT US AND RAISED A BROW. "THERE'S CLEARLY some coding going on here."

"Squalls are synonymous with Storms," Ben chimed in. "And Pinni is a dish often served back in my kingdom."

Dan nodded. "There's only one café I can think of that serves desert cuisine, and that's Javi's."

"Is Javi's located in Mahana?" Rob asked. "Whatever the hell that is."

"Mahana is a Rubian city," Ben explained. "It's located on Tikaree, the middle of the five islands that make up their archipelago."

"*Hades*, Ben, could you put it in plain fucking speech?" Rob scoffed.

Ben rolled his chocolatey-brown eyes but didn't bother to simplify what he'd said. Crissen's lips tugged up into a sexy half smirk.

"And, obviously," Cal added, pointing at the signature, "B & Z means Blane and Zane."

Dan nodded. "They must not want their parents or anyone else to know they're meeting with us, hence the bit of code and the neutral location."

"Assuming Rubio didn't already side with Blackwood," Ben reminded them.

Cal seemed to agree. "So, we leave now and sail for Tika-ree. How long is this trip going to take?"

Dan grinned devilishly. "With the Sea Prince as your captain? Less than an hour."

"Perfect," Rob declared, hopping from his seat and heading for the door. "Let's get the fuck out of here."

CHAPTER 21

SHER

"ADAM! ADAM! ADAM!"

The world swam around me as I aimed at the final cup. Cheers echoed in my ears from displaced competitors and partygoers who'd wandered in to watch. Confidence and nervousness warred as my dominant emotion.

If I make this cup, we'll go into overtime. If I miss, we're done. It'll all be over.

I stared at the little red thing as it split into two and then four, spinning in my vision like a wagon wheel. I blinked, and it once more drifted back to one. Gods, how much had I drank?

"Adam! Adam! Adam!" the crowd cheered.

"Shoot, pretty boy!" Dion shouted. "Sink that fucking cup! You got this!"

I took a deep breath, closed my eyes to keep the cup from spinning, and let my little white ball fly.

Cheers, groans, screams, shouts... so much sound entered my ears. It was like my brain was a cave and all the echoing was about to make my head collapse.

"You did it!" Dion cried.

I opened my eyes in time to see his fist pumping the air before he chest bumped me. I damn near fell on my ass, but the crowd behind me kept me on my feet.

"It's overtime, bitches!" Dion yelled out into the crowd. "*Whoop*!"

Heracles and Perseus were feeling the pressure and excitement too. They jumped up and down in place, shook out their heads and arms, and tried to focus their bloodshot eyes on the single cup remaining.

"Rules!" Dion shouted before Herc could throw. "We aren't making a three-cup pyramid or any of that shit. It's one-on-one. As soon as one team makes a cup, the other team has a chance to tie up. If they fail, the first team wins. If they make it, the next set of partners face off. The first of them to make a cup without the other team tying up, wins!"

The crowd went wild, and Herc once again stepped forward to take his shot. *Plonk*! The ball sailed straight into our cup.

Son of a bitch!

Dion drank every last drop of beer in it, cracked his neck, then quickly sank the other cup on the opposite side of the table.

Yes!

We were tied up again.

Percy grabbed his ball and got into place as Herc drank. He made a few practice motions before letting the ball fly... and he missed.

Whew! The pressure was off for a moment. I grabbed my ball, narrowed my eyes to keep focused, and launched it into the air.

"Yes!" Dion cried as a small plume of beer splashed from the cup I'd hit. "Herc's shit at countersinking. We got this in the bag now!"

I wasn't so sure. If I were a nail-biter, now would be the time for the clippings to start flying. As it stood, I just ran my hands through my feathery brown hair, trying to relax.

The crowd began chanting a new name.

"Herc! Herc! Herc!"

Heracles took a deep breath and exhaled slowly as he concentrated on our cup.

"Herc! Herc! Herc!"

He pulled his arm back, pushed it up, and sent the little white ball flying in a perfectly contoured arc. Then... ting! The ball hit the rim of the cup... and bounced onto the table.

"*Yes!*" Dion and I cried as one before the crowd swallowed us up whole.

No one seemed to care which team won, just that they'd been thoroughly entertained for the past few hours. And entertaining was an understatement—that shit had been *intense*.

All those bodies pressing in on me suddenly made me aware of how much alcohol I'd consumed and how badly I needed to piss.

I leaned over and shouted in Dion's ear. "I need to use the bathroom!"

He pointed in the direction we'd come from. "It's just out there and up the stairs! Don't get lost!"

I chuckled and shook my head.

"And don't end up in another paper towel kilt either," he threatened over the volume of the crowd. "I swear to the gods, I won't help your dumb ass next time."

I flipped him the bird, and he laughed heartily before once again basking in the glory of winning the tournament.

When I reached the top of the stairs, silence overwhelmed

me. Without the earsplitting noise, I actually felt a bit more sober. After pissing like a racehorse, I felt even better.

I exited the bathroom and stumbled into the hall, damn near smashing into a wall.

Okay, yeah, I wasn't perfectly sober, but still. At least I had enough wits about me to remember I needed to get the fuck out of this place and back into Blackwood. Except, I had no idea how the fuck to do that.

Alexis, Rob, and Dan had told us that when they found the arch in the Lunaley there was a party of sorts going on inside. A man had walked by and shut some sort of invisible door and then *poof*! No more magic.

When the Storm King dropped me off in chimera form with Ares and Dion, there was also a strange arch. He'd knocked on some invisible door, and then it had magically opened to this weird-ass place beyond.

I glanced up the hall, staring at door after door as they lined each side of the mansion as far as the eye could see. There must have been thousands of them. I blinked, and the world rocked like an ocean.

Okay, fine. Even *if* my drunk eyes were playing tricks on me and doubling my vision, there were still *a lot* of fucking doors.

What were the odds that they'd lead to various locations in *my* world?

I opened the first door on the right, revealing another bedroom—a guest bedroom from the looks of how sparse and tidy it was.

I turned left and opened the next door, and I was immediately blinded by blistering hot sunlight. I squeezed my eyes shut until the pain subsided, then shielded my gaze and tried again. The Obsidian Desert rolled on like a golden wave of shifting sands.

My thoughts drifted back to the strange old man we'd

encountered during our trip to the Ley. Had he appeared and disappeared so abruptly because of this doorway? Was there an arch nearby? And if so, did that explain why we'd lost track of time and reality for a bit that day? After all, it seemed like every time one of these doors opened, they leaked magic out into our realm.

I shut the door and kept walking, tiptoeing as silently as I could without losing my balance.

I opened the second door on the right and came face-to-face with the pink-and-purple-striped trees of the Lunaley.

This was... in-*fucking*-credible. My eyes and my smile were wide as I stared. This could solve everything. All I had to do was leave this doorway just slightly cracked, and the fae would have their magic back. There would be no need for war.

Alexis and the guys were going to freak when they found out.

I pulled the door nearly shut, leaving barely an inch of the striped forestry peeking through, then opened the next door, revealing a small towel closet. I turned right. Another bedroom. This one was decorated in red and black with a messed-up bed, clothes on the floor, and empty bottles of alcohol on the nightstand.

I went left again, opening a door to the middle of the ocean. There was nothing but sea in every outward direction, nothing but sky above, and below, nothing more than a single boulder jutting out of the water on which the arch stood.

Wait a second. Was that...? I peered closer, squinting my eyes to hopefully see a bit farther. Was that a ship on the horizon?

"You must be Adam," a dark, cunning voice said from the other end of the hall, freezing me to the spot.

I didn't have to look to know *exactly* who it was, but I turned around anyway. *Ares*, the fucking *War God*, stood at the top of the stairs looking absolutely lethal with his clenched fists, narrowed eyes, and his tightly set jaw.

Panic struck me like an ax to the chest.

Without a second thought, I impulsively leapt through the doorway and splashed into the ocean beyond.

CHAPTER 22

LEXIS

WE WERE IN A BOAT AND SPEEDING ACROSS THE SEA IN NO
time.

Dan stood at the front of the deck, holding his breath,
smoothing out the water beneath us while simultaneously
propelling the boat at incredible speeds. I clung to the side
railings as my hair whipped like crazy around my head. It
was only my second time on a boat, but I kind of wished it
was my last. As adorable as my "Sailor" nickname was, I was
certainly not fit for sea life. My stomach roiled, and I
concentrated on trying not to puke.

Meanwhile Cal, Ben, Rob, and Criss sat around talking
strategy and gods only knew what else as if the world weren't
rushing by us at breakneck speeds.

Clearly, they were insane.

As I white-knuckled the railing, I stared off into the
distance to where things weren't rushing by quite so fast.

Problem was, there was nothing but ocean for as far as the eye could see. Oh, and of course, a random stone archway in the middle of nowhere.

"Guys..." I called hesitantly.

They must've sensed the slight edge in my voice, because they came over right away.

I pointed to the arch. "Is that what I think it is?"

"*Another* magical doorway?" Cal asked no one in particular.

"How can this be?" Ben pondered aloud. "Unless the alternate dimension has threads tied to this world in multiple locations?"

"Dan!" Rob shouted. "Turn portside!"

Dan shot him a quizzical look but did as his brother asked. As the archway came into view, dawning crossed his features, followed by disappointment. "We don't have time for this!" he shouted back. "We need to meet Blane and Zane before they write us off and head back to Hydratica."

My heart sank. He was right, of course, but I hated to just leave it unchecked. It might've helped lead us to Asher somehow, and I missed him like mad. Was he okay? Was he lost? My stomach quickly twisted into knots.

Not now, Lex. We need to talk to the Hydratican princes first. Then *we can explore the arch.*

My little pep talk didn't help much. I still desperately wanted to go over there.

Suddenly, magical mist began pouring out of the archway like a flood. It raced across the surface of the sea like a heard of wild horses, charging in every direction. Dan tried to slow the boat down, tried to make a sharp about-face, but it was too late, the mist had already reached us.

I blinked, slowly becoming accustomed to my new hazy vision, but I felt half blind. Where were we? And why was it so foggy? I couldn't remember anything all of a sudden.

"Alexis?" a voice called from somewhere behind me in the mist.

I turned around, and Cal appeared a few feet in front of me. "I'm here."

"Thank the gods. Why don't you come sit with us until this fog passes?"

I frowned and looked all around, but I could barely see a thing. "What are we doing? Are we on a boat?"

Cal nodded. "So it seems. Maybe we were just trying to enjoy a carefree day on the water?"

Yeah, "carefree" and "Storms" didn't usually go together.

"Come on," Cal insisted. "The guys are waiting over here."

I had just turned to follow him when a faint sound caught my attention. I paused, listening harder. "Do you hear that?" I asked him.

Cal strained his ears, and his eyes went unfocused as he listened. "Is that a... *meow*?"

"A cat lost at sea?" I asked curiously.

"I remember there being an archway nearby," Cal muttered. "Or at least, I think I do. Maybe a cat accidentally pushed through?"

My eyes went wide. "We can't just leave the poor thing! It'll drown."

Cal immediately agreed. "I'll get a net. If we follow the sound and miraculously find it before it's too late, then we'll scoop it out and bring it aboard."

I nodded quickly. "Hurry."

Then I turned around to where the steering wheel ought to have been. I still couldn't see shit through all the fog.

"Dan?"

"Lexi?" he called back. "I can't see a damn thing. Are you all right?"

"Yes, I'm fine," I shouted. "Can you use your powers to sense a lost cat in the water?"

For a moment, I was met with silence. Then he finally answered. "I can try, but it's not going to be easy. The ocean is huge, and cats are pretty damn small."

"See if you can follow the *meows*," I added. "That might help you pinpoint it."

A moment later, Cal returned carrying a net. He had Rob, Ben, and Criss with him. The five of us grabbed onto the boat's railing and squinted into the mist, trying to glimpse the drowning cat.

"Ah, shit," Dan cursed. "Guys, it's magic. Use your powers and the effects should fade."

What was magic? The cat?

Cal, Ben, and Rob immediately did as Dan suggested, using their powers over the sky, the vegetation—which, in this case, meant seaweed—and the spirit realm. I had no idea if there were any spirits lingering, but I supposed if there'd ever been a shipwreck nearby, that might suffice.

Criss turned to me with panic in his hazel eyes. "I don't know how to use my magic. When I healed my nose earlier, that was purely instinctual. I haven't been able to call on it at will."

I nodded, understanding immediately what I needed to do.

I called on my own magic, smiling as the peachy-pink flames danced in my palm, then I glanced at Criss. "You ready?"

His brows furrowed, staring nervously at my fire. "Ready for what?"

"Look!" I cried, pointing to sea. "It's the cat!"

Criss turned around, and I grabbed his arm, scorching the ever-loving fuck out of him. He cried out in pain and jumped away from me. Instantly, his healing magic flared to life. It raced across his skin like a magical tide, washing away any signs of a burn and leaving behind nothing but perfect skin.

Holy shit, that was amazing.

"There," I said with an astonished smile, "all better."

He glared at me. "Gee, thanks."

I'd only used a small amount of magic, so my lust and desire weren't too gods-awful bad to deal with, but it had been enough to clear my head as Dan had said. I now remembered where we were—the Hydratic Sea. And where we were going—Rubio, to meet with Blane and Zane, the Hydratican twin princes. And where the mist had come from —the arch in the middle of the freaking ocean.

Meow!

And I remembered the drowning cat.

Thankfully the mewing was louder than it had been before, which hopefully meant we were getting closer to rescuing it. Once more, I scanned the ocean for any signs of feline life. A soft splashing sound came to my ears, followed by faint ripples in the water. I looked closer and gasped as I saw a tiny white head bobbing up and down in the water.

"*Meow!*" the poor thing cried before dunking under and popping back up.

"There, Cal!" I cried, leaning out over the rail to point to the white cat in the water.

He quickly scooped it up in the net and handed it over to Ben, who'd been waiting with a blanket in his arms.

"It's probably in shock from the freezing cold water," Ben explained. "We need to warm it up and dry it off as quickly as possible."

I was scared to death it might die before then. It was so much smaller than I'd been expecting—practically a kitten. Unsure of what else to do, I flared up my flames and held them out. "Here. This should help it dry."

Fuck, this was going to cost me *a lot* of lust. But whatever. It was worth it to save the poor creature's life. Besides, sex with a few of my guys below deck didn't sound too bad.

Talk about first-world problems.

Ben held the kitten still while Cal and Rob each grabbed an edge of the blanket and rubbed its fur. Their efforts, combined with my fire, eventually dried the little thing out into an adorable ball of white fluff.

When I was finished, I swallowed hard and put out my flames, glancing at Crissen from the side of my eye. The lust was starting to take over, and thanks to our tantalizing date last night, *he* was the object of my magic's desire.

Fuck. I needed a distraction. *Any* distraction so this didn't get worse.

"Oh my gods, this kitty is so cute!" I exclaimed, scooping it up into my arms. "It's been a while since I had a pet. Would you like to be my pet, little one?"

I *booped* it gently on the nose, but it was not enthused. It lashed out and clawed my hand faster than I could blink, which in turn caused me to accidentally drop it on the deck. Being a cat and all, it landed on all fours, but instead of darting away like I assumed it would, it stuck around and rubbed its head on my legs.

I put both hands on my hips. "You can't scratch me one minute and love me the next."

"*Meow*," it said, purring.

I decided to steal another glance at Criss since my whole body was yearning for him, but that was a very bad idea. If the intensity of his hazel gaze was anything to go by—and the swelling cock in his pants—then he was definitely feeling the pull too. *Shit.*

I turned away, focusing as hard as I could on the kitten that Ben had scooped back up.

Do not look at Criss. Do not look at Criss.

My heart beat faster, and my breathing shallowed out into desperate pants.

There was something so alluring about the cut of Criss's

jaw. The way the stubble there darkened his skin. His lips curved into a seductive smile, and my gaze slowly drifted up past his sharp nose and onto those gorgeous eyes. Pale blue, mint green, and just a touch of gold. They practically sparkled as they looked back at me.

Shit! I'm looking at him again!

I stared at the deck, taking in a deep breath and letting it out slowly.

"Alexis? Are you even listening?" Cal asked.

"Huh?" I glanced up, intending to scan the faces of Cal, Dan, Ben, and Rob, but I freaking honed in on Crissen again.

My lips parted when he took a step closer to me and heat swirled to life in my core.

"Nope. Not today, Aphrodite," Rob said, holding my hands at my sides and lifting me away.

The next thing I knew, I was being dropped overboard into the freezing cold water below. I was only under for a few seconds before a rush of water pushed me up into the air until I was once again level with the deck.

I was soaking wet and shivering, but the intended effect had been reached. I was no longer uncontrollably horny, and Crissen was no longer in my seductive trance.

The water deposited me onto the creaking boards; then Dan took a breath and released it.

"Thanks," I muttered, a bit embarrassed that it had come to that. As much as I wanted Criss, I wanted the guys to be good with it first. "I'm really sorry."

To my surprise, Rob came over and pulled me into his arms, planting a gentle kiss on my lips. "It's okay, Jewels. We know it's not your fault. I hope you're not mad at me though. For the whole throwing-you-overboard thing. I think you're still mad at me from before, so..."

I shook my head and wrapped my wet arms around his

neck. "No, I forgive you. For both of those things. But Cal's right—we need to have a chat about all this."

Rob nodded knowingly, but Cal interrupted. "Sorry, but we have better things to deal with at the moment."

I turned to him, surprised at the shortness in his tone, but he was smiling excitedly.

"What's going on?" I asked, turning to Ben and Dan who were also grinning a mile wide.

Criss still just looked kind of dazed from the spell I'd had him under.

Ben held out the kitten for me to take.

Without question, I grabbed it and snuggled it to my chest, rubbing my chin along its silky soft fur. But then Dan handed me a knife, and I started to get worried. As soon as the worry entered my system though, it was completely wiped out by hope. If they wanted me to kill an adorable little kitten, then that could only mean one thing...

I flipped it over and sobbed when I saw a gray spot under its chin—the only blemish in an otherwise perfectly white coat. It had to have been *him*. Ash was back!

And he'd kept his promise too—he was about to make me murder a *kitten*. The bastard.

I laughed and cried at the same time, wiping tears from my cheeks as they spilled down my face. I was so happy, I could puke. So happy I could stab a kitten. Neither of those things made sense, but I had a feeling they were both about to happen.

"Take him," I said, pushing kitty-Asher into Ben's arms once more.

I then ran for the side of the boat and puked over the railing. My fingers felt weak as they squeezed the wood. My legs were as mushy as seaweed. When I was finished spilling my guts, I took a deep breath and wiped my mouth.

"Ready now?" Ben teased, wiggling the kitten before me.

I snatched it back and laid it down on the wooden deck. Gods, this was awful. Even though I knew it was Ash, it still looked like a baby cat. Could I honestly kill an adorable, fluffy white kitten?

It stared up at me as I hesitated, and I swear I saw its amber eyes roll. It let out a low growl that I thought was supposed to sound ferocious but that came out as warm and endearing as ever.

I laughed one more time as the tears fell. *How fucked-up was this?* Then I reared back with the knife and, before I could chicken out, sank the blade deep into the kitten's chest. Scarlet blood soaked through its bright white fur and puddled onto the deck beneath it.

Seconds passed where absolutely nothing happened. The kitten didn't move. The guys didn't move. The magic didn't appear. I didn't breathe.

I was starting to think I'd legitimately murdered a real-life baby cat in cold blood, when *finally* the golden magic appeared and the kitten's tiny body slowly morphed into the hard-cut body of a very naked man. *My* naked man.

"Asher!" I screamed, falling into his arms on the deck.

He squeezed me tightly, almost so hard I couldn't breathe, but I couldn't have cared less. I was in his arms! After all this time, he was back with us!

He kissed me quickly then sat up, ending our reunion far too soon. "Sorry, guys, but we need to get the fuck out of here. I may or may not have an angry War God on my tail."

Cal, Ben, and Rob instantly demanded answers, while Dan merely sucked in a deep breath and sent the ship hurtling back into superspeed. I latched onto Ash as the wind whipped at my face.

"What are the odds you guys have any jeans?" Ash asked, glancing down at his nudity.

I glanced down too, and heat curled in the pit of my core.

STORM CHASER

"*Jeans?*" Ben asked intriguingly.

Ash smirked and then sighed. "I wish those borrowed clothes had survived the change. I looked so fucking good in them."

My gaze moved from his junk up to his handsome face. "I quite prefer you naked, actually."

As Ash chuckled, Cal offered to go find him some pants. When he returned with khakis and a white shirt, Ash quickly slipped into them and stood, reaching his hand out to Crissen.

"I'm Ash. You must be Criss, the guy who kept us alive back in the Lunaley."

Criss took his hand and shook it. "That'd be me. It's great to finally meet you. I know Alexis was worried sick."

"Our girl always fears the worst." Ash threw an arm around my shoulders and kissed the top of my head. "I wanted to thank you, though, for saving our asses and for helping to keep Alexis safe while I was gone."

Criss bowed his head slightly. "I'll always do what I can to keep her safe. No matter what."

Ash's amber eyes narrowed slightly before he turned to me and grinned. "You did it again, didn't you?"

I blinked. "Did *what?*"

"Captivated another Storm. He's in love with you too, isn't he?"

Heat burned in my cheeks, and though I wanted to turn away, I glanced up at Criss who was blushing too. "I have no idea," I muttered.

"Well, are you in love with him?" Ash asked. He didn't sound upset, which was a relief, but rather curious.

My face must've been as red as that kitten's blood.

"*Asher...*" I warned, trailing off because I honestly had no idea how I felt about Criss. I knew I liked him. I knew I wanted to fuck him. But did I *love* him?

"He's not part of the group," Rob said darkly, relieving me of having to finish that sentence.

Ash shrugged. "Okay, so what does he need to do?"

Rob crossed his burly arms. "What do you mean?"

"I *mean*, I had to jump from Dryroot Canyons to earn my place in the group. So, what does *he* have to do to earn the same rights?"

Cal hesitated. "Ash, we haven't *chatted* about this particular subject just yet."

"Then let's *chat*," Ash said, smiling shamelessly. "I have an assload of shit to tell you guys anyway."

CHAPTER 23

" *he gods are still around*?" Rob damn near shouted as Asher began telling his tale.

Ash nodded. "Yep. And they're fucking with us. We're like adorable little playthings to them."

"I'll do you one better," Dan said haughtily. "We *are* them."

Ash's brows furrowed. "What do you mean?"

Dan cocked his head toward me. "Alexis had tea with our mothers who saw fit to finally confess our true heritage. We're fucking demigods, bro. I'm not just a loose descendant of Poseidon—he's my real fucking father."

Ash's amber eyes went terrifyingly wide. He turned to Cal. "Zeus is your real father?" Cal nodded. He turned to Rob. "Hades is yours?" Rob nodded too. He twisted around to stare at Ben. "What about you? Demeter was a woman."

Ben chuckled. "Turns out, if you're a god, you can create life no matter what your sex is."

Ash pointed to himself. "So then, who are my parents?"

"Ashlynn and Hera," I filled in. "All gods have the ability to change shape, but Hera didn't want you to be as amazing as her, so she *only* gave you that ability."

"*Only?*" he asked with a grin. "I think it's pretty fucking awesome."

Cal closed his eyes and held up both hands. "Let's not get off topic here. What were you saying about us being the playthings of the gods?"

"Right," Ash said, getting back on track. "So, Ares and Dion—the War God and the Party God—made a deal with the Storm King, that if he can keep completing their ridiculous quests, they'll keep giving him vials of godly protection or some shit. They don't *need* him to fulfill the quests; they just think it's funny to fuck with him. You know why they wanted the chimera egg?"

"To create god-killing poisons?" Ben guessed.

The rest of us shook our heads since we were clueless.

"No," Ash replied with a grin. "Just to have a god-killer as a pet. They thought it would be funny. Or at least, Ares did. You know why they told the Storm King to get the Eye of the Sea?"

"You know about that?" Cal asked in surprise.

"Of course I know," Ash replied. "I was there when they made the deal."

Ben shrugged. "They need the Eye to look into the future?"

"No. They want it as a fucking fish tank decoration. *A fish tank decoration!* I mean, holy fucking Hades..."

Anger suddenly surged within me. Who did these assholes think they were, dicking us around like that? They allowed a tyrant to rule our kingdom with godlike powers just so they could have a cool pet? So they could have a cool fish tank decoration? Fuck them.

"When we get the eye," I said with a sneer, "we're *not* giving it to them."

"Fuck no, we're not," Rob agreed with a glare.

But Ash hesitated. "I don't know... If *we're* the ones who

hand it over to them, then they might just start helping *us* instead of the Storm King."

"What the hell makes you think they'd actually help us?" I countered angrily. "All they seem to care about is fucking us over for their enjoyment."

Ash nodded. "That's true. They really do love their fun and games. But I sort of befriended Dion while I was there. I think if we can prove to him that we're worthy by delivering the Eye, then he'll seriously consider helping us."

"And what about Ares?" Dan asked, taking a quick break from propelling the ship to breathe. "Didn't you say he was pissed off and possibly even following you into our realm?"

"Yeah," Ash replied. "Ares is going to be a problem. I think he's the real brain behind the operation. Because he thrives on war, he's always hoping to cause discord. What better way to cause discord *and* war than by supporting a tyrannical monarch?"

Dan shook his head, took another deep breath, and got back to boosting the boat.

"So, what's he pissed about?" Criss asked from where he was reclined on the ship's deck.

"He's pissed about *us*," Ash replied with cocky grin. "He hates the Storm Princes—and *princess*—" He winked at me. "—because we're directly interfering with his plans. We're a serious threat to the Storm King, and he hates that. If the Storm King loses, Ares doesn't get world war."

"He's already getting his war," Ben commented. "Timber-lune and Hydratica are out for our blood. Meeting with the twins is the only hope we have left for peace."

Rob shook his head. "Then all hope is lost. Hydratica will not stop until Sohsol is destroyed. Period."

Ash shrugged sympathetically. "Then we need to find the Eye and give it to the gods before the Storm King does."

Rob narrowed his gray eyes. "What's so special about the damn Eye, anyway?"

"No idea," Ash admitted. "But if we can somehow use it to our advantage, then we definitely should."

Cal nodded his agreement. "Ash is right. We find the Eye and strike a deal with the gods. If we can somehow take the Storm King out of the equation, then that's got to be our end goal."

"*Oh,*" Ash said, as if he just remembered something, "and I totally opened the portal to the Lunaley back up. As long as the gods don't notice the door is cracked, we should be good. Timberlune is probably already feeling the effects."

"You couldn't have *led* with that information?" Cal shouted. "We just had a horrible meeting with Bria where she basically told us all to burn in hell."

"Yikes," Ash said. His tone suggested he was not at all fazed. "Well, she'll be begging for forgiveness soon then, because Timberlune definitely has its magic back."

Personally, I was glad to hear Bria wouldn't be mad at me for much longer. She was more than just a potential ally to me; she was a friend—one of the few I ever had.

I glanced at Criss. It kind of seemed like our "chat" was coming to a close, and we hadn't yet discussed the terms of his involvement. I could tell neither of us wanted to be the one to bring it up though.

Luckily, Ben caught our secret glance. He smiled warmly and folded his hands behind his head. "Now, let's *chat* about Criss joining our group. I vote yes."

"I vote no," Rob grumbled.

Ash rolled his eyes. "You *always* vote no. I vote yes."

Dan, who didn't seem to want to exhale his latest deep breath, simply nodded his approval.

Cal sighed and eyed me with intent. "What do *you* vote?"

I swallowed hard and lifted my chin a bit higher. "I want

him in the group. He's already a part of us, whether you like it or not. He even has his own powers now, so he's not just a 'liability.'" I made air quotes to stress my point. "We need to start accepting him for the valuable member of the team that he is."

When Criss's gaze met mine across the deck, I could tell just how appreciative he was that I'd stuck up for him. Either that, or I could just *feel* his appreciation in the atmosphere around us.

Cal sighed. "Still. I vote... not yet."

Rob gave a little *whoop* of victory.

I glared at the two of them. "Then what would you have him do?"

Cal shook his head. "I don't know. We'll have to think about it."

"We'll know what he needs to do when the time comes," Rob added with a devious grin.

That sounded a whole hell of a lot like "it's never gonna happen."

My jaw ticked. "If you two haven't come up with something by the end of the week, then we're having another *chat* and *I'll* come up with the terms of his inclusion."

Before anyone could argue further, Dan let out a huge puff of air and sucked in a deep breath. Panting, he said, "We're here."

I peered up ahead and saw an island, filled with the vibrancy of a bustling seaside town. It must've been Tikaree, and the town had to have been Mahana. The island as a whole was a lot smaller than I was expecting. From end to end, it was probably less than half a mile, and I could see the other islands sprawled out on each side of it. It was beautiful though—pure white sands and crystal-clear waters.

Before we landed, Ash took my face in his hands and

kissed me. "I love you, Sweets. Time for me to disappear again."

I latched onto his shirt with clenched fists. "Stay with me this time. Please."

He grinned and kissed me again. "I'm gonna wrap around you like a snake."

Then his magic surged, and his body swirled into golden dust before curling around me and taking the form of... a *literal* fucking snake. It was long and white with yellow spots and beady black eyes. Its lower half wrapped around my waist, while its upper half coiled down my right arm.

"*Like* a snake?" I hissed indignantly. "You *are* a snake. I hate those little fuckers."

He flicked his forked tongue in my general direction, and I squealed, trying to hop away, but the bastard was wrapped around me, so he went where I went.

"I'm probably going to enjoy killing you this time," I muttered, leaning my head as far away from his as I could.

He stuck his tongue out again, and this time, I was fairly certain he was being bratty.

We moored the boat at an empty dock, then jumped onto the shore. My legs were wobbly from our time on the sea, but I was grateful to be back on solid ground—even if said ground was actually *sand* and, therefore, not all that solid. Still, it was the fact of the matter.

As we strolled through town, it became apparent rather quickly that Rubians were a stoic group of islanders. I didn't get the vibe that anyone was angry, and yet no one really smiled or paid us any mind. They lived a comfortable and peaceful life by the coast, even though no one seemed all that relaxed. They were too busy bustling about, doing this or that, to really even enjoy the sound of the surf. They were clearly overachievers with an incredible work ethic.

No wonder the Storm King wanted them as allies.

Dan pointed to our left. "That's Javi's."

The building in question was unique and beautiful. Made of sandstone and stucco—or possibly even adobe—it was a two-story structure with outdoor seating all along the wrap-around, open-arch porch. It had a definite desert ambiance that somehow seemed perfectly suited for its island location. Not too many people filtered in and out though, so I had to assume desert cuisine was more of a delicacy than a staple here.

We wandered inside, glancing around in search of the princes. I had no idea what they looked like. I was just sort of looking for two guys sitting together in a corner or something, but there were only a couple of tables occupied inside, and none of which were taken by twins.

"Let's check the porch," Dan suggested, leading us back outside.

The wings of the porch were each empty, but in the back, where the ocean rolled and crashed in full view, there was a single table that was occupied by three people. Two of which were men: tall and broad-shouldered with short, dark hair. And the other was female: short and delicate with long black hair. Her skin was olive, while theirs was more peach, and she looked familiar. *Very* familiar.

"Camilla?" I asked curiously as we approached.

She glanced up at us and smiled brightly. "Storms! So nice to see you all again!"

"What in the name of the gods are you doing here?" Ben asked, kissing each of her cheeks as we gathered round the table. His unusual greeting sounded more teasing than condemning, which I was certain had been his intention. No need to piss them off before we'd even sat down.

She grinned and gestured to the twins. "I'm officially courting Blane and Zane."

"Both?" I asked with a grin.

She eyed my snake warily but still leaned in so we could kiss each other's cheeks. "I figured I needed a reverse harem of my own," she told me with a wink.

The twins stood and began shaking hands with everyone. "I know there's a royal protocol for all this shit," one of the twins said, "but I don't really give a fuck."

I laughed and shook his hand instead of curtsying. "Sounds good to me."

"Please, sit," the other twin suggested, and we all took our seats. "We already ate since we didn't know when you'd arrive, but please, feel free to look at the menu."

I stared at the words on the parchment, but I had no fucking clue what any of the dishes actually consisted of. I shot a clueless glance at Ben who grinned.

"Don't worry, Sailor. I'll order for all of us."

Rob tossed his menu into the center of the table. "Thank the gods."

By the time our food arrived, all eight of the princes were ready to talk business.

Thankfully, my snake had unraveled himself from my body and curled up in my lap, allowing me to eat in some semblance of peace. But even still, each time he poked his scaly head above the table, it gave me the fucking creeps.

"So," Cal began with a charming smile, as he carefully took a sweet ball of pinni off our plate. "What can we do to just... make this war go away?"

One of the twin's laughed and draped his arm around Camilla's dainty shoulders while she preened like a peacock. "There is no 'making this go away,' Storms. Our father is set in his ways. He, like his father before him, has hated Sohsol since the dead first arrived. Any opportunity to wipe them out is a good one in his book."

Rob shook his head. "They're not just mindless zombies aimlessly roaming the frozen tundra. They're civilized and intelligent beings. I've busted my ass this past decade to create as much order down there as I could, and I think I've done a pretty damn good job."

The other twin nodded and, not to be outdone or excluded by his brother, slipped *his* hand around Camilla's waist. "You have done a superb job, and I commend you. It cannot be easy to create order out of chaos. But our father doesn't see it that way, and there is no changing his mind."

"Then why bother to meet with us?" Dan asked, his gaze slightly mocking.

The first brother smiled. "Because one day our parents will be dead and gone. And though we cannot stop the present, we do hope to establish a good rapport for the future."

My brows furrowed. "You want Blackwood as allies when you take the throne?"

The second prince's dark eyes twinkled. "Would you not like us as allies as well?"

Touché. He certainly had a point. Hydratica was a powerful nation, perhaps the only one strong enough to give Blackwood a run for its money. It would be wise to have them as allies.

"Plus, our lovely princess speaks highly of you all," the first twin added.

"And as long as she's with us," the second twin said, gazing at her adoringly, "she gets what she wants."

Camilla laughed breathily. "If my father even *thinks* about splitting us up, I'll tell him to go fuck himself."

They each grinned and kissed her cheeks.

Gods, this situation was fascinating. It was one thing to be in a polyamorous relationship myself, but it was something else entirely to watch it play out for someone else in front of my eyes. I found myself becoming personally invested in their romance, like I was reading a smutty novel and pulling for the ménage in the next chapter.

Cal sighed and did his best to keep the conversation on track. "We'll consider the potential for a future alliance."

"Consider it seriously, Storms," the first twin said. "It would be reckless and stupid to refuse."

"Why not just take the throne now?" I asked. "Then our alliance could begin right away and Sohsol wouldn't have to be wiped out."

"*Take* the throne?" the second twin asked in astonishment.

"Blane, *peace*," the first twin—who must've been Zane —said.

Finally, I had names for the pair of Hydratican princes— though, honestly, I still couldn't tell them apart. Even their voices sounded the same.

"Our father might be bullheaded," Zane continued, "but we love and respect him and would never seek to overthrow him. We will ascend to the throne when it is our due time and not a moment before."

Rob's normally plush lips were thin, and his brows were low. I had to wonder what he was strangling himself to hold back. No doubt, there were countless insults and threats seconds away from spewing from his mouth.

I decided to take a huge risk; I decided to open up and tell them the truth.

"Well, *we* do not love and respect *our* ruler," I said. "And we *do* seek to overthrow him as soon as humanly possible. When we do, can we count on Hydratica's support?"

Blane and Zane's eyes went wide, while Camilla smiled and nodded her approval.

"I hope you succeed," Blane said honestly. "The world would be a better place for it."

Zane nodded. "And, yes, when the time comes, Hydratica

will have your back... as long as you're willing to make our alliance official."

I wasn't sensing anything sneaky or deceitful in their emotions. I turned to Cal, wondering if he'd sensed any lies, but he silently shook his head.

So, they were telling the truth. They'd back us when we attempted to overthrow King Zacharias. That was *huge*. Possibly even a game changer.

"But like we said," Blane added solemnly, "not until our father has lived a long and robust life. We will not murder someone we love in the name of politics. That is not our way."

I nodded. I liked these guys. They seemed true and just, loyal and reliable. And also, I trusted Camilla's judgement. If she was enamored with them, then they must've been good men.

Ben smiled. After seeing how well my open honesty had been received, he apparently decided it'd be best to divulge a few more details to the twins.

"We're searching for the Eye of the Sea," he said nonchalantly. "Any idea where it might be located?"

Again, the twins' eyes went wide. "Why in the world would you be looking for *that*?"

"The Storm King wants it," Ben explained. "We're trying to make sure he *doesn't* get it."

Zane nodded and pinched at his bottom lip with his free hand. "We have no idea where the Eye is, unfortunately. But I can tell you this: our father has been searching for it as well —for *years*. It's the true reason we've been building up our armadas. Father has ships with nets and divers out probing for the Eye at all times."

So, they hadn't been building ships in preparation for war all this time? They'd simply been looking for the Eye, and we'd read the situation all wrong? I mean, all those ships were no doubt coming in handy now that war was imminent, but it was nice to know that wasn't their intention.

"What does *your* father want with the Eye?" Criss asked, speaking up for the first time. "What does it do? What's its significance?"

Blane lowered his eyelids and his voice and leaned forward. "The Eye of the Sea is the only object we know of that is powerful enough to rip tears into the fabric of our world. Our father wants it to create a portal to the underworld, to put the dead back where they belong, and get rid of them once and for all."

"That's bullshit!" Rob growled, unable to control his temper any longer.

But the twins seemed prepared for his reaction.

"Is it?" Zane asked calmly. "Do the dead not actually belong there? Would they not be happier existing in their final resting place?"

Rob looked reluctant to answer, so Dan answered for him. "Even if they *did* belong there, and if they *would* be happier there, it should still be their *choice* to go or not. They shouldn't be forced to leave."

Rob nodded his agreement.

Blane sighed. "Then let us hope that neither of our parents finds the Eye."

Shit. Now we *really* needed to find it first. Not only to keep it from the Storm King, but to keep it from the Hydratican king, as well—whatever his name was. Damn, I should have paid more attention in Professor Samson's class.

"What does the Eye even look like?" I asked. "Is it an actual eye?"

Blane chuckled and shook his head. "It's rumored to be one of the eight eyes of the four-headed hydra that lives at the bottom of the sea. But no one knows for sure, and certainly, no one has ever seen the hydra. Our father has scoured the ancient records though, and he believes it to be a *pearl* instead. So basically, it's a needle in a fucking haystack. Our currency consists solely of pearls, and the ocean is full of them. How he hopes to find one with magical powers is beyond us, and probably why he has failed thus far."

Ugh. Neither of those options sounded ideal.

Zane took Camilla's hand and brought it to his lips before turning back to us. "One more thing before we go. Since you have been honest with us, we will be honest with you: our father is planning on attacking Wessea as soon as possible. Once he has control of the Ebony Chateau, he'll blaze a southeast trail all the way down to Sohsol and the Onyx Fortress. There, he'll either open the portal to the underworld—assuming he's found the Eye—or he'll slaughter as many of the dead as he can."

"Use this information how you will," Blane added, as they rose from their chairs and prepared to leave. "But I'd recommend evacuating your cities in order to avoid excessive bloodshed."

"Don't take it personally when we counterattack," Dan warned darkly.

But Zane merely smiled and bowed his head. "Don't take it personally when you lose."

CHAPTER 24

*T**hwack!***

Rob stabbed a blade right through the center of Ash's snake-like head, sinking it deeply into the wooden deck below.

"I can't believe this whole trip was for nothing," he grumbled as he heaved the knife back out and wiped the blood on his pants. After our meeting with the princes, we were once again speeding across the ocean on our way back to Blackwood.

Ash's magic swirled to life a moment later, and soon he was back in human form, sitting right beside me on a bench.

I cocked my head in surprise. At least Rob had saved me the trouble of having to kill the slithery reptile myself. I might have hated snakes, but I hated killing Ash more—even though I knew it was just part of his magic and absolutely necessary for bring him back to us.

Cal sighed. "It wasn't for *nothing*. We have more potential allies now, at least."

Dan glared at him and exhaled loudly. "They're going to obliterate half of fucking Blackwood, Cal. They're definitely not our allies yet, and I wouldn't hold my breath about them being our allies in the future either."

Ironically enough, he then *held his breath* and continued propelling the ship.

I glanced at Cal then turned back toward the guys. "I didn't sense anything off in their emotions. They seemed genuine to me."

Cal nodded. "And there was no lie in their words. Not one."

"They were always pretty nice guys," Ash said thoughtfully. "Even when we were young."

"They actually gave us a lot of useful information," Ben added, seemingly agreeing with Cal, Ash, and me. "If we can evacuate the cities and find the Eye before either of the kings, then we might be able to stop this war before anyone even gets hurt."

It was so nice to have an inkling of hope to cling to.

Which was why it sucked so bad when it completely vanished.

Rob jumped to his feet on the ship's deck and scanned the horizon, breathing heavily.

"What's wrong?" Criss asked, climbing onto his feet too.

Rob shook his head. "I don't know. I just feel weird. Like there are *a lot* of souls nearby."

Dan exhaled again before sucking in a deep breath. "Nearby? We're damn near back to the Blackwood coast."

Cal's blue eyes went wide. "You don't suppose King Thane has attacked already..."

Wow. Thane, Blane, and Zane. Guess that's going to be easy to remember.

Dan's features went rigid with fear, and every muscle in his body tensed. He sucked in a huge gulp of air and pushed the ship as fast as he could manage. I had to cling to the railing to keep from blowing away.

Colors were the first thing I noticed on the horizon. Deepening shades of gray mixed with oranges and reds. Perhaps a strange sunset, I tried to convince myself at first. But then came the crackling sounds of fire and the terrifying buzzing of a screaming crowd. By the time the scent of smoke reached our noses, we were already in a panic. The closer we got to Dan's kingdom, the clearer the scene became —Ebony Chateau was on fire, and so was the city surrounding it.

Never slowing down, Dan crashed the ship into the shore, scraping the keel halfway up the beach before jumping overboard and sprinting toward the chaos.

The rest of us were right behind him. I didn't know what we were thinking or doing, running straight into a blazing city, but I knew we needed to do *something*. To help *somehow*.

The heat of the flames was like a physical force, pushing us back, but we shielded our faces and soldiered on. All around us, shops and buildings were on fire, billowing in putrid smoke. People stumbled through the streets, their skin char-coaled and bleeding, soot covering their tear-streaked faces. Others lay motionless on the ground. Boards creaked and cracked, foundations gave out and crashed to the ground, and Dan dropped to his knees in the middle of it all and sobbed.

"Alexis, you can control fire," he said, turning to me with the most gut-wrenching expression on his face. "Please, make it stop."

My freaking heart faltered. *Make it stop*? I'd never controlled more than a few blasts of flame from my palms. How the hell was I supposed to contain a raging inferno over a mile wide?

"I..." I was at a loss. "I'll try."

Then Dan turned to Criss. "You have healing powers? *Please*. Help my people."

Criss swallowed hard and nodded. I could tell he had no idea what to do either, but that, like me, he was going to try his damnedest anyway.

"I'll try to funnel it away," Cal offered. "Clear the smoke so they can breathe."

He jumped into the air, and his powers took over, allowing him to fly like a bird on the breeze. A moment later, he was swallowed up in the gray.

Ben put a hand on Dan's shoulder. "Get up, bro. You control the *sea*. Don't forget your power."

Dan sniffed one last time and stood. He took a deep breath of smoky air and immediately funneled in a swirling vortex of saltwater. The collision of fire and water made a fierce hissing noise and added a layer of white steam to the graying skyline, but it was a wonderful sight to see.

Criss jogged over to a sobbing woman carrying a little girl. The child had been badly burned by the look of her raw flesh, and I couldn't even tell if she was breathing. I'd never seen Criss look so pained. He splayed his hands out, closed his hazel eyes, and I watched him say "heal." As if responding to the pure agony of his soul, the power poured out of him and doused the little girl in golden magic. Seconds later, she was on two feet and running from the flames alongside her mother.

It was absolutely inspiring.

After that, he found another citizen in need and repeated the process. His magic didn't always seem to come easily, but he never gave up.

Smiling, I turned to the nearest blazing building and held out my arms. I normally had to speak the word "fire" in order to make the magic work, and when I was finished, I usually just clenched my fists to cut off the flow. This though... this was entirely different. The fire wasn't coming *from* me, so I couldn't make it stop, but maybe I could suck it *into* me somehow and still get rid of it?

"Stop," I ordered the flames.

They seemed to laugh at my weakness as they danced atop the rooftops.

Annoyed and seriously feeling the pressure, I solidified my resolve. "Stop!" I commanded once more.

This time the flames dimmed down and flickered.

Glad I finally have your attention, you little bastards.

"I said, *stop!*" The last time I shouted it was the most authoritative of all, and soon the fire smoldered out, leaving behind nothing but the charred skeleton of the building and a thin line of wispy smoke.

Yes! I totally considered that a win.

"Nice job, Sailor!" Ben cheered. "Ash and I can't use our powers against the fire, so we're going to go help people evacuate. Be careful and stay safe."

"You too," I said, feeling my heart splinter as they ran off into a wall of smoke.

They're demigods. They'll be fine. They're immortal. The bond will keep us alive.

Dan funneled in another wave of seawater, dousing the shop beside mine, and jarred me back into action. Jogging further up the street, I found the next burning building and got to work.

It went on like this for *hours*. Long after the sun had set, leaving the night sky to glow an ominous orange. Long after many quick dips in the freezing cold sea to cool my burning desire. Long after I'd used so much power that I was sure I'd simply shrivel up and die.

And then finally, it was done. The fire was out, we'd saved as many civilians as we could, the sky was mostly smoke-free, and the sun was just cresting the horizon. It had taken us the entire night, and we were all completely exhausted.

We trudged up the chateau steps, slow as molasses, talking quietly as we went.

"How are you feeling?" I asked Criss as we brought up the rear.

He ran a hand over his buzzed head then dragged it down his face. "I feel dead. Is this what death feels like?"

Rob chuckled darkly and glanced over his shoulder at us. "Death is peaceful. This chaos is *life* at its finest."

Cal looked back at us too. "So, you were able to figure out your healing powers, then?"

Criss nodded. "I think so. Every time I healed someone, I got a bit more tired. By the time I'd mended ten or fifteen people, I was so bleary-eyed I fell asleep in the middle of the street. A few times, I got dragged off to the edge of the woods because people thought I'd passed out from smoke inhalation."

"So, exhaustion is your price?" I asked, pausing midstep to catch my breath. *Seriously, fuck these stairs.* "And sleep is how you recoup?"

He nodded. "Seems that way. I didn't have to sleep very long though. Just a quick ten-minute nap was enough. I guess my new natural healing abilities kicked in while I slept and refilled my power stores automatically."

"That's awesome," I said with a proud smile. Since he was being so humble, it made it easy for me to feel pride and appreciation on his behalf.

Apparently, I wasn't the only one.

"Thank you, Criss," Dan said from the very front of our line. His voice was hoarse and raw and emotional. He then glanced from Cal to Rob with a blank expression. "If either of you still think he's not worthy of being in the group, you can go fuck yourselves."

Cal blinked, and Rob's mouth fell open, but Dan just

turned around and kept on walking. Pretty sure mine and everyone else's mouths were hanging open too.

Dan and Rob were best friends; they *never* spoke to each other like that.

"I'm going to go talk to him," I muttered, and fighting against the burn in my legs and lungs, I jogged to catch up. "Hey," I puffed as we crested the top of the stone staircase.

Dan reached out and took my hand, threading our fingers tightly. "Hey."

There was nothing truly consoling I could say. I knew he blamed himself for what happened. I knew there was nothing we could do to change any of it. So I told him the thing I thought he needed to hear most.

"I love you."

He glanced over at me with misty eyes and forced a smile. "I love you too, Lexi. You did amazing back there with the fire. I'm so proud to call you my wife."

His words touched me, and yet I started to understand more of where he was coming from, because I didn't feel like a heroine. I felt like a failure. Like I should have done so much more, somehow.

"I'm so sorry, Dan," I whispered through the tears puddling in my eyes. "I wish we could have saved them all. I wish this had never happened."

He nodded. "Me too, baby girl. Me too. But there's no changing the past. All we can do now is plan our next move."

Which I'm sure involved some heavy retaliation. I could feel his need for vengeance burning in the air. I didn't want to minimalize that need, but I didn't want to feed that particular beast either, so I stayed silent, offering him my love and support by simply standing beside him.

Edden met us at the door. "Your Highnesses, thank the gods you're all right."

Dan patted Edden's shoulder. "It's not us you need to worry about. How's your family?"

"They're okay, Highness. They were able to escape before the fires got too high."

"Thank the gods," Dan replied with genuine relief. "Go. Take the day off. Be with them."

Edden bowed deeply. "Thank you, Your Highness. Before I leave though..." He reached into his suit pocket and handed over some envelopes. "A few letters arrived this morning. They bear seals from Rubio, Werewood, and Valinor."

Dan's pale green eyes lit up. "Thank you, Edden."

As the servant left and the rest of the guys caught up, Dan led us all upstairs into his living room lounge. We made ourselves comfortable on the couches and sofas while he took a seat at the ornament desk in the back corner. He opened a letter and began reading silently to himself.

Nerves crept up my spine and swirled in my chest. I wanted so badly for him to read the note aloud, but I didn't dare push him—not when he was already so broken and upset.

Eventually, he heaved a sigh of relief. "Rubio will back us on the water—and *only* on the water—for a price."

"They didn't accept our offer on the finished metals?" Cal asked, standing up anxiously.

Dan shook his head. "No, they did. But it wasn't enough. They want Emory Isle as well, the last island in the chain on our side of the boarder."

Cal pursed his lips. "Do you think the Storm King will give it up?"

Dan shrugged. "I don't give a fuck. *I'm* going to give it up in exchange for some godsdamned help."

My brows furrowed. I supposed, to a prince, the idea of handing off an island seemed as simple as signing a piece of paper. But for the *people*? They were about to lose their homes.

"If you do that," I said, boldly speaking up, "then you need to offer aid to the citizens who are forced to relocate. Help them find jobs on the mainland and new homes."

Dan nodded slowly, mulling over my *suggestion*. Okay, fine, my *demand*.

"All right," he said. "We'll do it. Would you like to be in charge of the project?"

I'd never been "in charge" of anything, but if anyone knew how to help the people, then it was one of their own. I might be a princess now, but I'd never forget my humble beginnings as a peasant.

"Yes," I said with a nod. "I'll lead the relocation project myself."

Dan smiled. "Excellent."

He then ripped open the second letter and read it to himself.

"Same for Valinor," he said in a sigh. "They'll send reinforcements under a few circumstances. One, their soldiers won't ever be near or ever come into contact with any Rubians. Apparently, Akiko rubbed Veda wrong back in Blackwood. Two, any items they acquire during their stay in Blackwood will become their permanent property. I wonder if they're hoping to amass some jewels? And three, they still want Alexis to help with the volcanic issues they've been having."

I was suddenly very nervous. The relocation project seemed like a small but important thing. This would be an enormous undertaking, and I would almost certainly fail. I hated the thought of agreeing to something I couldn't come through on.

"I don't know how to control lava," I admitted. "I don't even know if it's possible."

Dan chewed on his lips. "You didn't know how to stop external fire until last night either. Maybe it's something you could learn? Would you be willing to try and help them in exchange for some of their soldiers?"

In other words, how far was I willing to go to protect my people? As a princess of Blackwood, I had the power to defend them and keep them safe... *if* I chose wisely.

I took a deep breath and scrounged up my courage. "Tell the Valinorians that I can't possibly promise to fix such a problem, but that I'll *try*."

"Thank you," Dan whispered on an exhale.

I hadn't even realized he'd been holding his breath.

He stared back down at the letter and tapped his fingers on the desk. "Keeping the Valinorians and Rubians separate won't be a problem since one will be on land and the other will be on the sea, but what about the permanent property clause?"

"I'd think that'd very much depend on what they were planning on pocketing," Criss said. "Perhaps if we define what 'find' actually means as opposed to 'steal' or 'take' and then specify what items are non-negotiable, such as jewels or coins, then we might be able to agree."

Cal nodded. "He's right. We can't just outright agree to that part. We can send them a counteroffer and see what they say."

Dan glanced out the chateau window and bit his bottom lip. "Do we have enough time to barter the details like this? Or should we simply settle?"

Ash studied him for a moment. "What if a Valinorian 'found' Alexis on the street? If you've already agreed to those exact terms, then she would technically be the property of Valinor."

Dan sighed. "I see the problem."

"So do I," I chipped in crossly. "I'm a godsdamned *woman*

not a piece of *property* to be found or owned."

"I love it when she gets fiery," Rob said, shooting me a devilish grin.

Dan grinned too before reading the third letter and summarizing it.

"Werewood will join the fight if they are provided with a constant supply of alcohol for the duration of the war—both for the soldiers they'll send to our aid *as well as* their citizens back home."

"Holy shit, how many distilleries do they think we have?" Ben asked.

Dan raised a brow. "Enough, I'm sure."

"Have you ever seen a drunk werewolf?" Ben countered. "It takes *a lot*."

"Nice word, lexicon," I teased him.

Ben rolled his brown eyes playfully. "Fine. It takes a massive volume of fermented fluids to inebriate a wolf shifter."

"*Any* shifter, really," Ash added, looking rather smug about his drinking skills. "You should have seen me at the beer pong competition."

"The fuck is beer pong?" Rob asked.

"Oh, bro," Ash replied excitedly, "as soon as this war is over and we get some free time, I'll show you how to play. You're going to love it."

"Can we stay on topic, please?" Dan asked, sounding an awful lot like a grumpier Cal. "Are we able to meet these demands or not?"

Ben stood and paced around the room. "Statistically, it's unlikely. But if we divert some of the non-warring civilians to the distilleries, then we could up our production substantially while still maintaining enough coin for the war efforts."

Rob raised a brow. "So that's a yes?"

Ben took a deep breath and glanced skyward. "*Yes*. Did

they have any other stipulations?"

"Yeah, one," Dan admitted, "but it's small. They wish to take credit for a major victory in the war. I think Prince Rafe wants to throw it in our dear father's face."

Cal scoffed. "Done."

My thoughts exactly. They could take credit for *half* the battles if it meant making the Storm King look like a fool.

Dan finished scribbling out the reply letters then rubbed at his temples. "All right, now, battle strategies."

"Hydratica has the entire sea covered in ships," Ben pointed out immediately. "There's little to no way of slipping between them, unless we hug the Rubian coast, which is now an option. I just wouldn't want to bring the battle to Rubio and wipe out our allies as soon as they joined the fight."

"You underestimate them," Cal replied. "Rubians are lethal in battle."

"Even still," Ben pressed, "they'd be outnumbered ten to one. Hydratica is *huge*; Rubio is a tiny chain of islands. The numbers don't lie, bro."

"Oh! I know!" Ash said, raising his hand in the air. "What if I turn into a bird and fly around shitting on our enemies, giving them all a severe case of Swamp Ass Fever?"

Ben looked utterly horrified. "I can't believe you'd even suggest that." But still, he paused. "Though, it might actually work..."

"What about the channel of Glite?" Criss asked.

The guys contemplated his question for a moment, while I tried to imagine where such a channel might exist on a map. Fuck me for not paying more attention in history and geography.

"No one's used the channel in years," Cal eventually said.

Ben nodded. "Because it's become too shallow to navigate. Even tiny boats end up having to be carried by hand for half of the journey."

"But it's the rainy season," Criss continued. "There might be just enough water for us to sneak in unnoticed and attack where they least expect it."

"But if there's not, we'd be fucked," Rob contended. "Our ships would be way too heavy to carry."

"You're all forgetting something," I said with a smile.

Cal folded his hands behind his back. "And what's that?"

I pointed to Dan. "*Him.* He's the *Sea* Prince, remember? As long as he can hold his breath, he can get our ships through the channel no matter how shallow the water is."

Dan nodded as if surprised that the idea hadn't come to him sooner. "She's right. And that'll definitely give us the element of surprise that we need."

He grabbed a scroll and unrolled a map, tracing the path we'd need to take.

"If we used the channel of Glite, we could hit Hydratica *here.*" He pointed to a port on the northern edge of the coast: Brineton. "Then we can slip right back through channel before they even know where we went."

"But," Rob said, coming over to study the map, "while we're attacking, we need to have our people evacuating along *here.*" He traced an invisible line from Ebony Chateau all the way down to Onyx Fortress. "Because I don't trust King Thane as far as I could throw him. It wouldn't surprise me one bit if he sent his troops inland while we were still out toiling on the sea."

"Then it's settled," Dan said, standing behind the desk. "We gather what's left of our sailors and soldiers and we counterattack as soon as possible. While we're gone, I'll send messengers to every town in King Thane's potential path. We'll evacuate as many cities as we can."

"Send a message to Southern Blackwood too," Rob said with a dark expression. "Tell them I'll be returning soon. Tell them to prepare for war."

CHAPTER 25

*W*e slept the rest of the day.

After being up all night, draining our power wells putting out fires and rescuing citizens, I supposed it didn't really surprise me. We were dead tired, and we needed our rest if we hoped to be of *any* help to *anyone* in the near future.

A knocking at the door was what finally woke me.

My eyes popped open and drank in the darkness of the room—we were still in Dan's lounge. I'd fallen asleep on the floor, along with Ash and Ben, while Cal and Rob were strewn out across a couple couches. An empty loveseat waited where Dan had once been sleeping. Footsteps shuffled across the floor. A door creaked quietly, and a thin band of ever-growing light scurried across the floor.

"General Madden," Dan said, his voice a bit groggy. "What news do you have?"

I saw the General's shadow bow in the hallway light.

"Just stopped by to update you on the status of the counterattack, Your Highness."

"And?" Dan asked, crossing his arms nervously.

"We're going to need at least one more day, Your Highness. Half of the men are wounded, and the other half are too exhausted to sail."

Dan sighed and scrubbed a frustrated hand through his sandy brown hair.

"Give us an extra day to recover and restock the food stores, Highness. After that, we'll attack with full force. I promise, we won't let you down."

Something about the General's words wiped away Dan's disappointment immediately.

"Of course, you won't, Madden. I'm always impressed with you and our military." He sighed one last time before nodding with conviction. "All right. One more day. Then we'll wipe Brineton Port right off the godsdamned map."

THE NEXT MORNING, I WAS THE FIRST TO RISE.

I hadn't slept well after Dan's midnight meeting with the General, tossing and turning between nightmares and dreams, but I still felt a shit ton better than I had the day before. I stretched out any kinks I'd gotten from sleeping on the sandstone floor, and I walked out onto the balcony to bask in the early morning sunshine.

We had one day. One day to relax, to recuperate, and to prepare for the journey ahead. How were we going to spend it?

A light flickered in my brain, and I realized I hadn't yet gone on my date with Dan. Yes, a date would probably seem trivial and petty next to the catastrophe that had recently transpired, but I also knew my Sea Prince needed to destress. He wouldn't feel up to doing anything normal or fun —he'd feel too guilty to even consider it—but he might be up for mixing some fun in with some humanitarianism.

Of course, now that Ash was back, I owed him some time too. Maybe we could do like Cal, Ben, and I had and make it a double date?

"Good morning, beautiful," Cal muttered, shuffling over to where I stood on the balcony with bleary blue eyes.

I smiled and kissed him. "Morning. I thought you usually woke up early?"

He chuckled, but the laugh came out gruff from all the sleep. "I usually do, but these past couple days have just been a blur."

I nodded my agreement. "So, what's on the agenda for today?"

Cal shrugged. "I don't know. Maybe helping the soldiers and sailors prepare for our voyage? Whenever that may be."

"Tomorrow," I told him, my voice suddenly solemn. "I heard Dan talking to his General last night. We head to Brineton as soon as the men are rested."

Cal nodded, staring out across the vast expanse of sea. "Good."

I tried to smile, but the thought of war had me feeling sick. "I'd like to take Dan and Ash on a date today," I told him. "Can you handle Dan's affairs while he's gone?"

"Of course I can, Peach. No worries."

His response warmed my heart. I reached over and wrapped my arms around his waist, snuggling my head into his broad chest. "I love you, Cal."

He kissed the top of my head and stroked my long dark hair. "I love you too, Alexis."

Soon, another set of bare feet shuffled onto the balcony and a different prince appeared on my left. Dan. He sighed and leaned his elbows on the stone banister, staring intently across the sea.

I slipped out of Cal's arms and curled up next to our newest arrival.

"Morning," I said quietly. I didn't dare say *good* morning, just in case it triggered any guilt.

"Morning," he muttered back, smiling faintly as he leaned in and kissed my cheek. "Sleep well?"

"For the most part." I tried to keep my tone light. "I was wondering if we might be able to have our date today?"

He smiled, but it looked pained. "Oh, Lexi, I wish we could. I just have so much shit to prepare for with this counterattack and with restoring the city... You understand, right?"

I nodded. "I do. That's why I thought we could spend our date helping the citizens."

He turned to me, pale green eyes filled with interest but also love and longing. "Oh yeah?"

"Yeah." I reached down and laced our fingers together. "I figured we could volunteer at the emergency food bank or the makeshift healing clinic. Then I thought we could gather the local children and play a game. Kids don't need to be experiencing the harshness of this world so soon."

Dan smiled for real this time before glancing over my head toward Cal. "Would you mind taking over my—"

"Already done," Cal informed him with a genuine smile. "She beat you to it."

Dan's gaze shifted back to mine, and his love for me filled the air around us, not even swayed by the gentle ocean breeze. "Thank you, Lexi."

I blushed and shrugged a shoulder. "You're welcome. Is it okay if Ash joins us? I haven't spent time with him either, and I kind of assumed this date would be more... platonic."

Dan nodded. "I think you're right. And, yes, Ash can definitely come. I've missed him too."

Gods, I loved that about them. There were times they got jealous, yes, but most of the time? They loved each other too much to be spiteful. They'd rather spend time together than apart, whether I had anything to do with it or not.

"Besides," Dan added in a low voice, "even if things miraculously get a little heated, you know I love to share."

He really did. I thought he enjoyed seeing his brothers take me as much as he enjoyed taking me himself. Just imagining the heated look in his eye as he watched Ash fuck me senseless had my panties growing damp.

"Let's wake him up and get going then," I replied, my voice equally as low and tempting.

We walked back into the lounge, and Dan threw a pillow at Asher's head. "Wake up, lazy ass. Time to rise and shine."

Ash grinned and used the pillow to block his eyes from the sunlight. "I'm still asleep."

Dan rolled his eyes and smirked. "Guess you're not going out with Alexis and me today then."

The pillow suddenly vanished from Ash's face as he whipped it across the room. "I'm awake."

"That's what I thought." Dan chuckled and led the two of us into his bedroom where all our suitcases had been stowed. "Grab a change of clothes. We need to hit the bathing pools before we go anywhere near civilization. We smell like smoke and sweat and staleness."

Ash laughed and shook his head as he rummaged through his bag. "I thought charm was supposed to be your second power? Telling people how awful they smell is rude, you know."

I grinned at Ash's teasing and pulled out a dress I'd never seen. It was one of those short-skirted, super-soft numbers that the beachgoers liked to wear, and it was a deep plum purple with lace around the edges.

Dan sighed heavily in Asher's direction. "Well, it's true. And after the night we had, it's not surprising. I'm not insulting any of us. I'm honestly incredibly grateful that we smell like smoke; it means we were out there doing as much as we possibly could to stop the fires. But now, it's time to look and *smell* like royalty. We need to show the people that we're strong and resilient. That we'll bounce back from this in no time."

He had a good point. The people probably did need as much encouragement as they could get.

I held up the dress and turned around. "Who put this in here?"

Dan smiled. "Ben. He's always mentioning gifts he wants to get you. He actually bought you a dress back in Northern Blackwood while we were staying at Nightshade. But since Bria had also given you a dress, he decided to save it for later."

I remembered that day. The very first date Ben and I had ever been on. We walked through Blackhaven, and I'd pointed to a shop where a beautiful gown hung in the window. He'd said it was probably ordered in special from his kingdom or Eristan, because the silk was so shimmery and rich.

I smiled at the memory as I hugged my new dress to my chest. Ben really was the sweetest man ever. I was going to have to think of a special way to thank him. On my knees underneath a table, perhaps...

"What's that devious look about?" Ash asked me as he slung his clothes over his shoulder.

I shook my head. "Nothing."

"Hey," Dan said with a raised brow. "This is *our* date. No fawning over Ben while you're with us."

I rolled my eyes but smiled. "I'll try not to. He's just so sweet."

"*Sweet?*" Ash protested. "I brought you sweets every time I saw you back in Blackleaf. If anyone's sweet, it's me."

I shoved his chest and strolled toward the door. "You haven't brought me sweets in years, Asher Storm."

"What about me?" Dan asked before Ash had a chance to protest. "I might not shower you in gifts, but I do shower you in compliments."

"Ha! You mean like telling me how stale I smell?"

He groaned. "Oh, come on, Lexi, you know what I mean. I'm always telling you how sexy and beautiful you are."

"*Sure* you are," I teased as we made our way downstairs.

Dan led us outside and over to a series of small pools that cascaded into each other. It looked like a private, tiered river leading all the way down to the coast. Steam rose from the surface of each pool despite the air already being quite warm.

The guys stripped totally naked without any of hesitation and waded into the water, waiting on me to do the same.

I raised a brow and put both hands on my hips. "I thought you said it'd be a miracle if things turned heated?"

Dan grinned devilishly, his pearly white smile making me weak in the knees. "We're just bathing, Sexy Lexi. Why don't you strip and get in the water?"

I pursed my lips, dithering only a moment longer before giving in. "Fine."

I tugged the dirty white dress up over my head and dropped it on the ground, fully aware of their darkened gazes as they roamed my naked body. Step by step, I waded slowly into the steamy pool and sat down beside them, the water coming up to my neck. I leaned back into the smooth stone wall and sighed. The heat felt amazing on my muscles, and the smell was fantastic, like roses, lilies, peaches, and papaya.

Dan and Ash sat too, but the water only came midchest on them, leaving their bulging pecks and dark nipples above water. It turned me right the hell on. I pressed my thighs together as Dan reached for a bar of soap sitting on a nearby stone. He lathered his hands up and cocked his chin my way. "Come here, Sexy."

I floated over and settled between his legs, my back pressed to his chiseled chest, his semi-hard dick poking into my butt cheeks. The soft slide of our slippery skin had my breathing going shallow, but when his fingers tangled in my hair, massaging my scalp with soapy bubbles, I freaking moaned out loud.

Ash took the bar once Dan was finished with it, and as his brother washed my hair, he rubbed my feet. My eyelids flitted shut, and I was sure I'd died and gone to Elysium. How else could I explain two sexy Greek demigods worshiping my body in a heated outdoor pool? I mean seriously...

Dan's fingers drifted lower, rubbing my neck and shoulders, while Ash's fingers glided higher, working the muscles of my calves and thighs.

Ash glanced up over my head and nodded, and I knew he and Dan must've just had some unspoken conversation. Then his hands moved even further up my legs, gripping my hips as he settled his torso between my thighs.

"I missed you, Sweets," he muttered, gliding his hands up my stomach and cupping my breasts. Bending down, he sucked my left nipple into his mouth, then moved right and suckled the other. My hips rolled on instinct, brushing into Ash's rock-hard erection in the front and Dan's in the back.

"I missed you too," I whispered. "I'm so glad we're all back together."

Dan kissed the side of my neck, making me shiver. As my nipples pebbled, Ash dipped down and took one into his mouth once more.

I moaned as lust washed over me like a tidal wave. I hadn't felt this horny without the prodding of my magic in a *while*.

Turning my head, I captured Dan's mouth in mine, and a

moment later, Ash slowly pressed his rigid length into me. And oh my gods, it felt amazing. I rocked my hips slowly as Ash slid in and out, and I flicked my tongue as Dan owned my mouth.

Sometime later—I didn't know when, I was in a blissful haze of oblivion—Dan's lips were gone and replaced by Ash's as he pulled me tight against his body. I wrapped my legs around his waist and slid my arms around his neck, deepening our kiss as Dan drifted off to the side, getting a better view of the action.

I stole a glance at Dan, pleased to find that same heated look I'd imagined blazing behind his sea green eyes. He loved this, watching me get fucked by his brother right in front of him. And surprisingly enough, I loved it too. It was so naughty and sinful, it made my toes curl.

Or maybe that was Ash making them curl?

He thrust up into me, harder and faster than before, his kiss intensifying with the pace of his movements. It wasn't wild and reckless though. It was intimate and impassioned. We were joined in as many ways as possible, our souls connecting as our bodies delved in and out of one another.

I had to break our kiss when my breaths started coming in panting waves. With my forehead pressed to his, I moaned that I was close. He responded by squeezing my ass and pumping in deeper, stroking me longer, and dragging out every last bit of pleasure from my body before I came apart in his arms.

As I shuddered, he growled and rooted himself deep inside me, holding that position until he finally finished coming.

The next thing I knew, Dan swept me out of Ash's arms and into his lap. In that position, the water just barely touched the tops of my shoulders. His cock was rigid beneath me, and his gaze was locked so intensely onto mine that everything except those sea green eyes just drifted away.

And then he started to move.

Slowly, inch by inch, he pressed up into me as I rolled my hips.

"What do you want, my queen?" he whispered so low I was sure Ash hadn't heard him. "I want to please you."

As his cock pushed further into me, grazing that elusive hot spot inside, I moaned and damn near saw stars. "Trust me, you *are* pleasing me."

Then the pool water started moving between us, swirling like fast rolling waves, or maybe pulsing like invisible bubbles trying to escape. The sensation moved from my breasts to my stomach and then down to my clit. From above, there was nothing strange to be see, but from below, it was driving me insane with need.

"You're doing that?" I panted in question.

He bit his lip and nodded darkly. "You like it?"

"Gods, yes."

It was like nothing I'd ever felt. Not as forceful as a finger or as carnal as a tongue, but still just as intense. Coupled with his cock reaming me, his fingers gliding up to roll my nipples, and the fact that I'd orgasmed once already, I was a fucking goner in seconds.

"Come with me," I begged him.

He groaned and did just that, letting loose as we both exploded into each other.

Once we caught our breath, I climbed out of his lap and leaned back into the rocky edge of the pool, gazing skyward with a lopsided smile on my face. Every muscle, bone, and cell in my body was content.

All that before our date had even officially begun.

Holy shit.

CHAPTER 26

"*D*id you ever consider bestiality?" Dan asked Ash as we made our way into town.

We officially smelled like roses—much to Dan's relief. And we were a fuck ton more relaxed. Literally, we'd fucked ourselves into relaxation. It was fantastic.

Ash blinked a few times before bursting into laughter. "*What?*"

"You know," Dan prodded, "like fucking her while you're a horse or something."

Ash glanced at me and raised a brow. "Hey, Sweets, you feel like getting railed with a horse cock?"

My eyes went wide. "Demigod cocks are quite massive enough for me, thanks."

"Oh, come on," Dan teased. "You don't want that sloth dick?"

I stuck my tongue out like I'd just licked a toad. "Nope."

Dan glanced at Ash. "Seriously? You never fantasized about fucking her when you were a sloth?"

"Oh no, I did," Ash assured him. "I just always pictured myself as a man when it happened."

Dan shook his head and tried to hide a grin. "I just can't help but feel like you're missing a really unique opportunity here."

Ash smirked and patted his brother's shoulder. "Sounds like you have some great new inspiration for your private jackoff sessions. Have fun with that, you creepy son of a bitch."

As they cracked themselves up, the emergency food bank came into view up ahead. Lines of hungry citizens stretched on for at least a few blocks, people who'd lost their homes, their possessions, and maybe even some of their family members—hard working people who probably despised having to ask for food.

My heart ached for them. But mostly, I was proud of them for even being there, for doing what they needed to do in order to survive when they could've just ended it all. They were true fighters. They'd endured much more than a brutal attack; they'd survived their own darkest thoughts.

I turned to Ash and Dan, who'd sobered up at the sight before them. "Are you guys ready?"

They each nodded solemnly. Clearly, they were as over-come as I was. I took each of their hands, and we made our way toward the entrance. The crowd parted as soon as we drew near, giving us a wide berth and a clear path to the building. They hung their heads in both respect and shame—I could feel it in the air around them.

It hurt so much to know that was how they felt.

I reached out and touched the nearest shoulder. The man quickly lifted his head, looking shocked and confused, while I tried my best to smile. "Life is like an ocean—it comes in waves. We can't always be strong. Sometimes we have to ask for help. And that's okay. Soon, another wave will come, and we'll be sturdy once again."

I touched another shoulder, that of a young woman.

"Don't lose hope. All highs become lows, yes, but on the contrary, all lows become highs as well."

As word spread of our arrival, the head volunteer soon met us at the door, curtsying deeply. "Your Royal Highnesses, how may we be of service?"

I turned to Dan, smiling. "Actually, we'd like to be the ones in service today. Do you need any help cooking? Or spooning out soup? Perhaps washing dishes?"

Tears filled the woman's eyes as she smiled gratefully and nodded. "You are too kind, Your Highness. But, yes, we could use all the help we can get."

I smiled as my own eyes went misty. "We'd be honored to lend a hand."

"Then, by all means, please follow me."

She led us to the kitchens in the back and rearranged the volunteers so that Dan, Ash, and I were the ones spooning out soup. I assumed she'd thought it'd bolster the masses to see us serving them face-to-face. At least, that's what my train of thought had been. If they could see their own princes and princess serving soup to the needy, then perhaps they'd feel less ashamed of being needy in the first place? We were one in this thing—war, life, whatever—whether royal or not.

With us captaining the ladles, we moved through the lines rather quickly. However, *because* it was us, the lines also grew considerably. People who never would have willingly joined the line were filing in, anxiously awaiting the chance to meet the Blackwood royals.

By the time lunch was over, the head volunteer—named Addy—thanked us over and over for our service. We assured her it was our absolute pleasure, but still, as we exited the door, she prayed that the gods would bless us and any children we had for generations to come. It was a sweet sentiment, but with the Storm King's demand that I become pregnant in the back of my mind, it felt more like a warning.

When was the last time I'd had my period anyway?

Panic struck me like a lightning bolt, knocking my heart out of rhythm. Oh my gods, how long had it been? A month? Two? Was it even possible that...

No.

I couldn't allow myself to think about such terrifying things. I'd rather face a world war head-on than deal with pregnancy right now. My period would come soon, I was sure of it. Until then, I'd beg and plead for the blood to flow.

"What's the matter, Sweets? You look pale."

Ash took my hand in his as walked down the street toward the temporary healing clinic set up at the edge of town.

I shook my head, feeling the nervous sweat beading along my brow and the nape of my neck. "Nothing. Just—"

"Please don't lie to us, Lexi," Dan murmured, taking my other hand. "There's something wrong. You look petrified."

I swallowed hard and wished I was less of an open book.

"She prayed that the gods would bless our children," I muttered. "I'm not ready to be a mother."

Ash smiled warmly. "That's okay, babe. We'll deal with that when the time comes."

"Unless..." Dan began, clearly catching on faster than Ash. "Are you...?"

I shook my head, and tears welled in my eyes. "I have no idea. I can't remember the last time, I—"

Suddenly, Dan had me in his arms, his face flush against mine. "Hey, it's okay. Please don't cry. No matter what happens, you will always have us to help you through it. I swear."

Ash came over and wrapped his arms around us too. "We love you, Sweets. We're not going anywhere."

"But what if I am?" I asked as tears rolled down my face.

Dan chuckled almost happily. "We're a bit older than you,

Lexi. I think you'll find we're not as terrified at the idea of fatherhood as you think."

"We're almost thirty," Ash agreed. "That's, like, *ancient* in the must-produce-a-royal-heir department."

I chuckled despite the tears and quickly wiped my cheeks. "Well, I'm like a baby in the I-have-so-much-more-life-to-live department. I'm not ready for my life to be over."

Dan sighed and shook his head as if my fear was kind of adorable. "Kids aren't the end of the world, babe, and certainly not the end of your *life*. It'll be okay if you are. And if not, that's okay too. We're here for you no matter what."

"No matter what," Ash agreed, and they finally put me back on my feet.

I sniffed out a laugh despite myself. "You guys are fucking amazing."

"No, *you* are," Dan assured me. "You've proven it over and over since the day I met you, and again today by coming out here to help our people. I couldn't ask for a better queen."

Ash smiled and wrapped his arm around my waist. "Neither could I—you know, as soon as I take my kingdom back from that dick-headed imposter claiming to be our father. Oh, and as soon as I can marry you like everyone else seems to have."

I cocked my head as remorse filled my heart. "I'm so sorry, Asher. I know you've wanted to marry me the longest."

He kissed my forehead and squeezed me tightly. "It's okay. I was gone. I get it. But as soon as this war's over, I'm making you mine too."

Happiness welled inside of me, filling me with hope and anticipation.

"I can't wait for that day," I told him, and I absolutely meant it.

At the clinic, things got intense once more. We ran around helping doctors and healers work their nonmagical "magic." Antiseptic here, antibacterial ointment there. A few stitches in that wound, a layer of gauze on that one. There were so many people with injuries to attend to, they must've felt like the patients were never ending.

I know *I* did, and I'd only been there a few hours.

We sterilized equipment and restocked shelves and bins. We changed sheets and made beds, disposed of trash, and spoke to each incoming patient, offering words of encouragement and praise.

By the time we had to leave, only a small dent had been taken out of the line. I felt awful that we couldn't help them all, and yet I was glad that we'd at least been able to help some. *Some* was better than *none* any day. *Some* would eventually add up to *all*. And that's what kept my spirits lifted as we moved to the camp where the homeless but uninjured had gathered.

We found a handful of unofficial leaders and approached them.

"Good afternoon, everyone," Dan said, smiling brightly. "You all know me, I would hope. This is Princess Alexis, and her guard, Adam. We're here to play a game with the children, if you don't mind?"

Mind? They were ecstatic.

Less than a half hour later, we were in a field with a couple fallen logs separating us into teams—Ash and Dan had carried them over from the woods. I was on one side with quite a few hearty teens and a handful of little ones, while Dan and Ash were on the other side with mostly uncoordinated toddlers—to make it fair.

"All right," Ash yelled, gathering everyone's attention. "The goal is to hit as many opponents as possible."

One of the kids on his team tugged on his shirt. "What's an o-po-men?"

Ash smiled wide and put his hands on his knees, getting

on the kid's level. "People on the other team. They're you're opponents, okay?"

The kid said nothing, just grinned and nodded.

"If you get hit," Ash continued, standing back up, "then you're out. If one of your teammates catches a ball, you can get called back in. The last team standing wins." He glanced around the group with a playful smile on his face. "Any questions?"

Dan raised his hand, making me giggle.

"Yes, Prince Daniel?" Ash asked with a grin.

"What if you're hit by your own team member by accident?"

Ash chuckled and most of the kids giggled. "Then you're safe."

Dan raised his hand again. "What if you cross over the logs in the middle?"

"Ooh, good question," Ash commended. "If you cross the logs, you're out."

Dan raised his hand yet *again*.

Ash sighed. "Last question, Dan."

The Sea Prince chuckled. "Can I use my magic?"

"No way," Ash decided right away. "That'd be cheating, and cheating is a definite no-go, okay? If you see someone cheating, you better call their asses out."

The kids thought that him swearing in front of them was the funniest thing ever.

"All right," Ash said, grinning, "battle starts on the count of three. One... two... three!"

Suddenly balls were soaring all over the place. People were being hit like crazy and dropping like flies. I dodged balls sent from both Dan and Ash, sticking my tongue out as they missed me. Which, of course, made them want to take me out even more.

The longer we played, though, the better people got at

understanding the game. Kids were soon catching flyway balls and calling their sidelined team members back into the game. Shouts and giggles echoed off the trees and the soot-covered buildings beyond. Adults gathered to watch the game and cheer their children on. Even tiny toddlers were tossing balls a few feet then picking them up and trying again.

By the time night fell, neither team had won, but both teams had thoroughly enjoyed themselves. I watched as Dan ruffled the hair of a five-year-old boy and said good night. Then I turned to watch Ash high-fiving a group of kids as they headed back to camp. A few of the children even came over to me, offering me quick hugs before shyly running away.

The joy that filled me at the end of that day would never be replaced. What we'd done for the people had affected more than just them—it'd affected *us*. The act of giving, of helping, of coming together and uniting as one was powerful.

I hoped they'd remember this day for as long as they lived...

Because I knew I would never forget it.

CHAPTER 27

The following afternoon, we were ten ships strong
and sailing down the channel of Glite.

It'd been a strange trip up till then, full of tension and
eerie silence. It made me nervous.

I glanced up at the tall, rocky cliffs on either side of us
and held my breath. It was a *very* narrow channel. We
supposedly had the element of surprise, but something still
felt off. I kept waiting for everything to go wrong. I imagined
getting ambushed from a above or hitting a rock at the
bottom of the channel and ruining the boat or the walls
caving in and burying us alive.

Every ten minutes or so, we'd have to pause and allow
Dan to catch his breath, and every time we stopped, the
water levels lowered drastically. The more he used his power,
the more it cost him, and at that slow rate, we'd already been
in the channel for three hours. Luckily, the end was near. I
could see up ahead to where the channel widened out and
met with the sea once more.

Birds flew through the dreary gray sky, but they never
chirped or cawed. The wind didn't blow, though it seemed

like a storm might be moving in. All I could hear was the soft lapping of the water at our ship's hull and the nervous breathing of our crew.

And again, that sense of fear and nervousness gnawed at me.

I thought about vocalizing my concerns, but I didn't want to cause any unnecessary panic. Just because I was scared didn't mean I needed to freak everyone else out too.

As our ship slowly drifted out of the channel and into the ocean, a soft rumbling met my ears, like a far-off roll of thunder. Only, it didn't feel like thunder. The vibrations didn't seem to be coming from the sky or even the ground; they seemed to be coming from the *sea*, as if the water beneath us were trembling.

I glanced at Dan, who's pale green eyes were squeezed shut in concentration as he held his breath. Then I turned to Cal, who was standing at the front of the boat, his hands clutching the rails tightly as we slowly crept forward. Ben, Rob, Ash, and Criss were the only ones sitting nearby, and they all looked as solemn as I felt.

"Did you feel that?" I whispered to them.

"Feel what?" Rob asked, standing up and instantly becoming more alert.

I shook my head. Was I imagining it? I mean, there was clearly a storm brewing on the horizon, so the probability of it truly being thunder was likely.

Then the sea rumbled again, and I felt a tiny pulse in the deck beneath my feet.

"That," I hissed.

Suddenly, Dan's eyes snapped open wide.

"Turn back!" he shouted to the ships following us. "Turn back and follow the backup plan!"

The backup plan? Sailing close to the Rubian isles and hoping that Hydratica didn't see us? But we were already at the very end of the channel. If he was telling them to turn back, then...

"Something's here," Dan said as he and Cal ran over to us. "Something *big*. In the water. If we can't get back to the shallows immediately, then I don't know what the fuck's going to happen."

"What do you think it is?" Ben asked. "A whale? A shark?"

Dan shook his head and swallowed hard. "I don't know. It just feels... bad."

He then sucked in a huge gulp of air and began pushing all ten of our ships backward through the channel. But it wasn't fast enough. At least, not for us. We were now the last ship in the line, so when a motherfucking *sea creature* reared its ugly head out of the water, we were the first target it laid eyes on.

The creature opened its razor-like jowls and screeched so loud it rattled stones loose off the cliffs. The rocks plunged into the channel behind us, splashing water high into the sky. Then another head emerged from the murky depths, and another, and another.

My jaw dropped to the fucking floor as I stared, wide-eyed and terrified, at the *four-headed* creature that I was pretty sure was a godsdamned hydra. Its skin was scaly like a snake or lizard, but its eyes—all eight of them—were opaque, almost as if they were blind or something.

I turned around to see how the other ships and their passengers were faring, but I found a wall of rocks separating us from them. The hydra's roars had apparently collapsed the channel walls behind us.

I prayed to the absentee gods that none of our sailors had been caught in the landslide.

When I turned back around, I was just in time to see one of the hydra's massive heads crashing into the side of our ship, busting it into splinters.

"Jump!" Dan shouted as he raced to the opposite end of the boat and dove overboard.

He didn't have to tell us twice; we were all too panicked to do anything more than obey.

I crashed into the sea below, sinking a few feet underwater before frantically kicking and clawing my way to the surface above. Air filled my lungs as I gasped, followed immediately by water as I slipped back under the waves. I coughed and spluttered, alternating between bobbing up above the water and sinking down below. It was a fight I knew I wouldn't win on my own, since I'd never learned how to swim.

Suddenly, the sea itself pushed me forward, and I was once again taking in deep gulps of air while coughing and gagging on the sea water pooling in the bottom of my lungs.

"It's okay, Lexi," Dan called to me from across the choppy surface of the sea. "I got you. We just need to get to shore, and it'll all be okay."

The water pushed me over to a broken piece of ship and deposited me on top.

"Find some debris!" Dan shouted at the guys. "I'll do my best to float you to shore!"

"*Shore?*" Rob cried as he scrambled onto a chuck of wood. "There's nothing but mile-high cliffs as far as the eye can see!"

The hydra leaned its heads back and screeched into the sky as it pummeled into the remaining half of our sinking ship, obliterating it completely.

Dan pointed to some distant chunk of brown on the horizon. "That's Brineton Port! If we can get there, we might have a chance."

"Brineton is in Hydratica," I protested as I clung to my makeshift raft. "If we wash up there, we'll be taken as prisoners of war!"

"Better than drowning at sea," Dan shouted back.

And I guessed if those were my only two options, then Brineton it was.

Still, we were miles away from the coast, and we had a giant fucking hydra attacking us. Our odds for survival did *not* look good. And this time, all six of us were in peril. There was no Crissen waiting in the wings of Blackwood Palace taking on the brunt of keeping us alive—he was there, right beside us. If we all went down, then we all went down... for real.

As soon as we all found boards to hold onto, Dan held his breath and propelled us through the water. We started gaining speed and distance, but the hydra didn't seem to like that. It screeched and dipped underwater, resurfacing a few seconds later right at our heels. One of its heads smashed into the water between us all, scattering us in turbulent waves.

I barrel rolled through the sea, eventually resurfacing with my raft still clenched tight beneath my fingers. As I coughed and gagged, Dan floated over to my raft, facedown in the water.

"Oh my gods!" I shrieked, scrambling to paddle over to him.

I tried to lift him onto my raft, but I damn near slid off into the water beside him.

"Stop!" Cal shouted. His raft was the closest one to mine. "He's okay, because we're okay, remember? And as the Sea Prince, he can breathe the water with no ill consequences. He just got knocked out."

"Well, what are we going to do?" I shouted back. "We can't leave him here, and we have absolutely no chance of paddling back to shore with this hydra on our asses."

Rob climbed back onto his piece of wood and ran a sopping wet hand down his face. "I say we kill the fucker. It might be the only way to make it out of here alive. Running from it clearly isn't going to work."

"You mean *swimming* from it?" Ash asked with a grin, trying to lighten the mood.

Rob glared at him. "Why don't you turn yourself into something useful and counterattack?"

Ash thought for a moment before his amber eyes lit up. "On it."

Then he sank beneath the sea and his golden magic took over. When he resurfaced, he was in the form of a massive hydra with white and gold scales and giant copper dots under each of his four heads.

"Yes!" I screamed in excitement.

Talk about fighting fire with fire.

"Now, let's go!" Cal shouted. "Swim for shore while Ash has it distracted!"

I scrambled into action, paddling as hard as I could while the hydras clashed behind me. Their fight kicked up monstrous waves that threatened to overturn my little board at every chance, forcing me to hold on for dear life instead of rowing.

I turned toward the guys and found they weren't faring any better. "This isn't working!"

"Fuck it," Rob decided when he realized I was right. "Let's help Ash take it down. As soon as it's gone, we'll be able to get to shore easier."

At that, the Spirit Prince closed his eyes and eventually started shivering.

Ben followed suit, reaching down below and pulling up a rope of seaweed and winding it around the bad hydra's legs.

"Careful," Cal warned him. "If you lose all five senses, you're fucked. Dan's not awake to give you fresh water."

Ben rolled his chocolaty eyes. "It's almost as if we're surrounded by water."

Cal glared. "You know as well as I do that you can't drink saltwater."

"Not to survive," he agreed, "but to sustain my magic for a few extra minutes? Possibly."

"It's a risk," Cal stressed.

"A risk I'm willing to take." Ben yanked on the seaweed rope, and the hydra was forced a few feet back away from Ash. "I don't know how long I can hold it though, so you guys better work fast."

Suddenly, Rob started talking to some spirit we couldn't see. "Hey, so glad you and your crew were nearby. Do you think you could lend us a hand?"

Whatever the spirit's reply was, I couldn't hear.

"That's the one," Rob said in agreement, making me think the spirit must've dealt with this hydra before. "Yeah, don't touch the white one though. That's my brother." There was a pause and then Rob chuckled. "No, I'm not crazy. He's a shifter." He nodded as he listened to the spirit's silent words. "All right, I'll tell them. Thanks."

He blinked his gray eyes a few times, adjusting his vision as he came back to the real world from the astral plane. Then he turned his gaze toward us.

"Captain Brinewurst says to aim for the eyes. They don't enable the creature to see, but they *do* provide it with its energy and lifeforce. If we can dislodge all eight of them, it'll die."

"And how does the good captain know this?" Cal asked a bit sarcastically.

"Because that's how he died," Rob said flatly. "Fighting this ugly bastard."

I turned and stared at the hydra once more and realized one of his eyes was, in fact, missing. It only had seven instead of eight. "What happened to the *eye* that Captain Brinewurst dislodged?"

No one missed the suggestion in my tone.

"You think the hydra's missing eye is *the* Eye?" Cal asked. "The Eye of the Sea?"

I shrugged. "I think any of the eight could be 'the Eye.' If what the captain said is true, then they each hold a magical energy that's probably strong enough to open a portal."

"So, we don't need to find the elusive lost Eye," Criss said, putting the puzzle pieces together in his mind. "We just need to get one of the seven remaining?"

I nodded. "That's my guess."

"It's more than a guess," Ben told me with a wink. "I'd classify that as a theory, at least."

I grinned as I bobbed on my board in the waves. "Why, thank you, Mr. Lexicon."

He grinned back. "You're welcome, Mrs. Lexicon."

Rob rolled his eyes. "Let's just take this thing down first. We'll deal with individual body parts later." Then, out of the blue, his attention was focused elsewhere. "What do you want?"

Since no one was there, I assumed he was, yet again, speaking to a spirit.

"Oh really? And you know this how?" Rob asked mockingly.

All at once, the smug expression dropped off his face and he listened more intently.

"How'd you get it?" Rob asked him, and I immediately perked up.

"Get what? Is he talking about the Eye?" I asked eagerly, but Rob shushed me.

The silence carried on for a while, so I figured the spirit was telling him a story of some sort. Well, not *silence*-silence. The hydras were still battling it out in the background, screeching and splashing and causing all sorts of a commotion. I had to grip my wooden board extra tight to keep from slipping off in the waves.

"And where is it now?" Rob asked. There was a brief pause, during which his expression turned sour again. "Yeah, humans are dicks."

"What happened?" I asked him.

He glanced back at the spirit and nodded. "Thanks."

Then he turned back to us.

"The spirit that just left says he was in possession of a magical pearl a few years ago. He set the pearl in a ring, then paid Captain Brinewurst some coin to take him across the sea to Hydratica, where he intended to sell the item of jewelry for a small fortune. Along the way, however, the ship was attacked by a hydra—*that* hydra. The entire crew drowned, passengers and all."

I immediately locked eyes with Ben. "That's the one!"

He nodded quickly in response, an excited smile spreading across his tanned face.

"What one?" Cal asked, looking from person to person almost suspiciously.

"The fae who traded the faerie lights for the pearl," I told him.

Rob cocked his head. "How'd you know the spirit was a fae?"

I sighed. "Because Ben and I were talking to the man who made the trade with him."

"Where's the Eye now?" Ben asked anxiously.

Rob shook his head. "He says it was looted by some human fisherman. It could be anywhere now."

"Son of a bitch," Ben muttered, just as I shouted, "Fuck!"

"Yeah," Rob agreed grimly. "So, we're back to plan A: kill this fucker first, then worry about the Eye later."

Unfortunately, that plan only looked good on paper.

When it came to the execution, it was much more difficult than we imagined.

Rob's spirits attacked the hydras from the air, but they kept forgetting and attacking Ash too. Ben's hold on the seaweed didn't last forever, and soon he could no longer see, hear, smell, taste, or touch. He had no idea what he was doing, and he eventually fell right off his raft and into the ocean. Cal swam over to help him, but the pair got caught in the hydras' scuffle and ended up headbutted by the damn thing. They were soon floating on water like Dan, who was just starting to come to.

"Wha—?" Dan asked as his bleary eyes began to focus. "What happened?"

Rob pointed skyward. "A hydra happened."

Dan's eyes bugged out of his head. "*Two* hydras!"

"Oh, that's just Ash," Rob said, brushing his brother's fear away like dust on the breeze. "But now that you're awake, we could really use some help."

I'd been zapping balls of fire at the four-headed asshole, but its skin was thick and slick, and my flames only seemed to irritate it rather than damage it.

Suddenly, a loud screech tore through the air and a stream of blood rained down on us. One of the bad hydra's heads was latched onto one of Ash's necks, its teeth tearing into his white-gold flesh.

"No!" I shrieked in horror.

Crissen didn't hesitate. He dove into the water and swam right up to Ash's side. When his hands touched the hydra, healing magic instantly jolted through the sea creature's skin, rushing to the neck where the wound was still dripping blood.

By the time he was finished healing Ash, he passed out right where he floated, slipping silently into the sea.

"Criss!" I shouted, leaning so far over the edge of my raft that I damn near flipped it.

"I got him," Dan said, using the water to lift not only Criss, but Cal and Ben as well, to the safety of a nearby board.

Now that he was healed, Ash attacked the other hydra with renewed strength. Their heads flailed wildly, teeth snapping and gnashing, and the waters grew perilous once more. Waves far taller than me rocked my board and flipped me over, plunging me into the sea.

Dan raised me up so I could breathe, but just as I resurfaced, another wave knocked me back under. From beneath the surface, I watched a hydra head smash into a board before Rob's motionless body crashed into the water in a frenzy of tiny bubbles.

Fighting hard, I clawed toward the surface once more. When I found some air, I took a huge inhale, but as the water sucked at my body, I felt myself getting pulled closer to the fight.

No, no, no, no!

I kicked and splashed harder, struggling against the tug of the current, but if I couldn't swim in placid water, then I sure as hell couldn't swim in *this*.

Dan surfaced right beside me and wrapped his arm around my waist. "It's all right. I got you."

I noticed Rob was now stacked on the board along side the other three, and none of them appeared to be waking.

My heart hammered and tears formed in my eyes. This was really and truly *it*. We were going to die out here on the ocean, fighting a losing battle with a mythological creature. There was no way to survive this. The chances were just too slim.

"Come on," Dan said as he swam in the guys' direction. "There's another board over there for you to hold onto."

But we never made it.

A loud screech ripped through the air, and just as I turned back to see what had happened, a fucking hydra head smashed down into us, instantly turning my whole world black.

CHAPTER 28

 EMMA

The sheets stirred, and Tristan kissed me before climbing out of bed.

Most of the time, I slept right through that part. But every once in a while, I became conscious enough to crawl out of the warm covers and visit with him for a few minutes before he set sail.

Dragging my sleepy ass into the kitchen, I filled a metal pot up to the brim with some freshwater we'd collected from a nearby stream and placed it beside the fish stew over the fire. While that heated, I sleepily ground a handful of coffee beans into a course powder and dumped them into a metal filter. When the pot finally whistled, I removed it from the flames and dropped in the coffee filter, smiling as the fresh scent of caffeine wafted up to my nose.

Ah, the nectar of the gods.

I poured Tris and me each a cup just as he came around the corner clad in his stained plaid dress shirt and those ass-fitting pants I loved so much. I reached around and squeezed his butt, but the damn thing didn't budge an inch. He was so ripped it was glorious.

Our lips met, and I smiled against his mouth. "Want to head back to bed for a few more minutes?"

He chuckled. "The pants did it for you again, huh?"

I nodded vigorously as I waggled my brows. "You're just such a sexy fisherman, Tris. And your ass looks even better *out*side of the pants than it does *in*side them. It only makes sense."

He took the coffee cup from my hands and set it on the counter before hefting me up into his big, strong arms. "Is that right?"

It was still dark outside, but the moonlight that filtered in lent a definite sort of mischief to the twinkle in his eyes.

"Uh-huh." I giggled as he spun me around and headed back toward our bedroom, but that's when I saw the most disturbing thing ever out the kitchen window: bodies. Some tumbling in the surf, some already beached on the shore, none of them moving. "Tris!" I yelped, pointing out into the night.

He quickly spun back around and peered through the glass. "*Hades, Zeus, and Hera,*" he cursed as he set me back down on my feet. "Are those seals? Or are they human fucking corpses?"

I squeaked as I shook my head. "I have no idea."

"Shit." He grabbed his boots and hurriedly slipped them on.

Panic hit me like a hammer to the chest. "Oh my gods, Tris, what are we going to do?"

He grabbed my shoulders and stooped down to my level. "*You're* going to wait in here where its safe. *I'm* going to go out there and see if anyone is still alive."

"No, wait!" I cried, reaching for him. But he was already out the door.

I wanted to tell him he couldn't just go examining dead bodies on his own. That he was practically begging to be a murder victim in some unsolved mystery novel. I mostly read romances, but I'd read enough horror to know that this was a very, *very* bad idea. I'd also read enough of it to know that, if I was dumb enough to go out after him, we'd *both* end up hanging from a fishhook in some psycho's underground root cellar.

No fucking thank you.

Instead, I watched nervously from the kitchen window as Tris ran around checking the corpses necks for pulses or signs of life. By the time he was finished, there were six of them all lined up in a row.

He jogged back and opened the door. "They're alive. I think you need to see this."

I shook my head adamantly. "Nope. No thank you. Blonde haired white girl will *not* be the first to go due to stupidity. Not this time."

"Babe, what are you talking about?" he asked in exasperation.

"I've read a *lot* of books," I told him confidently. "And this is something straight out of a horror novel. If I step foot outside that door, I'm going to take a sickle to the chest or some shit."

"*Hades*, Gem, you need to not read shit like that anymore."

"I don't," I assured him. "I much prefer steamy romance to pissing myself."

He took my hand and tugged me toward the door. "Well,

good. Now come look at these people. They look really familiar to me."

My eyes went wide, and I dug my heels into the floor. "Wait. *How* familiar?"

There were six bodies lying on the beach, and six harem ladies back home. Had the Storm King killed the queens and sent them as a message to me? A warning that I was going to be next? Oh fuck, I wished I'd never read those scary books as a teenager.

"Like, *Blackwood princes familiar*," he stressed. "And a *princess*."

I gasped.

Alexis? My very best friend in the whole wide world had miraculously washed up on the shore outside my illegal immigrant residence? That didn't seem strangely coincidental or anything.

Ah, fuck it.

Horror novels be damned, I rushed right out the door and down to the beach.

Dawn was just breaking over the oceanic horizon, lending a gentle bronze glow to the bodies so they didn't look quite so lifeless and creepy. Sure enough, Tris was right. Those were most definitely the bodies of the princes and Lex. But what had happened to them? And how had they ended up *here* of all places?

"There's another one over there!" Tris called, drawing my gaze further down the shore.

I jogged over to him and studied the face in the sand. He looked slightly familiar, maybe… But I definitely didn't remember ever meeting him.

"I don't know this guy," I admitted to Tris. "Do you?"

He shook his head. "Nope."

I gasped once more. "Oh my gods! What if he's their would-be murderer? What if his evil plan was foiled at the last second and he was injured along with them?"

Tris's eyes went wide, but this time he didn't tell me to stop reading horror novels. "Get some rope then. We'll tie him up just in case."

I nodded. "Good idea. When Alexis wakes up, we'll find out who he really is."

I ran to the dock and grabbed some extra rope from one of the poles. When we finished tying the would-be murderer up, we dragged him through the sand and up to the side of the house where we hid him in the dunes.

Tris glanced up at the sky, which had brightened significantly into a gentle shade of pink. "We better drag the rest of them up here too before any of the locals find them."

"Another good idea," I complimented him. "You would have made an excellent detective in a novel, you know that?"

He chuckled and shook his head. Thank the gods I'd found a man who understood and appreciated my particular brand of weirdness.

By the time we dragged the last body up the beach, I was sweating like Zeus's nut sack.

That's when they all started to stir.

"Oh, come on!" I cried in frustration, a hand on my hip. "You couldn't have done that *before* we dragged your dumb asses up the beach?"

Lex's eyes popped open immediately, and she sat up so quickly they spun around in circles. "Gemma? Oh fuck, we died. We're in Elysium."

I threw my head back and laughed. "You're not dead, you royal asshat. You just washed up on my beach. Care to tell me how that happened?"

She stared at me like I had two heads. "But you're dead, and Rob's the only one who can see and speak to spirits, so..."

Clearly it wasn't adding up for her.

"Lex, I'm not dead. Tristan and I faked our deaths to escape the Storm King."

"You *what*?" she screeched, pushing up onto her feet. "All this time I've been mourning you, and you were *alive*?"

She looked angry at first; then she tackle-hugged me into the sand, sobbing uncontrollably.

"Oh my gods, Gem, I'm so happy you're alive."

I patted her back. "I'm happy, too, Le—"

But she cut me off. "I missed you so much."

"Yeah, me t—"

"I hate myself for bringing you to the palace with me."

I sighed and rolled my eyes. "Lex, it's oka—"

"I've blamed myself every day for your death."

I scoffed. "Now that's a little—"

"I swore I'd avenge you. I swore I'd kill the king."

Just as I was about to tell her to shut the fuck up, her last words entered my brain and messed up my train of thought. "And did you?"

She sniffled. "Did what?"

"Did you kill him?"

She shook her head. "Not yet. But we're getting closer."

"*Oh!*" I suddenly remembered the would-be murderer tied up in the dunes. "Speaking of killers and all that fun shit, I have a guy I need you to see."

Lex's brows furrowed, but she carefully followed me over to the side of the house.

I jabbed a finger at the sleeping criminal with a proud smile. "Does this bastard look familiar to you?"

She gasped and dropped down onto her knees. "Oh my gods, Gem, what happened to him?"

"We tied him up," I said smugly. "So he couldn't get to you guys and hurt you again."

"Hurt us?" She looked astounded. "Gemma, this is Asher Storm. Ashlynn's son."

My mind screeched to a halt. "Wait. Ashlynn's long-lost son? The one she told me about that night in the woods?"

Ash groaned then and cracked open a single eyelid. "What the fuck?"

Oh, shit. Now it was all coming together. Why he looked so familiar even though I'd never met him. He looked just like his mom. Shame I didn't see it sooner.

"Why the hell am I all tied up?" he asked in confusion.

"Shit," I cursed again as I quickly unraveled his bindings. "I'm so sorry. I thought you were the reason Alexis and the guys were half dead and washed ashore."

"No, the *hydra* is the reason for that," Lex explained. "*Ash* is the reason we're even remotely alive right now. He shifted into a hydra and fought the other one off."

I blinked. "Holy shit, that's badass."

"Right?" she asked with pride on his behalf.

I could tell she loved the guy already. But there was something else about him that seemed familiar to me. Something beyond the fact that he resembled his mother. I just couldn't quite put my finger on it.

"Have we met before?" I asked him, even though I was pretty sure that we hadn't.

He grinned. "Not exactly. I tried to stay away from Alexis when she was hanging out with you. She didn't really have many friends besides us."

Ding, ding, ding. That rang a bell.

"Oh my gods, you're Adam!" I shouted, pulling him into a hug. "*The* motherfucking *Adam*! The one Alexis was in love with. The one that broke her heart and left her to wallow in tears and sadness for the rest of her days."

Wait a second. Why was I hugging him again?

I threw him off me and shook my head. "You should be ashamed of yourself."

Alexis laughed and laughed. "Gemma! He didn't leave me

and break my heart. He turned into a sloth to avoid being spotted by the Storm King or any of his guards, and then I found him and made him my pet before he had a chance to turn back into a man."

No. Fucking. Way.

"You're *Speedy* too?" I asked, flabbergasted.

This shit was beyond fucking weird.

My brows scrunched together nervously. "You're not going to tell me you're actually my dad too, are you? Or Alexis's long-lost father? I couldn't handle that."

He laughed and shot Lex a funny look. "What's up with this girl?"

Lex latched onto me and squeezed. "She's quirky like me."

"*Ah*," Asher-Adam-Speedy said as he stood and dusted the sand off his pants. "Makes sense then."

"Wait," I said, because apparently, I wasn't done being stupid just yet. "I thought the Storm King killed you? Like, twice." Once as a man many years ago, and then as sloth just a couple months ago.

He nodded. "That's what everyone's supposed to think. Keep the secret and you'll be fine."

I scoffed and rolled my eyes. "Any other secrets I need to know about?" I asked Lex as we followed Asher over to the other Storms.

"Probably," she admitted with a grin. "Like, where did his pants come from? Shouldn't you be naked from the shift, Ash?"

"If you don't know, then I'm not telling," he teased over his shoulder.

And that's when Crissen's eyes locked onto mine. He hopped up like someone lit a fire under his ass and he pointed straight at me. "You!" he cried.

"You," I said back, just for shits and giggles.

"You're alive? How?"

Dear gods this was going to be a long day of repeating ourselves over and over again.

I sighed. "Why don't you all come inside, and we can reminisce over some coffee and a steaming hot bowl of fish stew?"

CHAPTER 29

LEXIS

As soon as we entered the beach house, my nerves buzzed with energy.

The excitement of finding Gemma alive had clearly gotten to me.

I sat there listening in awe as she told the story of their escape, and I found myself absolutely floored by her bravery and strength. Without even knowing it, she encouraged me to be a better person. A stronger leader. A braver princess. A fiercer friend.

And a more lethal enemy to the Storm King.

I'd seen how she perked up when she thought I'd killed him. I'd heard the relief in her voice. Felt the repose of her emotions as they settled around me.

I couldn't wait for the day when I told her he was dead and it was the honest to gods truth.

She spooned us all some soup, and after we ate our fill,

she made us all some coffee. I wasn't a natural born coffee drinker—I generally preferred tea—but who was I to turn down caffeine after the night we'd just had?

I blew the steam away from my mug and gingerly sipped at the boiling hot beverage.

"So what about you?" Gem asked me excitedly. "How'd you guys get washed up on our shore?"

I took a deep breath and blew it out across my coffee, hoping that'd help to cool it. "That's a long story."

She glanced at wooden clock hanging on the wall. "We've got time."

I supposed we had *some*. It was only midmorning, after all. But still, I knew we couldn't stay long, not with the world falling to shit so quickly back home.

I summed it up as best I could. "The Storm King sent us to retrieve a magical object called the Eye of the Sea. On our quest to find it, we were attacked by a hydra."

"Actually," Dan cut in, "we were on our way to attack Brineton, but we were separated from the rest of our fleet."

"Brineton?" Gemma blinked, her neck straightening up in surprise. "That's just down the coast from us."

"How'd you get separated?" Tristan asked. He was sitting in a chair at least three times too small for his burly frame, and Gemma was cozied up in his lap, looking three times too small for him as well.

Why either of them asked about *Brineton* and our *separation from the fleet* before asking about a mythological fucking *hydra* was beyond me. That would have been the first question out of my mouth. Followed by, *what the ever-loving hell is the Eye of the Sea?*

"The hydra separated us," Dan told him. "The bastard caused a landslide in the Channel of Glite. I'm hoping our crew survived and regrouped back home, but we haven't been able to make contact, so I'm honestly not sure."

Gem glanced between Dan and me with an uncertain expression. She seemed to have lost some of her vivacious-ness since I'd last seen her, and that made me sad. No doubt the Storm King had beaten it out of her. I hated him so damn much.

"So, which is it?" Gem asked hesitantly. "Were you attacking a port or looking for the Eye of the Sea? I don't understand why either of you would lie about it."

"Neither of us were lying," I assured her, taking a sip of my blazing hot coffee and burning my tongue. "They're both true. We've been on a search for the Eye since we arrived in Western Blackwood. But Hydratica just attacked Ebony City, destroying everything in their path. We were about to retal-iate when everything went to Hades."

"And what exactly *is* this Eye?" Tristan asked skeptically.

"According to a spirit hanging around a shipwreck"—Rob ran a hand through his dark hair—"it's a magical pearl."

I nodded my agreement. "According to a bartender in Western Blackwood it's a pearl too."

"But in all actuality," Cal cut in, "it could be *anything*."

"But given the vast majority of the evidence," Ben argued, "it's most likely to be a pearl. A bluish-purple one."

Gem's bright blue eyes went wide.

Cal sighed. "I've never heard of a bluish-purple pearl, *Benson*. They're usually ivory, champagne, or pink. Some-times blackish if they've been dyed. If *I* know this, then *you* definitely do."

Ben nodded. "Which is just another reason why this particular pearl is special."

"You mean, *this* particular pearl?" Gem asked, reaching into her apron and pulling out three tiny orbs. She plucked the only bluish-purple one from the bunch and held it up between her thumb and forefinger.

I couldn't help but gasp, accidentally spilling a splash of

scalding hot coffee into my lap. As the brown liquid stained my once-white dress, I quickly set down my cup and clasped my hands together tightly, trying to contain my anxiety.

Could it really be the Eye of the Sea? My nerves were already buzzing with excitement. Or maybe that was *magic* making my nerves go haywire? I remembered feeling that same buzzing sensation as soon as I entered the house. I'd attributed it to the excitement of finding Gemma alive, but maybe it was the pearl all along?

She deposited the little bead into Ben's open palm, and he proceeded to examine it. He rolled it around between his fingers, stared at its coloring, tapped it to test its density, and even held it up to his ear to... I don't even know what. Listen for vibrations maybe?

Either way it was pointless—the longer he held it, the surer I became. I could feel the energy from across the room. Just like the night I found the alicorn in the glade, I knew beyond a shadow of a doubt that there was magic in this pearl.

"I think this is it," Ben muttered breathlessly, passing it to Cal.

Squealing in pure delight, I hopped up and down around the room. There was so much elation and exhilaration bubbling inside of me, I couldn't possibly hope to contain it. Jumping for joy was apparently contagious though, because soon everyone was jumping around, cheering and hugging. It was sort of odd. The guys weren't opposed to showing emotion or anything, but they weren't normally so hyper about it. It was almost as if my happiness had somehow infiltrated their systems, compelling them to feel what I felt.

If that was the case... was it because of the *pearl* or because of my secondary power of *empathy*?

Maybe my empathy went beyond me sensing other people's emotions? Maybe I could project my emotions onto them too? And maybe *that's* why other people got horny when I did?

Talk about a revelation.

I forced myself to sit down and calm down, so that I could test my theory. Sure enough, as soon as my emotions calmed, everyone looked around in confusion and awkwardly stopped jumping around the living room.

Shit. Hopefully that only happened when my emotions were extreme. I had a feeling it didn't happen all the time, or else I would have noticed it by then. But still, I kind of felt bad knowing I could affect people like that.

Tristan and Gemma curled up once more in a wooden dining chair. Rob, Dan, and Cal took comfortable seats on the couch. And Ash and Criss sat down on the floor next to the coffee table.

"You guys," I said, grabbing my coffee before opening up the latest can of worms, "I think I can project my emotions."

"Is *that* why we were dancing around like crazy people?" Dan asked, apparently relieved that he hadn't acted so ridiculously on his own.

I bit my bottom lip and took a sip from my mug. "I think so."

"Are you sure it doesn't have something to do with the pearl?" Ben asked, his tone slightly skeptical.

"No, I'm not," I admitted. "I contemplated that option, but then, the empathy thing would also explain—" I glanced at Gem and my cheeks warmed a bit. "—my magical *side effects*."

Ben's brows rose and he nodded, considering my words.

"What will you do with the pearl?" Gem asked. "Will you give it to the Storm King?"

"Fuck no," Rob grumbled, crossing his arms on the couch.

Cal sighed, hanging his hands between his knees. "Our goal is to keep the Eye away from the Storm King and King Thane long enough to get it to the gods."

"And what will they do?" Tristan asked.

"Depends on which god," Ash admitted. "Ares would just turn around and help the Storm King like he's been doing."

"*What?*" Gem blurted out with tight lips.

"Yeah," Ash agreed. "But if we get it to Dion, I think he'll help *us* instead."

Tris raised a brow. "So, your whole plan hinges on the possibility of getting help from a party god?"

"No," Cal assured him. "The main thing is to keep the pearl out of the wrong hands. If the Storm King gets it, he'll remain untouchable for at least another month—and we need him weakened if we hope to take him down. If King Thane gets it, he'll open up a portal to the underworld."

Gem sat up straight in Tristan's lap. "Why the hell would he do that?"

"To get rid of my people," Rob spoke up. "He's hated them since the Sohsol Apocalypse. He feels they don't belong on our plane."

"Hasn't he thought about the consequences though?" she asked seriously.

I cocked my head to the side. "Like what?"

"Like the portal going both ways and *more* dead things coming through?" she asked with a shrug. "Or the portal opening up to someplace that *isn't* the underworld? Or the magic backfiring and killing everyone around it? I mean, come on, don't these people read books?"

I chuckled but immediately felt a deep sense of shame. I liked to consider myself an avid reader. Why the hell hadn't *I* thought of those things?

We continued talking and catching up like that for the rest of the day. Telling stories, exchanging news, and taking turns recounting tales of what we'd all been up to since we last saw one another. Some of it was light and happy, some of it was dark and depressing. But no matter what the subject matter, I was grateful to be conversing with my best friend again. The only thing that made me sad was that our visit would soon be over.

I sighed as the sun drifted lower on the horizon, casting its shadow across the beach.

"You have to go now, don't you?" Gem asked with delicate smile.

I swallowed hard. "Yes."

There was an unmistakable sadness in that raspy little word. But as sad as I was that I was leaving her behind, I was equally as glad that she had survived and found a way to be happy again.

Be strong like Gemma, Lex. You can do this.

"I love you, Gem," I told her as I wrapped her in a hug. "Take care of yourself."

She squeezed me back and rocked me side to side. "I love you too, Lex. Stay safe. And kill that dickbag, will ya?"

I chuckled as a single tear slid down my cheek. "I will."

I will, Rory. I will, Gem.

"Go," Gemma said, wiping a tear from her own smiling face. "Do what needs to be done. When it's all over, you know where to find me."

I smiled back and nodded, unable to speak without sobbing. I waved at her as tears flooded my vision; then I turned and walked out the door.

The beach was dusky, and the sea breeze was cool and welcoming against my heated cheeks. It soothed the sting of the tears and helped dry the salty trails they'd left down my skin. Breathing deep, I filled my lungs with the peace and tranquility of the ocean air and exhaled all the fear, sadness, and doubt that had somehow invaded my mind.

I turned to the guys and smiled. "I guess Brineton is over that way," I said, pointing. "We could try to acquire a boat?"

"Or," Ben said with a glimmer in his eyes, "now that we're on land, I can simply build us one."

He held out his hand and trees darted over from their homes in the woods, splitting and splintering until they molded themselves into the concave shape of a boat. He then held out his other hand and seaweed curled out of the water, tying itself around the joints of the boards and winding itself along the masts for use with sails.

Ben dropped to his knees, wobbling, but his magic continued to flow. Leaves floated over from the forest and braided themselves together until they formed giant sails attached to the seaweed vines. And after that was done, a stream of tree sap drifted over and filled up any cracks that were left in the hull and deck.

What we ended up with was a very natural, very exquisite-looking ship that would easily fit all seven of us for the journey to the archway and then back home to Blackwood. We were also left with a senseless Storm curled up into a ball on the beach with his eyes open, staring at nothing.

"I got this," Dan told us, before funneling some sea water and spinning it like a whirlpool. Salt separated and flew through the air like raindrops. When he was finished, he funneled the now fresh water into his brother's mouth until Ben finally came back to his senses and stood up.

Taking a deep breath, the Sand Prince put his hands on his hips and marveled at his creation as it floated on the surf. "I outdid myself this time."

Ash chuckled and patted his brother on the back. "That you did, bro. That you did."

"All aboard," Criss said, gesturing for us climb on the ship and get moving.

Cal and Rob were first in line. But instead of boarding right away, they paused and shared a knowing look.

"Criss," Cal said with a sigh. "I want you to know that my vote is yes. I don't know what's going to happen when we reach the arch and come face-to-face with the gods for the first time, but I want to do so knowing that we're a *team*, that you're a true Storm brother, and that you're officially a part of the group."

Criss's brows knit together, his throat bobbed like he couldn't quite swallow, and his lips tugged at the bottom like he was maybe getting choked up. "Thank you, Cal."

Cal smiled. "Call me bro."

Oh my gods, I was going to cry again. This was everything I wanted and more.

Rob punched Criss in the shoulder and grinned. "Likewise, bro. In case something goes terribly wrong at the arch, at least you'll die knowing you're a part of the team, right?"

I breathed out a laugh as I wiped the tears from my eyes. My Storms were a team. They'd finally all come together. My heart was completely full.

Dan stepped in line next. "*Six* dicks and a set a tits," he clarified, glancing back at me. "Team tattoo. Happening the next time we port. *For real.*"

I shook my head and rolled my eyes. "No tits and dicks!"

Criss and Dan chuckled as the last two princes got in line.

Ben and Ash took turns giving Criss fist bumps and hugs. "Welcome to the group, brother."

"Thank you, guys." Criss's smile was huge, his eyes were misty, and the love and happiness he radiated was almost enough to knock me over.

Catching my balance, I walked up to him and stared into his hazel eyes for a long time.

"You weren't always one of us," I said, trying to find the words for how I felt. "But you've *become* one of us. If you climb on this ship tonight, you're going to be *mine*. Are you sure you don't want to heed Bria's warning and run for the hills while you still have a chance?"

Criss smiled and pulled me into his arms.

"There's been no chance of me running since the moment I met you, Alexis. I fell in lust with you on that dance floor back in Nightshade, but I fell in love with you this week on the beach. Every moment I spend with you, that love grows a little bit deeper. And now..." He brushed a strand of hair behind my ear, but it didn't stay. Stupid fucking wind. "Right now, I'm so deeply in love with you that I'm never getting out, and I wouldn't change a thing."

His lips met mine in a kiss so sweet I'd swear I was floating on air.

Actually, I *was* floating. Or rather, Rob was pulling me up by my hips onto the ship's deck.

"Sorry, Jewels," he said as he sat me on my feet. "He might be an official part of the group, but I'm not ready to witness any sloppy make-out sessions just yet."

"We weren't *making out*," Criss protested as he climbed aboard. "I barely even kissed her."

"One step at a time," Rob assured him with a protective glare.

Dan chuckled and raised a brow. "Everybody ready?"

As soon as we all nodded, he took a deep breath, and we were speeding across the sea once more.

IT DIDN'T TAKE LONG BEFORE THE SUN SET THE REST OF THE way, the moon rose high into the sky, and countless shadows appeared on the horizon. They were interesting shadows. Almost shaped like...

"Ships," I gasped, pointing in their direction. "Hydratican ships!"

Dan quickly steered our boat to the left, but more vessels appeared out of the dark, blocking our path. We turned around and went right, but the same thing happened. Our only other option was to head back to shore, but when we ultimately tried that too, we found Hydratican ships behind us as well. They had us surrounded.

"Hand over the Eye," someone from the ship closest to us boomed. They must have been using some sort of a horn in order to project their voice like that. "I know you have it."

The fact that he said *I* instead of *we* made me wonder if the voice didn't belong to King Thane himself.

"What are we going to do?" Dan asked us. "We can't let them get the Eye, but there's nowhere to run and nowhere to hide."

I knew immediately what needed to be done.

"*You* take the Eye," I told Dan, handing the pearl to him. "Slip underwater and swim away beneath all the ships. Get it to the arch, and we'll catch up as soon as we can."

He shook his head, torn between his duties. "I can't just leave you all to fight an armada of Hydratican ships on your own."

"We'll be fine," Rob assured him with a cocky smirk. "Kicking ass is an old pastime of ours, remember?"

"Besides," Ben added, "as long as one of us is alive, we all stay alive. If you and the Eye are safe, then we all are."

Criss nodded. "That's true."

Cal patted Ben and Criss on their backs. "What they said."

Still, Dan hesitated.

Then the voice boomed again. "You have until the count of three to give me the Eye, or I'll take it by force. *One*!"

"Go!" Cal hissed at his brother.

Dan kissed me quickly then turned to leave, but a terrible thought crossed my mind, one that pretty much ruined my original plan. I reached out and latched onto his arm.

"Wait!" I cried. "What about the hydra?"

"*Two!*"

"I'll just have to take my chances," he said, glancing around the group.

"What if you lose the Eye?" Criss asked.

Dan shrugged, but his expression was pained. "Better at the bottom of the ocean than in the hands of King Thane or King Zacharias."

Wasn't that the fucking truth.

"*Three!*"

A battle cry invaded the air like a swarm of angry bees, and soon there were ropes and ladders stretching over to our ship from all sides. They were going to board.

Dan slipped quietly down the side of the boat and entered the water as the rest of us ran around pushing ladders away and untangling ropes. It'd be easier for Dan to escape if we could keep the enemy distracted, presuming that we really *did* have the Eye and that we were trying to protect it at all costs.

My power simmered anxiously beneath my skin as I shoved a foreign ladder into the sea. But I held it off. So far, no one had made any overly violent moves, and I didn't want to be the one to throw the first stone.

Keeping the Hydraticans at bay was a futile endeavor though. Every time we pushed one rope or ladder away, three more would take its place. Soon, they'd be swarming our tiny vessel and it would all be over.

My magic itched to ensure that didn't happen.

Suddenly, a cannon sounded, the *boom* echoing into the night like thunder, shattering the last layer of peace between our ships like a broken window.

As soon as that first shot was fired...

All hell broke loose.

CHAPTER 30

*H*orns sounded in the distance, more cannons fired, and the ocean rocked in an unsteady rhythm.

My brain worked overtime to try to figure each event out, while simultaneously shooting fire at every ship I could find.

Horns? Where are they coming from? Is Rubio here to back us up?

I found a ship and shouted, "Fire!" Then I watched the reflection of my flames in the dark, choppy water until my target lit up like a bonfire.

Why are they shooting cannons? They're clearly not aiming at us—no lead balls dropped through our ship's deck or even landed in the water beside us. So, who are they shooting at?

I spotted another ship. "Fire!" I yelled, and sent a fireball soaring right at it. I silently cheered as it too went up in flames.

And what's up with the ocean? It's rocking like mad, like some-thing's disturbing it. Does it have something to do with Dan? The hydra? The Eye?

It was impossible to tell.

But, damn, I was getting horny...

Suddenly, Dan lurched from the sea and landed belly-up on our ship's deck, soaking wet and clutching the Eye with white knuckles.

He looked delicious as sin, all wet and wild and sexy as hell.

"The hydra's back!" he shouted, momentarily knocking me out of my haze of lust. "I can't escape through the water. Not with that thing on my ass."

"Son of a bitch," Rob cursed. "I'll try to call Captain Brinewurst and his crew back. Maybe they can help again."

I turned to Cal. "We can't get the Eye to safety by land, ship, or sea, but can we get it there by *air*?"

Dan passed the Eye to Cal and leaned back, trying to catch his breath. I wanted to crawl on top of him and steal his breath in a different way.

"I'll see what I can do," Cal said. "I'll head for the arch. Meet me there if you can."

I tore my eyes away from Dan and nodded. "We will."

Cal kissed me; then he jumped into the night air. As soon as his body was surrounded by sky, his powers kicked in and propelled him high and away from us.

I exhaled a shaky breath. This was our last hope. I had no other ideas after that.

Splash! I gasped and shivered as a bucket of ice-cold water streamed from my head.

"Sorry, Jewels, but we don't have time for an orgy."

I glared at him. Rob, *cockblocker extraordinaire*, had saved the day, yet again.

"Thanks," I muttered dryly.

He chuckled as if my irritation amused him. "No problem."

A shrill screech tore through the air, and I didn't have to *see* the four-headed beast to know that the hydra had just emerged from the water. More cannons sounded, and I hoped the lead balls were being directed at the sea creature this time, rather than us or our allies.

Ash shook out his limbs and prepared to shift. "Here we go again," he whispered.

But I stopped him immediately. "No way. The Hydraticans won't know *you* from the real deal. They'll attack you both."

Ash shrugged. "So? What's the worst that can happen? I die and have to turn back into a hydra again?"

I pursed my lips and contemplated his words, but he didn't give me much time to think.

He kissed me quickly and jogged to the side of our boat. "I got this, Sweets."

Then he jumped, disappearing in a swirl of golden dust.

"Damn it, Asher!" I shouted at the empty air.

Horns sounded again, louder this time. I turned in their direction and, by the ginger light of a burning Hydratican ship, I saw a new fleet of vessels sailing closer. They had ruby red flags waving at their sails.

Rubians! Thank the gods. They really had come to our aid.

The Rubian ships opened fire on our enemies, just as Ash emerged in hydra form and attacked the other four-headed sea beast. Their fangs and claws clashed, the cannons *boomed*, the ocean churned, and the burning ships snapped and crackled. The battle raged on in a continuous push and pull of victory and defeat. Who would come out on top in the end? As long as Cal got the Eye to the arch, then *we* would be the victors.

That thought no more than crossed my mind when Cal came soaring down from the sky. He landed with a *thud* on one knee and quickly strode over to us.

"I can't get through."

"What do you mean, you can't get through?" Dan asked, joining our circle.

"I mean, I can't get fucking through," Cal growled. "There are harpies all over the sky. They attacked me at every turn."

"*Harpies?*" I repeated in surprise.

I mean, yeah, okay, I knew that Eristan wouldn't support us after my marriage to Ben and Rob. And, yes, I suppose I knew Camilla was courting the Hydratican princes, Blane and Zane. But for some reason, I never really put two and two together and assumed that Eristan would actively serve as our *enemies*.

Fuck, this was bad.

I shook my head and stared at the fiery destruction I'd caused. One of the ships masts creaked and crashed to the deck beneath, breaking a hole in the planks and sending embers sparkling into the night.

"We're just going to have to go through," I decided. "If I burn enough ships, they'll eventually sink and make a path for us."

Rob held up his bucket. "I'm on cool-off duty."

I stuck my tongue out at him. "You would be."

"Hey, *somebody* has to make sure rule number one gets enforced." He cocked his dark-haired head to the side. "Speaking of, what's the score right now?"

"The score says it's my turn next," Criss butted in. "Because I'm at zero."

"The score doesn't matter right now," I snapped.

They both chuckled as if my impatience was adorable, but they at least shut the hell up.

I scanned the horizon in search of my next target. "Fire."

A wave of curly peach flames shot from my palms and crashed into my intended ship with enough force to rock it side to side. Its hull quickly caught fire, the flames spreading up onto the deck, sending its crew into a panicked frenzy.

Splash! Rob doused me in seawater.

I growled and shot him a deadly glare. "You could at least wait until I'm actually feeling horny."

He shrugged. "I'm thorough, what can I say?"

I rolled my eyes and focused on another ship, blasting it with my power. Then another and another. I made my way in a circle all around us, lighting up ships one by one until the entire Hydratican fleet was ablaze.

When the last ship caught fire, Rob doused me in water for, like, the fifteenth freaking time. Growling, I spun around to give him a piece of my mind, but a group of harpies carrying Hydratican soldiers landed on our deck. One of which wore a royal blue robe and a crown with sapphire jewels and pearls. He was tall, broad shouldered, and had dark hair and dark eyes like Blane and Zane. There was no doubt that this was their father, King Thane.

The harpies and soldiers parted, creating a path for the Hydratican monarch to walk right up to us. His expression was dark yet amused as he held out his hand. "Give me the Eye."

I'd half-assed forgotten which one of us had it, until I saw Cal clench his fists tightly behind his back.

"We don't know what you're talking about," Cal lied.

King Thane chuckled. "Yes, you do. Hand it over and live or die trying to keep it. I'd much prefer the prior option, wouldn't you?"

Live, yes. Hand over the Eye, no fucking way.

In a last-ditch effort to save our asses, I shot a fireball straight at the king. A Hydratican soldier jumped in front of him at the last second, sacrificing himself to the flames instead of his ruler. Screaming and flailing as his skin burned, he jumped into the sea.

King Thane's dark eyes got suddenly darker. "You will pay for that."

The next moment, Cal launched into the air, followed by a hoard of angry harpies. As he made one last beeline for the arch, the rest of us started fighting on deck. I tried to pay attention to everything, the soldiers as they swung their swords at me and the guys, Cal as he dodged the harpies in the shadowy sky, Ash as he fought the hydra in the inky sea... but it was difficult. A few times, I ended up sliced in the arms, cringing as blood raced like a stream down to my hands.

"Rob!" Cal shouted from up above, and he tossed the pearl to his brother.

Miraculously, Rob caught it—I had no idea how—and he quickly handed it off to an invisible spirit, the pearl disappearing into thin air.

Yes!

But before I could even blink, a spear lodged into Rob's chest, and he dropped to the floor in an angry growl. King Thane's boot came down hard on his chest and pinned him to the wooden deck below. "I suggest you get that back. *Right. Now.*"

He twisted the spear, and Rob cried out in pain.

Suddenly, we were all crying out in pain as the connection of the blood bond dropped us to our knees. Cal fell from the sky and splashed into the waters below. The white-gold hydra screamed from all four heads and thrashed wildly in the water, taking out enemies and allies alike.

As Rob's strength wavered, so did his power over the spirits. The pearl flickered in and out of view as it undulated between the astral plane and the real world.

Gritting my teeth against the ache in my chest, I forced myself to stand. I needed to get the damn thing before King Thane did. That's all I knew in that moment.

Without any further thought, I lurched into the air, swiping my hand as the tiny pearl briefly flickered into view. As soon as I made contact, it smacked to the ground and rolled over to Dan.

"Go!" I cried.

A second later, Dan and the pearl were once again darting through the ocean toward the arch. Only this time, the hydra was occupied, so he actually stood a chance.

Or so I thought.

King Thane smiled wide, and his eyes lit with madness, a look of victory smeared onto his arrogant face. "We have him now."

Fear consumed me. *Why? Why does he think they've already won?*

And then, I got my answer.

A thousand freaking *heads* suddenly rose above the surface of the water. Their skin was dark, perhaps blue or green, and it shimmered like scales in the firelight. As soon as they opened their mouths and started to sing, I knew we were fucked.

Sirens.

Of course there'd be freaking sirens, this was *Hydratica* we were talking about—an entire kingdom of people ranging from human to full-blooded siren and everything in between.

I'd been so preoccupied with the hydra that I never even thought about there being another threat in the sea.

Stupid, stupid, stupid!

I covered my ears, smashing my head in an effort to block out their music, but my brain felt like mush. I couldn't concentrate; I couldn't see straight. My whole world tilted and wavered, and I tottered dizzily across the deck.

Cal, Dan, and Ash were still somewhere in the water, but Ben and Criss were stumbling along the deck just as drunk and delirious as I was, while Rob remained pinned beneath King Thane's foot.

Time passed in snippets. Standing one minute, floundering on the deck the next. Boots filled my vision, stomping closer. Then all at once, they were gone, drifting farther away across a backdrop of early morning sky. Ships blazed on the water one minute, and they were gone the next, sinking to the bottom of the sea. Two hydras. Then one hydra. Then none. A sea full of sirens, then an empty ocean, calm and sparkling in the light of the rising sun.

I blinked, and ever so slowly awareness came back to me. A killer headache swirled around in my skull, muffling my memories and distorting my focus, but it eventually subsided enough for me to sit up and stare blankly at the peaceful waters around us.

Gulls cawed and glided across the peach and pineapple sky. Our boat bobbed gently on the waves. All six princes slept peacefully on the deck—even Dan, Cal, and Ash—though I had no idea how they'd gotten there.

Rob was the first to stir, sitting up and wobbling in a sloppy circle until he finally straightened out and stared at me.

"They took the Eye," he said, his tone dull and lifeless. "My kingdom will fall. My people will be destroyed. There will be nothing left."

He ripped the spear from his chest and threw it into the water. Blood gushed from his open wound, but he didn't seem to care. It was almost like he couldn't even feel it.

We rocked on the sea in silence for a moment before I shook my head. "No. We won't let that happen. We'll stop them."

"How?" Rob asked, and he didn't even sound angry, just defeated.

I reached out and took his hand, desperately trying to

squeeze some hope and confidence back into him. "By never giving up. You can fail a thousand times, but if you don't stop and you don't quit, then you will still win in the end."

He stared at me with pained gray eyes. He wanted to believe me, I could feel his hope hesitating in the air around us, but he was scared. Scared for his people and possibly even scared for us.

I clasped his hands tighter. "I promise you, Rob, we will *never* give up. We Storms are tenacious little fuckers."

That, at least, earned me a small chuckle from him. He pulled me into his lap, with me carefully avoiding his injury, and we stared out across the glittering sea.

"I guess we better get to Southern Blackwood as fast as we can," Rob muttered. "We have another Sohsol Apocalypse to prepare for."

I sighed and nodded slowly.

Apocalypse. Revolution. Annihilation. Transformation.

There were a million words to describe the terrifying events to come.

One way or another, though, the world as we knew it... *was about to end.*

THE END of book three

Continue the story with the short, sweet, and hilarious novella, Snow Storms!

OR

Finish the perilous and captivating adventure **RIGHT NOW** in the series finale, Perfect Storms!

AFTERWORD

I hope you're as addicted to Alexis and her sexy Storm Princes as I am! Watching them live, love, fight, fail, and try again is just... amazing—even to me. LOL. I'm so excited for you to see how it all ends in the series finale—*Perfect Storms*!

If you liked this book, I hope you'll consider leaving a review. It would mean so much to me!

To stay updated on new releases and everything bookish, feel free to join: *Elle Middaugh — Reader Group*!

ACKNOWLEDGMENTS

A huge thank you to everyone who helped make this book possible! I love and appreciate each and every one of you.

A big thank you to my alpha, beta, and ARC readers! You guys rock!

A special thank you to Ann, who is not only a phenomenal writer, but also an extremely kickass developmental editor! I don't know where this series would be without you! ♥

Standalones

Siren Awakened

CONNECT WITH ELLE

Website:
www.ellemiddaugh.com

Newsletter:
www.ellemiddaugh.com/newsletter

Facebook Group:
www.facebook.com/groups/ellemiddaugh

ABOUT THE AUTHOR

Elle Middaugh is a USA Today bestselling author living in the Pennsylvania Allegheny Mountains with her wonderful husband and three beautiful children. She spends most of her time raising kids, writing stories, playing video games, reading, and attempting to keep a clean house.

She's a proud Navy wife, a frazzle-brained mother, a fan of health and fitness, a lover of tea and red wine, and a believer in happily-ever-afters.

Sassy. Seductive. Spellbinding.
www.ellemiddaugh.com

 facebook.com/ellemiddaugh
twitter.com/ellemiddaugh
instagram.com/Ellemiddaugh

Made in the USA
Columbia, SC
03 October 2020